REJECTED BY HEAVEN

REJECTED BY HEAVEN

THE UNBELIEVABLE MR. BROWNSTONE BOOK TWO

MICHAEL ANDERLE

DISRUPTIVE IMAGINATION

Special Thanks
to Mike Ross
for BBQ Consulting
Jessie Rae's BBQ - Las Vegas, NV

Thanks to the JIT Readers

James Caplan
Kim Boyer
John Ashmore
Sarah Weir
Peter Manis
Daniel Weigert
Joshua Ahles
Paul Westman
Larry Omans

If I've missed anyone, please let me know!

Editor
Lynne Stiegler

To Family, Friends and
Those Who Love
to Read.
May We All Enjoy Grace
to Live the Life We Are
Called.

James sat in the passenger seat of Shay's Fiat as they drove to her place. Recent events replayed in his mind.

He didn't give two shits about killing Walt Anderson. Even most bounties he had gone after had more honor than that man. The greedy little bastard'd had a wife who'd given up everything for him.

And he still wasn't satisfied.

Vengeance hadn't fulfilled James as much as he would have liked. Killing was easy. Living was hard. He'd miss Leeroy for the rest of his life, like Alison would miss her mother...he supposed.

He never had a mother, that he could remember.

Shay glanced at him. "I don't know what crawled up your super-armored butt, but shit happens, Brownstone. You gotta shake it off. This can't be the first time something's gone south for you?"

"My life has gone south from the beginning," he replied matter-of-factly.

Shay made it sound so easy—and she was right—but the recent convergence of events had disrupted his perfectly ordered and simple world. Nothing was the same now, and he couldn't pretend it was.

"I mean, look, we've both got our issues," Shay continued, "but you did the right thing back there. And you're doing the right thing with the girl. And you got revenge for both of the Anderson women."

He looked out the window of her car. "I wasn't supposed to get revenge. I was supposed to bring Nicole back to her daughter."

Shay shook her head. "We were both supposed to bring her back, but we didn't make it in time. That's the cold reality. You got some time-magic mojo in your warehouse, Brownstone? Otherwise it doesn't matter, and beating yourself up over it isn't going to help." She sighed. "You know the real difference between men and women?"

He grunted. "Dicks and pussies?"

That pulled a snort from Shay. "That too. No, it's that women understand—like on the level of our DNA—that not everything can be fixed. That sometimes you just have to roll with it. But men? Oh, you men...somewhere you're always thinking, 'I can fix this shit. Just give me a big enough tool.'"

James chuckled. "Maybe there is a bit of truth in that, but things are still weird."

She made a quick left, and a horn blared behind her. "Fuck you!" She flipped off the other driver. "It's Los Angeles traffic, asshole!" She pushed a wisp of hair out of her face. "Given some of the shit I've seen you do, I'm surprised to hear that. Weird is relative, you know?"

He shrugged. "Kicking ass, I get. Bringing in the bad guys, I get. Taking care of a girl, Shay? Especially one who's half-Oriceran? What if I fuck her up?"

She clicked her tongue. "Can't do worse than the dad, who tried to sell her to a group of gangsters who were torturing her mom."

He winced. "Yeah, I guess so."

"Don't overthink it, Brownstone. Kicking ass is your strength." Shay grinned.

The Spider pulled up to a nice two-story brownstone townhouse with an attached garage. The well-kept lawns and upscale houses in the area were a sharp contrast to James' rougher neighborhood, where fresh paint was as rare as hope. Shay's neighborhood was the kind of place the head of the gang lived, rather than his foot soldiers.

"Nice place," James mumbled, looking it over.

Shay smirked. "Hey, Brownstone, how do you like my brownstone?"

He eyed her sideways. "You've been probably waiting to say that for days." He snorted. "You should quit the tomb raider gig and do stand-up comedy. I'm sure there's some magic that would actually make you funny."

"You know I'm as funny as I am hot." She pressed a button on a garage door opener connected to her sun visor, then pulled in and parked the car. A sober look settled over her face. "I'll let you take the lead on whatever you want to tell Alison."

James' only response was a nod as they got out of her Spider.

The field archaeologist tapped a code into a pad near the door, and then leaned forward for a retinal scan.

The door clicked open.

"Actual security, see?" Shay pointed to her setup. "On the whole house, not just the Red Room of Pain."

James followed her inside. Two earth-toned loveseats dominated the open-plan living room, and a huge TV hung on the back wall. Fine white carpet covered most of the floor. A quartz-topped island stood in the center of her kitchen. The overall vibe he got was clean and modern, yet comfortable.

"Whatever you do, don't look in my refrigerator or my cabinets," Shay commanded.

"Why? You got body parts in there?" he asked.

"Nope. Because nothing's organized." She laced her fingers together, then pulled them apart. "Your OCD will explode."

"I don't have OCD. I just like to keep things si—"

"Simple," Shay finished as she walked into the kitchen, clicked something in there and came back out. "Sure." She snickered. "And let's not even get into my bedroom." A few beats passed, and she added in a sultry voice, "Unless you ask nicely."

James plopped himself down on a love seat and didn't say anything in response. He didn't want to get into another stupid conversation that ended with her accusing him of being gay.

He was still trying to wrap his mind around Alison being a more permanent part of his life.

Shay would have to take a number.

"You're so boring," the woman mumbled.

"Better boring than annoying," he responded.

She pursed her lips, then nodded. "You're that, too."

Light footfalls came down the stairs. Alison tightly gripping the bannister as she took each step. The girl stopped at the bottom and looked toward James, her eyes slightly unfocused as always. Now that he knew what to look for, he could easily see that her eyes didn't track people and objects.

His face twitched under her scrutiny. "What?"

A huge smile spread across her face. "You're glowing brighter. It's so beautiful. I wish you could see it."

James shook his head. "I... I'm gonna be straight with you, kid."

Alison's face fell. "Nothing ever good follows a sentence like that."

He took a deep breath. "We found the place where your mom was, and we, uh—"

She interrupted him. "I listen to the news, Mr. Brownstone. I know you think I'm just a kid, but I'm not an idiot. I heard about what happened. It's kind of a big deal, even on national news. They are calling it 'World War G.'"

"'World War G?'" Shay asked.

She nodded. "World War Gangster."

James rubbed the back of his neck. "A lot of that... violence...took place when we went in. We found your mom, but she was already in bad shape by then."

He didn't see any point in telling her that her mother had been brutally tortured. The perpetrators had been punished, and it'd do nothing more than give the girl nightmares.

Alison's lip quivered, and she gave a curt nod. "She's dead, right?" She swallowed.

"Yes. I'm sorry."

The girl sighed. "I kind of knew, I guess. But I don't understand why all this happened."

James paused for a moment to gather his thoughts.

He leaned forward in his chair, his hands clasped together as he tried to figure out the right words. "You're special, and she was special. More than you realize. Your mom wasn't from around here."

Alison retorted. "A lot of people aren't from California."

James managed a chuckle. "Your mom was two hundred and twelve years old, Alison. She was Oriceran; some sort of Drow princess."

Her face scrunched. "What's a Drow princess?"

Shay and James exchanged glances before he continued. "We're not totally sure on that, and we'll have to ask around, discreetly. We're gonna keep it to ourselves for now, so no one else comes after you."

Alison made her way to a love seat. "I guess that explains a lot of stuff, like why I can see what I can see, and my hair."

"Your hair?" James looked at it. Looked the same as it always had: black with frosted tips. "Did it change?"

While he hadn't had many girlfriends, he knew from his male friends that not noticing a girl had changed her hair was somehow breaking the unknown Eleventh Commandment.

Relationships with females violated the KISS principle.

"I don't dye my hair, Mr. Brownstone, and I know there are white parts. It didn't used to be like this. Dad told me to dye it all black when it started changing, but Mom wouldn't let him force me. Now I get why. It must be a Drow thing."

James thought about everything Nicole and Walt had said. He needed to tell the girl everything he knew.

"You'll probably get darker as you age; your skin, I mean. And, yeah, your hair will get lighter. Your mom had incredible magic, so maybe you'll get that, too. I just don't know."

Alison bit her lip and nodded. "What happens from here? I can't go back with my dad even if he wanted me."

James let out a breath he hadn't even realized he'd been holding. "I'm gonna take care of you. At least for now."

The girl looked down, her breathing shallow. She'd gone from having a family to having no one in a very short period. She was an orphan, something James knew more than a little about.

He'd been pondering whether to tell her about the wish ever since he'd learned about it. It was her birthright, but it was also a hell of a head trip. Considering the girl had just lost her mother, she didn't need more stress.

Nicole had suggested that James would know when the time was right. The bounty hunter was confused about the Drow people and Oriceran—let alone wishes—but something in his gut suggested the girl didn't need to know about it yet.

"You don't have to stay with me if you don't want to," James continued. "I'm not good with kids. If you have some other relatives, I can help you track them down. I'm not good with anyone, really, but I have space, and I'm clean." He was trying to at least sell the one part he might figure she could appreciate.

"Very fastidious," Shay muttered from the kitchen. She started filling a glass of water.

James let the verbal poke slide.

"I don't have any relatives that I know of." Alison smiled. "I wish to stay with you."

He stared at her for a moment, wondering if the word choice had been coincidental, or if there was some deeper meaning.

Guess I'll find out the hard way.

"Okay, kid, your funeral," James told her.

Alison laughed and looked towards the kitchen and Shay. "Is she gonna be my new mom, then?"

"WHAT?" Shay choked on her water, spewing the liquid onto her countertop. "No, no, no! I'm not old enough to be a mom. Uh, I'll be the aunt." She nodded, wearing a satisfied look on her face. "Yeah, that sounds perfect. I'm the aunt. Or the hot older sister."

"I like 'aunt' better," Alison declared.

James shrugged. "That's more than what I was going to ask. At least now when I ask you to babysit it'll be your niece, so you can't bitch too much."

After he finished speaking, he realized he might have to try to cut down on the amount of cursing he was doing, at least in front of the kid.

Alison frowned and shook her finger at him. "I don't need a babysitter. I'm a teenager, not a little girl."

And so it begins. He groaned mentally.

"Whatever. We'll figure it out later." James shrugged. His phone buzzed, and he pulled it out. "Oh, I almost missed it. Hey, do you mind if I watch some Barbeque Wars? With all this fun we've had lately, I don't even know what's happening on my favorite show."

"Be my guest," Shay offered. "The voice recognition's on for the TV."

"Don't you have a remote? I fuc—" James glanced at Alison and sighed. "I don't like voice recognition systems. They always have trouble with my voice. It's like they think I'm background noise or something."

Shay rolled her eyes. "You have the weirdest problems, Brownstone."

After thirty minutes of listening to James explain the finer points of sauce ingredient counterpoints and the advantages of different cooking temperatures, Alison excused herself and headed up to the guest room with a faint smile on her face.

Shay watched the girl as she walked up the stairs. The minute her back was turned, her smile had disappeared.

"I've got to go check on something," Shay announced. "I'll be back in a few minutes."

"Sure, okay." James barely nodded. He was too engrossed in one of the judges' acerbic takedowns of the perceived failure of a contestant's experimental "Divine Sauce."

"There's only one real God Sauce," he muttered. "And that's at Jessie Rae's. Fool shouldn't have stepped up if he couldn't really bring it."

Shay resisted a snort and hurried up the stairs and down the hall. When she stood in front of the guest room door, she knocked lightly.

"Come in," Alison called.

Shay opened the door. Alison was hugging the pillow on the bed, her eyes tear-streaked.

"Thought so," the older woman muttered. She sighed. "You don't have to hide if you want to cry about your mother, Alison."

The girl shook her head. "I didn't want Mr. Brownstone to see me like this. It'll make him feel bad, and he's already done so much."

Shay came in and sat next to her on the edge of the bed. "He may only have two settings when it comes to showing emotion, 'Asshole' or 'Clueless,' but that doesn't mean he expects you to be like that, too."

"You don't understand, Shay." Alison sniffled. "That's not what I'm worried about."

"Then explain it to me. I know about pain, Alison. I can't say I've always dealt with it well, but I do know what it can do to your heart and mind."

"I don't want to cry and make him feel worse." The teen sucked in a deep breath. "I can tell by the way he's talking and his energy that he blames himself. That he thinks he let me down, or something. I wanted my mom back, but it's not Mr. Brownstone's fault. It's my dad's, and those Harriken guys. I was happy when I heard about them being killed on the news."

Shay stared at Alison, taken aback by the girl's insight. They would have to stop underestimating her.

"Don't worry about Brownstone. Worry about yourself. He's the adult..." she waffled a moment. "well, adult-ish person, and you're the teenager. No one's gonna blame you for being sad over your mom dying. It's what we'd expect."

Alison nodded, but then her face twitched and she

threw her arms around Shay. The girl's restraint shattered, and she buried her face in the woman's chest.

"Mom," the girl sobbed.

They sat there on the bed like that for several minutes, Shay stroking Alison's hair while the girl cried a tsunami of tears over all that she'd lost. The tsunami became a mere wave, then finally a shallow trickle.

"Sorry," Alison sniffled out, her cheeks and eyes red. "I...I told myself that I wasn't gonna do this. I told myself I was gonna be strong."

Shay pulled away and smiled. "Leave the stone-faced attitude to Brownstone. You'll have years to learn to bottle up all your emotions in a screwed-up way like the rest of us. For now, revel in the fact you're still allowed to feel."

The sadness vanished from Alison's face, replaced by fiery anger.

Shay blinked, wondering if she'd said something to piss her off. Normally she wouldn't care, but kicking a grieving kid while she was down wasn't her style.

"I wish he hadn't let him go," Alison finally admitted.

Shay's eyes narrowed. "What are you talking about?"

"Mr. Brownstone. He let my dad go. He'll come back for me."

Shay snickered. "Don't worry about your dad. James made sure he would never come after you again."

Alison looked up with a question on her face, but no words emerged from her mouth. The girl exhaled softly and nodded.

Be glad you're not asking, kid. Sometimes it's better not to know for sure.

2

J ames took a deep pull of his Irish Stout and shifted on his stool, looking around the Leanan Sídhe. The place wasn't all that crowded that evening, which suited him fine.

He had come for the beer, not for drunken singing.

"Looking for Father O'Banion?" the bartender asked, as if reading his mind.

James shook his head. "Nah. Just haven't been in for a few days. Lots of crap has happened, and it makes you think. Trying to, you know, appreciate what I have and all that shit."

The bartender chuckled. "You need to get a few more beers in you. Then you won't have to worry about thinking, and you'll appreciate every second."

James raised his glass. "Working on it. You keep 'em coming, and we'll go until I can't think anymore."

A large man sat down next to James even though most of the stools were open, and the bounty hunter turned his head to check out the new arrival. Surprise washed through him as he realized it was Sergeant Mack.

The cop was in street clothes, which suggested he wasn't there on business.

"Sergeant Mack?" He eyed the man to make sure he had the right guy. "I don't think I've seen you around here before."

The cop looked around with a grin. "Yeah, this place isn't my vibe." He squinted for a moment as he read a sign on the wall. "Home of the Original Bard of Filth Competition." He looked at James.

The bounty hunter shrugged.

Sergeant Mack held up a hand. "You know what? I don't even want to know." He reached into his pocket and pulled out his phone. He tapped the screen a few times and held the phone up. Displayed on it was an image of Walt Anderson's fake confession.

"I should care about this because…" James asked.

"Let me give you a little hint, Brownstone," Mack told him politely. "You're good at going after bounties, but investigating crime is different."

James shrugged. "Not disagreeing. I've always said you guys have the harder job."

Mack chuckled. "Anyway, people generally leave behind suicide notes, not murder confessions right before they… um…shoot themselves. When they do confess, they like to do that shit face to face." He tapped his finger on the screen. "Plus, you didn't get all your DNA off this bad boy. You're a great bounty hunter, but a shitty criminal. Don't quit the day job, man."

James resisted a snort.

The cop sighed. "Next time don't leave this shit behind, okay? It makes it difficult to not follow up."

James locked eyes with Sergeant Mack. He'd fucked up, and the cops had caught him. There wasn't much he could do about it. He wasn't about to hurt a bunch of police officers.

"Just tell me that he deserved it," the cop requested.

"Does a man who gives his wife to the Harriken to be tortured deserve it? Does a man who plans to sell them his daughter for the same deserve it?"

"Guess we now know what was going on at Belmont House." He held up a hand to stop James from trying to explain. "The drones were conveniently jammed, so don't say anything to make me wonder. As far as we're concerned, a bunch of gangsters and mercs got into a shootout."

"Someone, not saying who, told me that Nicole Anderson was there but didn't make it. Because they tortured her for days." James curled his hands into fists.

Sergeant Mack's nostrils flared and anger flashed in his eyes. "Why did Anderson do it? I mean, I've seen wives murdered, but it's usually just to get rid of them to avoid an expensive divorce or insurance payout—not handing them over to gangsters for torture."

"Anderson found out his wife was Oriceran. Some other shit happened, but that seemed to be the main thing driving all this crap. He felt betrayed, and he obsessed about his daughter being a 'half-breed,' as he put it. Guy had issues."

Sergeant Mack looked down, his jaw rigid. "Jesus. You see so much shit in this job, but there's always someone ready to take it to the next level." He looked back up. "We followed up on the note, even though we knew it was bullshit. We've got DNA from that Harriken torture chamber. We could have tied him to it, you know. I'm not crying that he died, but it didn't have to go down that way."

James gulped down some beer. "Sometimes the wheels of justice turn too slowly, and we both know that it can be hard for some of these interspecies crimes to be successfully prosecuted. Hell, there was that guy who murdered that Light Elf kid a few months back… He got off with self-defense by claiming he thought the kid was cursing him. You also have assholes like the Humanity Defense League stirring up shit now."

"The HDL are just a bunch of loudmouths." Mack scoffed. "There's only so much they'll risk. I mean, you never know if you're dealing with some guy you can take down easily or a guy who can melt your brain, when it comes to fucking with Oricerans."

James let a feral grin take over his face. "An armed society is a polite society, and now anybody can be armed."

"Yep."

"Point stands," James continued. "The man who'd send his wife and kid to be tortured is less than a cockroach, and I don't give a shit about his reasons."

"Not saying I disagree, Brownstone. I'm just trying to make sure we're both on the same page on this."

"Whatever. We're on the same page." James finished his beer. "So what happens now?"

Sergeant Mack chuckled. "Nothing."

"Nothing?" James narrowed his eyes.

"I think you've misunderstood, or I guess I could say you've forgotten something."

James had no clue what the cop was getting at.

"Enlighten me," his gravelly voice ground out.

The cop stood and pushed the stool back into place. "Sometimes people get killed during bounties. I'm sure by the time I next check, I'll find out there was a bounty on Walt Anderson. I'll even go so far as to guess that the bounty was originally posted a week ago. The system, you know; it's shit, and has so many problems. It's gotten out of sync. As far as we're concerned at the station, Walt Anderson got killed during a retrieval gone bad."

James nodded slowly. If the cops were willing to look the other way, he wasn't going to make a big deal out of it. Society needed both his kind and their kind to function anymore.

"Understood." He shrugged. "I'll try not to make trouble for you in the future."

"We'd appreciate it. Only one last thing before I go: what about the girl? She's got no dad, no mom. Who is taking care of her?"

"Me. I'm watching her for now, and we'll go from there. Probably adoption."

It was Mack's turn to eye James. "Damn, Brownstone! Since when have you become such a family man?"

"Since her dying mother asked me to take care of her," He looked at Mack. "Allegedly."

Mack nodded slowly and shrugged. "Good enough for me. Just keep her safe." He turned to leave, then stopped and looked over his shoulder. "I'm having a little get-together this Sunday. Barbecue. Thought you might like to stop by."

"We friends now?" James wondered.

"Something like that. I think you're a man I want to get to know better."

James waved. "Then I'll be there."

A few days later, Alison and James were sitting together on his couch and the bounty hunter handed her a document. Shay watched from a chair, her legs crossed.

The girl scanned the paper with her fingers for a couple of minutes before looking up. "I don't understand what all this means."

"Don't worry. I had to have someone explain it to me, too. The short version is, after the house and property are sold, all that money will go into a trust for you. Once you turn eighteen you'll have full access to those funds, but before then the money can only be spent on things that are for your use and upkeep. Not that I planned to do anything else; it's for your protection." James took the document from her and set it on an end table. "I'll take care of getting everything sold, but you'll need to go through the house and figure out what things are worth keeping."

"Okay, I understand." Alison still looking a bit confused. "It's just... Wow. I don't even know where to start. I never thought I'd have to do this sort of thing until... Well, I guess it is what it is."

"I stopped by and did an initial evaluation," Shay told them.

Alison and James both asked. "You did?"

She winked at James, but spoke to Alison. "If there's one thing a field-archaeologist-slash-treasure-hunter is good at, it's quickly identifying valuable things. Mostly it'll be a matter of you figuring out what has sentimental value." Her grin vanished. "That said, I spotted some items that I'm pretty sure are magical artifacts."

Alison's eyes widened. "Magical artifacts? Seriously?"

Shay looked at James, and he nodded. They needed to give Alison as much control as possible in this situation.

It was her life.

"I can easily sell them for you, if you want," the woman offered. "We can get some good money for anything magical, even if it's not super-powerful. I can also make sure they only get sold to decent people and not scumbags."

"But from selling the house and everything, I'll have good money anyway, right?" Alison asked. "I mean, it's not like I'll need more money, if I understand all this."

"Nope," James answered, the conviction in his voice removing any doubt Alison or Shay might have had.

The girl sighed. "Then I don't want to sell them. They must have belonged to Mom, and I want to keep them. If it's okay?" She looked toward James, her eyes pleading.

"Your choice, kid. We'll keep them safe for you."

"Not in the warehouse," Shay muttered. "I don't like that place."

"You have a warehouse?" Alison asked.

"Not exactly," James replied. "But the stuff would be safer there than in a bank."

Shay glared at him, and he shrugged.

"Okay, okay." James put up his hands. "We'll set up a

safe deposit box and get a key for you, Alison." He took a deep breath. The next part was the bigger deal. "In any case, you'll have more than enough money to take care of you, but I don't think that's the most important thing we need to talk about."

Alison frowned. "What do you think is the most important thing?"

"Your mother was powerful, which means you're powerful—or at least half powerful, and that's still pretty damn impressive, considering what she was capable of. I've looked into it, and I found a place I think might be good for you. The government's pretty shi— Not great about handling a lot of this Oriceran stuff, but they do seem to know that control of power is better than suppression of use."

"I don't understand. What are you talking about?"

"There's a school. It's called the School of Necessary Magic. It's a place where you could learn to control and manage the powers you have. A place where you'd be safe, and around kids your age."

Alison's face fell. "You want to send me away?" she asked, the tremble in her voice revealing that she was scared.

James shook his head. "You'll have vacations, summer breaks, and parent weekends. You'll spend those with me, or I'll be there with you. I don't want to send you away, but I can't help you learn to control your magic. This school can, but it's your decision in the end."

Alison looked down and gave a shallow nod. "It's kind of weird." She chuckled. "I can see souls—and I never thought that was weird because I grew up with it—but the idea of going to a magic school kind of freaks me out a little. My mom made me read all the Harry Potter books and the Arcane Academy series. They made magic schools seem so dangerous."

James laughed. "Just stories, kid. This is the real deal. And Los Angeles is plenty dangerous as is." He shrugged. "You'll do great, and I'll be always ready to help you out."

"Me, too," Shay told Alison.

"And like I said, it's your decision," James said. "If you hate the school, you can come back and live with me full-time."

Alison moved closer and threw her arms around James, squeezing him tightly. "Thank you, Mr. Brownstone. Thank you for everything."

He patted her on the back. "You're welcome, kid."

James sat out on his back deck, looking up into the stars and sipping a beer. He couldn't help but wonder what the stars looked like from Oriceran. Astronomy had never interested him much; he'd always taken the stars in the sky for granted.

Shay slid open the door leading to the deck and stepped out, closing the door. "You're a damn good man, James Brownstone."

He grunted. "I think there are a lot of Harriken who'd disagree."

"I'm not all that interested in the opinions of ruthless gangsters who tortured a tied-up woman," she told him, taking a seat near him. She grabbed his beer from his hand

and took a swallow, the whole time daring him to say one word. She leaned back over to give it back to him.

James didn't miss a beat. "Just sayin'. The line between me and some of the guys I catch is pretty thin."

"You're a guy who is helping a girl who needs it," Shay told him firmly. "Just take the compliment, Brownstone. It's not the end of the world if people actually like you and think you're a nice guy."

"I'm just not sure about a lot of things. When it's just me it's easy, but with a kid everything will be different." James sighed.

"Welcome to parenthood." Shay shrugged.

"Do you think I'm doing the right thing, sending her to that school?"

"I think that if she's one-tenth as powerful as her mother she'll need a safe place to explore that power, and that school sounds like the best place for that." Shay pursed her lips. "Less concerned about that than the wish. When are you planning to tell her?"

James shrugged. "I honestly don't know. This was something her mom wanted for her, so that means I have to think about it like a parent. I'm playing this all by ear. I was an orphan raised by the Church. I don't really know what it means to be a parent, let alone a parent who controls an actual freaking wish."

Shay chuckled darkly. "My parents were shit, which is probably why I went down the path I did."

James took a swallow of his beer as he gazed into the heavens. "I had no parents, and yours were horrible, Shay. With a bar that low, I don't see how we can do worse."

3

James Brownstone eyed his foe.

He'd told himself he'd stop after annihilating the last nine, but he couldn't help himself.

He snatched a tenth pot sticker and threw it in his mouth, letting the savory flavor linger. Chinese food didn't match the glories of good ol' American barbeque, but no one could say it wasn't tasty.

"Damn, Brownstone." Shay eyed him from across her dining room table. "I don't get why you're not fat, considering the way you eat." The woman brushed a few rogue strands of dark hair out of her eyes.

He covered his mouth. "Ass-kicking burns a lot of calories. It helps."

"True enough."

James glanced at the stairs. Alison had wandered to the guest room for some sleep about thirty minutes prior.

He wanted to make sure that impressionable teenage ears did not overhear the conversation to follow.

The girl was still getting over the loss of her mother

and the betrayal of her father, and what she needed now was stability and continuity. James was determined to provide that, although he was probably the last person who should be taking care of anyone.

Even though he was still figuring out the whole foster parent/guardian role, the bounty hunter knew that showing weakness or uncertainty in front of the girl would only make her worry.

He'd failed to save her mom from the Harriken, but he damn well wouldn't fail *her*.

"You said earlier you wanted to talk about the School of Necessary Magic," James said, his deep and rumbling voice as intimidating as ever.

To most people, at least. The woman on the other side of the table didn't seem to mind.

Shay nodded. "I decided to look into the school from my side of things."

"Why? You think I didn't do a good job? I know how to check into shit, Shay. I'm a bounty hunter."

She eyed him with her lips pressed together. "Don't get your panties in a twist, Brownstone. I don't think you did a shitty job. I used to kill people for a living, so I have some dirtier sources of information than you might."

James offered a curt nod of acknowledgement.

Shay's new life as a field archaeologist was earning her money and a good reputation.

She'd been reluctant to admit the truth about her past, but she now seemed a lot more comfortable discussing it with him. It was as if a weight had been lifted off her shoulders.

"What'd they find?" he asked.

She moved her fork in a circle. "Nothing really. The government is supporting the school...in a good way."

He eyed her. "What would be a bad way?"

Shay shrugged. "Using it to manufacture magical super-soldiers. MK Ultra II, that sort of thing."

James responded with one of his trademark grunts. "Okay, so it's not a bad place. Seems safe."

He frowned.

Xavier's School for Gifted Youngsters had been a safe place too until they'd attacked it.

"It's not a hidden school for hated mutants or anything," Shay interrupted his thoughts. "Too many kids there from powerful and important families. People might have issues with Oricerans, but at the end of the day everyone wants every advantage, and there's no bigger advantage out there right now than magic."

James stared at Shay, not caring about the explanation as much as her first sentence.

"How the hell did you know what I was thinking?" He scrubbed his face with a hand. "Wait, did you pick up some sort of mind-reading artifact on your last job?" The last thing Shay needed was unfiltered access to his mind.

Shay snickered, a faint glint of amusement in her eyes. "It's because you're not that complicated. Did you forget that I was here for your stupid classics of super-hero cinema marathon last week?" She shrugged. "Though I agree with you... The originals, except for the third one, are way better than the remakes. The point is, Brownstone, I know how your mind works."

"Thinking you know and knowing are two separate things."

"Sure, sure. Keep telling yourself that." She took a bite of her food. "Anyway, I was thinking about this the other day. I think I should go with you."

James furrowed his brow. "To the school?"

"Yes, to the school." She pointed her knife at him as if she were using it to make a point. "You don't know how to act around normal people, Brownstone, or even non-normal people. You'll probably insult someone and get turned into a toad or something." She went back to eating.

He grabbed another pot sticker, number eleven. "I'm not the person who beat down a random guy in the bar the night we met."

Shay glared at him. "That guy grabbed my ass. We aren't talking a random accident, we are talking full-bore pinch-an-inch. He got what was coming to him." She held up a hand. "Let me rephrase my earlier statement. I'm coming with you. Alison needs all the help she can get, and as her aunt I insist I go."

He grabbed number twelve. "Whatever. The more, the merrier. I'll have to let them know you're coming. They were clear about specifying exactly who would visit, and said if I didn't do that we wouldn't be able to find the school."

"Huh?" She looked up and grabbed the last pot sticker before Cro-Magnon Man snagged them all. "You mean you wouldn't be allowed in?"

James shook his head. "Nope. They said I wouldn't be able to find the school."

Jiro Ikeda walked down the dimly-lit hallway. Tattooed men in dark suits lined the entire length; his brothers, fellow Harriken.

Every man bore a wakizashi at his side, ready to engage any who dared attack their organization by blade or bullet.

His pulse thundered in his ears, and his stomach churned.

It'd been three years since the last full Executive Meeting, and the man had no doubts about why they'd called this one. Few such meetings ended without punishment. The only question was whether that punishment would be fatal.

Two enforcers at the end of the hallway bowed to him and opened the broad wooden double doors.

Jiro stepped inside. A low table had been placed in the center of the large room, and a single floating orb provided the only illumination. The magic lighting was new. Perhaps Grandfather wanted to demonstrate his increasing power.

The man bore no actual relation to Jiro, but as head of the Harriken, he'd earned their ultimate title of respect.

Thirty men knelt in front of the table and Grandfather sat in a chair, both literally and figuratively above them all. Unlike the other men in the room, he wore a purple kimono instead of a suit.

"How wonderful of you to join us finally, Ikeda," Grandfather said in accented English.

Jiro bowed deeply and then knelt at an empty spot at the table. The slight of Grandfather greeting him in English didn't go unnoticed.

Failure harmed the Harriken, and anything that harmed the Harriken would be destroyed.

"Good, we are all finally here," Grandfather said, shifting into Japanese. "I apologize for forcing you to travel so far on such short notice." His cool gaze locked on Jiro. "Events in America have forced this gathering, and I thought it important that everyone be present as we explore the recent failures that have harmed our organization and our future."

Everyone turned to stare at Jiro, who steeled his features. Failure was part of life. The important thing was to learn from it.

Though he might not survive to do that.

"Explain yourself, Ikeda," Grandfather said, his voice still as calm as a spring breeze. "Explain why so many of our men lie dead in Los Angeles and one of our buildings was a burned cinder. You are responsible for American operations, so the failure of the men in Los Angeles is your failure. You've seriously crippled our expansion plans."

Jiro bowed his head. "What I set in motion should have increased the strength of the Harriken, even if there were some...operational failures."

"Strength? Strength comes from killing your enemies, not from dying." Grandfather tilted his head, resting his elbow on an armrest and his head in the palm of his hand. He looked more like a bored teenager than the head of a vicious international criminal group.

"The men in Los Angeles... That is, we came into possession of something unusual; special. Oriceran. A woman, a Drow princess."

Even if he hadn't been running the operation directly,

his responsibility for it dictated that he must speak as if he had been directly involved. Anything less would lessen the respect of the men in the room for him.

Grandfather's lip curled in a sneer. "Foreigners are disgusting enough. These alien creatures are even more so. What do I care for Oricerans, royalty or otherwise?"

Jiro saw his chance. Tradition would always fall before greed. "This Drow princess possessed the ability to grant a wish. It is powerful magic."

"Interesting. And how did you contain such a creature if she was so powerful?"

"We acquired rare and special rope that drained her power through black magic. For us to gain the wish, she had to give it up willingly." Jiro gave a light shrug. "She proved reluctant, so we tried to force it out of her through torture."

Grandfather drummed his fingers along the side of his chair. "But you failed."

"There were...complications. She proved surprisingly resilient."

"Elaborate on these complications. If you had this woman restrained, that implies there were additional issues?"

Jiro took a deep breath. "There were no survivors from the attack on the location where we kept the Drow princess, but there was a single survivor from the first attack. He gave us information, and I had a few other local Harriken subjected to...aggressive questioning to confirm what had happened. I also discreetly inquired around the area."

Every man in that room understood that Jiro had

ordered those Harriken tortured, just as he understood he was on the verge of torture or death for his failures as the leader of the American branch.

Grandfather continued to look more bored than angry. "And what did your questioning reveal?"

"The Los Angeles branch under Takahashi involved outside forces; a bounty hunter named James Brownstone."

The other man quirked a brow. "You expect me to believe a single bounty hunter killed that many of our men?"

"There...was a woman with him, I believe."

Grandfather jumped from his seat, his face red with rage. He stabbed a finger at Jiro. "A man and a woman would not have been strong enough to butcher our men!"

Jiro looked down, swallowing and awaiting the execution order. A dozen guards lined the room, cloaked in the shadows in their dark suits. A word from Grandfather would end his life in seconds.

"This Brownstone," Jiro continued when the word didn't come. "He's not normal. He's some sort of ogre or evil spirit. He apparently has a reputation for unusual strength. They call him 'the Granite Ghost.'"

Grandfather smoothed his features and gave Jiro a cold smile, all trace of the rage gone. He sat back down before he spoke. "Interesting. Maybe he is another sort of Oriceran, or has availed himself of the magic that has returned. Why would such a creature involve himself in our dealings? Was he an ally of this Oriceran woman you tortured?"

"Two of the Los Angeles men were sent to capture the woman's daughter to force her cooperation, but Brownstone was there. He stopped the men, and..." Jiro sighed as silently as possible.

"Finish," Grandfather commanded. "My patience runs thin."

"The local branch... We decided to teach him a lesson, so our men went to his home, killed his dog, and left it there for him to find. He reacted more extremely than had been expected, and from what we can tell, all his later involvement was because we killed his dog."

Grandfather burst into a hearty laugh. The other Harriken exchanged glances, confusion on their faces. Jiro kept his head down, waiting for his superior to finish.

"A dog?" Grandfather scoffed. "We lost all those men because of a fucking dog?" He shook his head. "You, will of course repay Mr. Brownstone, Jiro. Please make sure he joins the dog he loved so much very soon."

"Yes, Grandfather. There's another matter as well."

The man leaned forward. "Tell me, Ikeda."

"A unit working for the Grayson company was involved in the second battle. They were wiped out as well."

"By Brownstone and this woman?"

Jiro nodded. "We're unsure how to best handle the situation with Grayson. The mercenaries knew the risk, but they are pressuring us for more information on what happened to their men."

Grandfather leaned forward. "How much were they to be paid for the job?"

"Ten thousand dollars a man."

"Tell them that if they kill Brownstone, we will make up every one of their deaths at a price of twenty-five thousand a man. A million to kill one man. Very generous, I think, especially since they too proved incompetent."

"Yes, Grandfather."

For the first time since entering the room, Jiro allowed some hope to enter his heart. If he was receiving orders, that meant he wouldn't be killed.

Grandfather let out a long sigh. "There is one last matter, Ikeda. A failure below reflects a failure above."

Jiro's jaw tightened. "It is as you say."

"Are you left-handed or right-handed?"

"Right-handed."

Jiro locked eyes with Grandfather. This was the time to show his bravery. He could still make up for the failures in Los Angeles. He shoved his left arm out, resting his arm on the table.

Grandfather paused, staring at the hand offered before nodding to someone behind Jiro. A huge guard stepped forward, sword in hand.

"You will pay for your failure with your left hand. Next time, I won't be so generous."

"Yes, Grandfather."

The guard lifted the sword and brought it down in a powerful stroke.

Jiro didn't scream as his hand parted from his body.

Brownstone pushed his way into the Leanan Sídhe.

Customers jammed the Irish pub, chatting, drinking, and laughing. It was busier in the bar than James had seen it in the last few weeks.

A quick look around the bar located his target, an attractive if slightly pudgy older man in the back. The Professor, aka Father O'Banion, aka Dr. FJ Smite-Williams, sat alone in a booth.

The bounty hunter navigated toward the Professor through the happy and not-so-happy drunks who filled the bar. The white-haired man waved to him, and James slipped into a seat across the table.

"I've got good news, lad." The Professor's eyes were slightly red. "That's why I asked you to come."

He spoke clearly and his face wasn't red, which suggested the Professor hadn't downed that many drinks yet. Had he done so, Father O'Banion would have been unleashed. Two beer-filled glasses sat in front of him, so the night might have just started.

To James' surprise, the Professor slid one of them across the table.

"What's this?" he asked.

"Irish Stout. It's on me," he answered. "Enjoy it."

James picked up his glass and took a sip of the beer, enjoying the roasted barley flavor. "So what's the news?"

"I might have access to that certain item you asked me about. It took some doing, let me tell you."

The bounty hunter stared at the Professor for a moment, trying to judge his tone. There were few people better when it came to information about magical artifacts —and the man hadn't steered James wrong so far—but it didn't hurt to be careful.

"And?"

"Reciprocity, lad. Reciprocity. I can get it to you, and in

exchange, I need something. I need your help, along with that of the fair Ms. Carson."

James shook his head. "I can't speak for Shay, only for me."

The Professor sighed. "Sometimes, lad, the two who need to see reality are the two who don't have a clue."

James' eyes narrowed. "What the fuck does that even mean? I'm not in the mood for riddles."

The Professor chuckled. "That means you need more beer in you." He picked up his glass and took a sip. "It means, tell Shay I'll pay her to help you get this item. If you agree, send me a text, and we'll have another little chat here about what the service might entail."

James grunted. "It's not like you to be so mysterious."

"The problem is, I'm not drunk enough to give a shit." The Professor picked up his glass and swallowed some beer before wiping a bit of foam off his smiling face. "Time to remedy that!"

4

J ames stared at the single medium-sized pink suitcase in his living room.

It didn't seem like nearly enough for a girl about to start a new life at a magical boarding school.

Maybe they had some secret street where students bought all their shit on the first day?

He looked at the suitcase, then at Alison. "This is it? You sure? I paid for the flight upgrade, so you can bring whatever you need."

Alison shrugged. "What do I need more for? I can't see my clothes, so I don't care much about having a zillion different outfits. I have my phone and my adaptive braille reader."

James nodded.

Alison's ability to perceive living energy and souls made her movements different than a normal blind person's. Sometimes he'd go a whole day and forget that she couldn't see. For that matter, she couldn't even use a notepad and pencil.

She looked down. "And I don't want to risk bringing all those special things that Shay found. I want to keep them in the safe deposit box for now. Maybe I'll pick them up later."

"Your choice, kid. I can always send them by mail or special courier or something."

Alison nodded quickly.

"Well, we should at least get you a backup reader and backup braille phone," James said. "Shi... Do you know a good place? We have plenty of time for a little shopping before the flight."

The great thing about booking first class on a super-sonic flight and paying the upgrade fee was that they'd be able to get through the lines quickly. The ridiculous price of the tickets might almost be worth it.

"I do know a good place." Alison grinned. "Want me to drive there?"

He looked at her. "Very funny. Just tell me where, and let's get going."

"Shay's still coming with us to the school, isn't she?"

"Yeah, she's coming. We'll pick her up after we buy your stuff."

Alison looked at him, her eyes unfocused as usual, but the curiosity on her face telling him everything she was thinking.

Here it comes. More matchmaker bullshit.

"You don't seem happy, Mr. Brownstone. The mention of Shay always gets you worked up."

"I'm fine, kid."

A coy smile appeared on Alison's face. "Sure. Forget I asked." She gave him a mock salute.

First the Professor, and now a kid is busting my balls about Shay? Fuck.

The trip to the store went quickly, which was fine by James. Shopping for anything other than barbecue-related items didn't excite him much.

Money wasn't a concern when a man lived simply and caught as many high-level bounties as he did each month. That still didn't save him from sticker shock over the prices of the devices.

The pair had piled back into his polished black extended-cab Ford F-350 and almost reached Shay's house when he let his surprise finally get to him.

"Who knew all this braille-tech crap was so expensive?" James muttered.

"*I* knew," Alison told him. "You could have just asked me."

"Sorry, kid. I didn't mean anything by it. I was just surprised."

The teen sighed and looked down. "You sure it's not a big deal? My dad used to tell me if I ever broke any of my devices I'd never get a new one."

James gritted his teeth.

The last person he wanted to be compared to was Walt Anderson. The sonofabitch had turned his wife over to the Harriken to be tortured, and tried to give his daughter to them to steal the wish owed the girl.

The wish James now controlled.

Not a good time to tell her. *I'm gonna have to trust my gut on this.*

"Money's not an issue," he told her. "Don't worry about it. I don't want you to worry about anything but what you need. We've got plenty of money for you in the trust, and I've got plenty of money myself."

"No offense, Mr. Brownstone, but you live in a pretty crappy neighborhood for a guy with a lot of money. I don't get why that is."

James snort-laughed. "I like my house. It keeps things simple, and if my work ever follows me home, the people in the neighborhood have the common sense to stay the fu—"

He sighed. Controlling his mouth around the girl was harder than he'd ever expected. "They know to stay out of the way. Some rich idiot might poke his nose into trouble, and the last thing I want is for somebody to get caught up in my stuff."

"Ever thought about stopping?" Alison asked quietly.

"Stopping?"

"Bounty hunting. You have a lot of money, right? I'm betting you could never work a day again and not have to worry about money. All you ever do is sit at home watching cooking shows, or going to that dumb bar with their perverted song contests."

"Huh? How do you know about that?" James grimaced. "And I don't participate."

Alison scoffed. "They advertise it on their website. 'Bard of Filth Competition?' Gross."

"Stay off shady websites," he told her. "And anyway, I

don't hunt for the money."

"Why do you do it then?"

James turned left. They were almost to Shay's house.

"I do it because Harriken garbage try to kidnap kids like you, or some shifter decides he likes to hunt prey who walk on two legs. Or some jerk who just likes blowing stuff up. This is a big world. It's beautiful and ugly at the same time, and I'm trying to pretty it up by taking out the trash."

James spared a glance the girl's way. She was looking down with a worried look on her face.

"I can't help you if you don't tell me what's on your mind, kid."

Alison sighed. "I just worry, Mr. Brownstone."

"About what?"

"About you getting hurt or killed."

"I don't get hurt, kid. Bad guys get hurt."

"There's always someone bigger and tougher, Mr. Brownstone. What if some dragon comes to Earth and starts stirring up trouble?"

"Then I'll change my name to 'Dragonslayer.'" James made the final turn onto Shay's block. Her townhouse stood at the end. "I can't quit, kid, but I can be careful."

They pulled up to the curb in front of it.

James snickered as he took in the small but carefully manicured lawn. This was the kind of neighborhood Alison probably would have preferred he'd live in.

Shay's door opened, and she stepped out and waved before setting her security.

She carried a silver metal briefcase as she hurried to the truck. The field archaeologist opened the back door and hopped in, setting the briefcase at her feet.

James glanced over his shoulder at Shay and nodded. The briefcase wasn't his business, and if the woman wanted it to be, she'd tell him.

That didn't mean he couldn't wonder. He only worried that she'd have some trouble getting it past security at the airport, but then he remembered who he was dealing with.

A treasure hunter with a past as a professional killer wasn't the kind of woman who'd get caught by some bored TSA agent.

"This won't take long," James assured them, pulling up in front of a church. "Just have to talk to Father McCartney for a quick moment."

"I'm fine. Not going into a church," Shay muttered.

"I wonder what kind of religion my mom believed in," Alison said.

James and Shay both looked at the girl.

She'd grown up believing her mother was just another normal human, and not secretly a two hundred and twelve-year-old Drow princess with insane magical powers. Fitting in with human society had probably meant not flaunting beliefs that weren't common on your planet, let alone your neighborhood.

Even now Alison looked normal enough, the only external hint of her otherworldly heritage the natural white ends on her dark hair.

"Maybe that's something you can find out at the school," Shay suggested. "There are Oricerans there. Some of them might be as old as your mom was."

Alison smiled. "I hadn't thought of it that way."

James patted the girl on the shoulder and stepped out of his truck. The teen still seemed very hesitant about going to the School of Necessary Magic, so it was good for her to at least see some advantage to it other than learning to control magic she hadn't even known about a few weeks before.

He stepped into the church, spotting a few familiar faces and giving them a polite nod. An elderly man he didn't recognize gasped when he saw James, but didn't say anything.

Not a big surprise. With his mottled skin and ridges, he had a visage only a dog could love—and now even his dog was dead. His tattoos probably didn't help.

Hey, Jesus walked among the sinners, pal.

James threw the guy a smile as he strolled toward the confessional. He'd confessed many horrible sins in that booth, so the man was probably right to assume he was about to admit to some violence or evil crime and beg for forgiveness.

With that thought in mind, the bounty hunter slid open the confessional and sat.

A few moments later movement on the other side caught his attention, and the grate was pulled back.

"Forgive me, Father, I'm not here to confess any sins today."

"Then why have youse come to the confessional, child?" The strong hint of Father McCartney's native Jersey accent hinted at stronger irritation than normal.

Must have been having a bad day.

James could understand. It had to be frustrating dealing

with a bastard like him, but he wanted the priest to understand he wasn't disrespecting God's house.

"I wanted to talk to you about helping you out, and I felt more comfortable doing it in this booth than your office."

The priest chuckled and some of the tension left his voice. "This booth is like a second home for you. You spend more time here than any other member of the parish. Fine, what is it, then?"

"I wanted to give you something to help with the parish's money problems." James pulled out his phone and tapped a few keys. "Check your phone."

The rustling of cloth was the only noise James heard for a few seconds. It always gave James an anachronistic jolt when he saw the priest in his vestments pull out a smartphone.

There was a pause before the father finally spoke. "I don't understand what I'm looking at. You've transferred me ten thousand packets of experimental barbecue sauce?"

James laughed. "No, it's shares of stock in a specialty sauce company I invested in a long time ago. Very low volume, so the stock price is kind of all over the place, but I've got a good feeling that if you hold them for about a week the price might go up, and then you can sell. Just be patient. I'm pretty sure it'll pop to a decent share price soon, at least twice the current amount. Then you'll have plenty of money for the parish and the orphanage that doesn't come from bounties."

"I see. I'm not much for the stock market, but I'm very, very grateful for this. I'll do what you say and watch it for a week."

"I have a good feeling about this stock, Father."

The priest murmured, "This is a generous gift, James."

James shook his head. "I bought it when it was super-cheap. Just been lucky, and wanted to share my wealth to help the church and the orphanage."

"Go with God, then. I thank you, and I'm sure the children will thank you."

James slid open the door and stepped out of the booth, giving the suspicious guy another grin before striding out of the church. He wasn't sure if fucking with people's minds in a church was a sin, but he figured he'd bring it up at his next confession.

Once outside, he slowed his pace and pulled out his phone. He scrolled through his contacts and finally dialed a number.

"Hello," answered the man on the other end. "This is Stephen."

"This is Brownstone."

"It's been a while… Does this mean…" His swallow was audible over the line. "Wait, how the hell did you even get this number?"

"I'm a bounty hunter, numbnuts," James retorted. "I'm actually just interested in some stock action today. You're a stockbroker. You can do that, can't you?"

"Technically. You know I'm not licensed anymore, Brownstone. It'd be against the law for me to help you."

James scoffed. "Are you in the game or not?" He paused outside his truck, lifting a finger to Shay to let her know he would still be a moment.

"Okay, okay. A man's got to make a living, right?"

"Sure. The problem comes when you making a living

includes helping some bastard apocalypse-worshipping cult launder a shit-load of money, and that cult is able to use their cleaned money to stockpile the crap needed for a massive terrorist attack."

"I didn't fucking know what the Children of Fenrir were up to, Brownstone," Stephen hissed. "I can't go to prison. If I do, those fuckers will have me dead within a week. They have access to serious magic!"

"Some would say the real magic is financial fraud, but that's all the more reason to stay out of prison. So maybe you should play nice with me."

"Wait...you're not coming for me? I thought you told me if you ever called me again, it was because I was going down."

James chuckled. "No, I just need you to drive up the price of a penny stock. I own a bunch, but I'm going to buy a bunch more shares to drive up the price. Can you spread those buys out through the...friends you told me about before, so it doesn't all look like it's coming from me?" He rattled off the ticker symbol for Experimental Sauces, Inc. "This week about ten thousand shares of the stock are going to be sold, and I need the price to be high as possible before that happens."

"Wait, you're going to sell those shares?"

"No, not me. Someone else."

Stephen sighed. "Don't you get how this works, Brownstone? You should sell right now. If you don't, the price is going to drop once those shares are sold, especially..." he paused for a second, and James assumed he was looking up the stock "with a volatile micro-cap penny stock like this. I can set up a stop order for you so at least you don't take a bath on what you have, but I recommend you sell right now, not double-down like a dumbass."

"No, no. You don't get it—I don't want to sell, even after the price drop."

Stephen groaned. "What is this, some sort of weird tax write-off thing? You hoping to lose money? Because you're about to shovel in a bunch of money to prop up some stock and then not exit. It's supposed to be a pump and dump, Brownstone, not pump and hold. It's the opposite of savvy investment."

James wanted to rub his eyes. "I'm keeping my stock in that company. Someday they are going to be the biggest star in sauces. I just need this temp spike to help somebody else out."

"Why? I don't get this. How does this even benefit you?"

James glanced at the worn stone church behind him. "Because my church has fallen on hard times. So you need to get this done."

"Church, huh? I wonder if this little stock scheme will get me brownie points with God."

"I'm sure God knows when you're doing shit just for points, Stephen. Don't worry about God, just worry about yourself and staying out of prison."

"Okay, okay. I'll get it done, but are we square?"

James snorted. "Hell, no. I just won't come looking for you right now. So you do what I need, and do your family right. They are the only reason I let you go before. Understand?"

"I do. And thanks."

The call ended.

Not blood money, Father. Just me robbing myself to pay Paul.

5

"I had a reservation for a truck," James grumbled.

"Are you still bitching about that?" Shay snickered. "Afraid someone's gonna question your manhood if they catch you in a mom car? Plenty of big strong men drive around in family SUVs, Brownstone."

"I like the car," Alison chirped from the backseat. "It's comfortable, and it's not as hard to get into."

"My truck is comfortable," James muttered. "Even if it is tall. Besides, the whole point of having a fuc— Having a reservation is that they are supposed to *reserve* the vehicle for you. The word is in the actual other word."

The teen giggled, and the bounty hunter decided to drop his complaining for now. There were worst things in the world than being forced to drive a light silver Chevy SUV around. Not many, but they did exist.

They pulled off the main road onto a curving side road. The flight from LAX to Richmond International had gone smoothly enough, even with Shay insisting the male flight attendant in first class was checking her out the entire time. He wasn't about to let her kick someone's ass on a plane.

Dealing with the security would have complicated things.

The closer Charlottesville airport couldn't handle supersonic flights, which forced them to Richmond and added another hour to the trip—but that still beat taking a regular flight directly into Charlottesville by almost four hours. It might have not been a cost-efficient travel plan, but it was definitely a time-efficient one.

Rolling green hills dotted the lightly forested area, with only the occasional recessed home or mansion in the distance at the end of a private road. There wasn't a skyscraper or graffiti-covered alley in sight.

James hated it. It was all too bright and natural.

The air even smelled fresh.

"We're almost there, according to the GPS," James told them.

"Is it bad that I'm nervous?" Alison asked.

He shook his head. "Change can mess with people, kid. It's understandable. And you've been through a lot."

"You'll do fine," Shay added. "Everyone here is special, just like you."

A tall and elaborate wrought-iron fence extended past both sides of the road ahead. An imposing gate sat in the center, bisecting the drive leading up a hill. Dense trees clogged the verges.

James slowed the SUV as they approached the fence, looking for some sort of security guard. A man in an ill-fitting suit walked away from the gate, a camera with a large telescopic lens hanging around his neck.

James pulled up beside the man and rolled down his window. "Is this the school?"

The man blinked at him. "The school. Yes, I was supposed to...something about taking pictures at the school. What was I doing here again?"

Way too early to be drunk, pal. Even Father O'Banion waits until nighttime. Sometimes, at least.

The man with the camera shook his head and continued trudging up the road and muttering to himself.

"Okay, that was weird." Shay watched the guy wander off.

James shrugged and drove up to the gate. "They didn't say anything about who to call. I assumed there'd be someone here."

"Maybe it'll magically know who we are." Shay laughed.

The gates swung open as if pushed by invisible forces. No obvious mechanism was visible.

James glanced into his rearview mirror, in which the man's silhouette was still visible. The school had been rather insistent that he let them know exactly who was coming.

He suspected some sort of passive magical defense the school needed to explicitly disarm. Judging by the camera, the poor man in the suit was probably a reporter trying to write a story about the school, and he hadn't planned on dealing with that kind of spell.

James resisted frowning. That was serious magic. Then again, such magical knowledge was the whole reason they were bringing the girl there.

"Guess you'll have to get used to that kind of thing, Alison."

"What?"

"Oh, sorry, kid. The gate opened itself. I'm assuming it's some sort of magic thing." James pulled through the gate, which swung closed behind him.

Their trip took several more minutes, until a large building surrounded by a few smaller buildings appeared in the distance. The trees grew sparser.

Alison gasped and jerked her head to the side. "Wow. The energy is... It's so beautiful."

James glanced to the side to see what had caught her attention. "You've got to be fucking kidding me," he murmured.

A white unicorn tromped along the side of the road. He would have sworn faint sparkles surrounded the thing.

There was movement on the opposite side of the road as well. Another hoofed creature floated among the trees, eyeing the car with wide reptilian eyes.

A lightly flaming halo burned around it.

The creature looked like some sort of strange cross between an elk and a small dragon. It had jade-colored scales covering its body, antlers protruded from its head, and a soft mane of white fur around its neck.

"What the hell is that?" James asked

Shay stared at the creature and shook her head. "Not sure, but I think it's a Kirin. Kind of like the Asian version of... Hell, I don't even know what to compare them to. They are supposed to be wise and benevolent and all that."

"Its soul is as beautiful as the unicorn's. The other thing was a unicorn, right? The energy shape kind of seemed that way."

"Yeah." James shook his head and took a deep breath. "Welcome to magic school, I guess."

They didn't spot any more bizarre creatures before they arrived at the main school, a huge extended Georgian manor surrounded by a constellation of smaller buildings. Teens of various ages in uniforms wandered the grounds, some with backpacks. Pointed ears protruded from more than a few of the students' heads.

Two students who looked a year or two older than Alison appeared to be balancing scintillating balls of pulsing light on their hands. Another girl, a Light Elf who looked like she'd only recently made it out of grade school, leaned over and shook her finger at what appeared to be a ferret.

James refused to believe it *was* a ferret. Normal animals didn't stand on two legs or wear rodent-sized suits and top hats. Hell, *humans* didn't even wear top hats anymore.

Why did everything magical have to be so freaking complicated and weird?

Alison smiled brightly, and James took a deep breath. She could see the true nature of the place—the very souls of the people and creatures around them—and if she thought they were okay, that had to count for something.

He parked in a circular drive surrounding an elaborate fountain resembling a bird on fire. A phoenix, he assumed.

You're not the only one who's read a book or two, Shay.

Smaller roads led off in a couple of directions and he wondered if there was a parking lot, but the email they'd sent him indicated had that he should park in the circular drive.

They filed out of the car, with James surveying the area.

Tactically it didn't seem well-defended, with lots of blind spots infiltrators could take advantage of, let alone a forest that could hide an entire mercenary battalion.

Of course, that same forest was filled with Kirin, unicorn, and God knew what else. If he was right about the gate, it might be hard for normal humans to even get close to the main school grounds.

James rubbed the back of his neck, trying not to frown. If anything, all the fantastical displays proved that the School of Necessary Magic would be able to help Alison learn to control her abilities.

"Good afternoon, sir," said a student, a fresh-faced Light Elf.

"Uh, yeah, same to you," James rumbled back.

A few of the other kids waved, and he nodded. If he could make it the next thirty minutes without cussing or insulting anyone, he'd be doing okay.

Shay helped Alison grab her single suitcase from the back.

The teen had only taken a few steps when an older boy with his head buried in a thick book bumped right into her. Alison fell on her rear and winced, and the boy's book fell to the ground with a thump.

James growled and took a step forward. "Time for a little appropriate punishment. Not going to let you knock a blind kid around, punk."

The boy's eyes widened. "I-I'm so sorry. I just... I wasn't looking." He held up his hands.

"You try a spell, kid, it'll be the last thing you do. I've taken down a lot more impressive wizards than you."

Shay laughed and placed a hand on his arm. "Dial it down, Brownstone. He's not a bounty. He's just a kid."

James glared at the boy, who yelped, grabbed his book, and scurried off.

Alison pushed herself to her feet and rubbed her butt. "I'm okay, Mr. Brownstone, really. I wasn't paying much attention myself. A lot of the energy here is different than what I'm used to."

"Yeah, I can see that. Maybe not *that*, but I get the idea," he admitted.

The first adult he'd spotted since arriving, a distinguished-looking older woman with short hair and dark glasses, marched toward them.

"You must be Mr. Brownstone," the woman called as she made her way to them. She smiled at the teen. "And Alison."

"Am I...supposed to bow or something?" James asked.

Shay slapped a hand to her forehead, rolling her eyes. "Seriously, Brownstone?"

The woman laughed and extended her hand. "How about I just offer you my hand? I'm Eleanor Hudson. I teach magical history and basic spells here. The headmistress was called away on an urgent matter, so she asked me to help Alison with her orientation."

James shook the woman's hand as he looked her up and down. "You're human."

"Yes, a human witch. I can assure you that every species here will be able to help Alison learn magic."

She looked at Shay to keep her in the conversation. "Well, I do hate to be rude, but I'd like to get Alison's orientation started. In the beginning, many things about the school may be overwhelming to new arrivals, so the orientation is critical to integration."

"Okay. Yeah, sure."

Alison walked over and threw her arms around James. "Thank you for everything, Mr. Brownstone. You'll be at the parents' weekend in two weeks, right?"

He placed a hand on her back. "Yeah, but before I let you go with Ms. Hudson here, you sure you have everything? Your phone?"

She nodded. "Yes."

He raised an eyebrow. "Your backup phone?"

"Yes," she answered.

"And the burner phones I gave you at the airport?"

Alison rolled her eyes. "Yes." She held up her hand to stop him from continuing. "And the five one-use cards, Mr. Brownstone. I'm...fine."

James' shoulders sagged and he let out a sigh. "I'll miss you, Alison." He gave her a hug. "And I think by now you've earned the right to call me James."

A soft smile appeared on the girl's face. "Okay, James."

Eleanor offered James and Shay a polite smile. "I assure you, she'll be in the best hands on this planet."

James resisted spewing out what he wanted to say. Alison starting off her school career with her guardian threatening to kill one of her teachers if she messed anything up probably wouldn't be great for the teen's chances of fitting in.

"I'm sure she will," he replied instead.

"Come along," Eleanor told Alison. She offered the two adults a final nod and turned on her heel.

Alison waved to James and Shay and hurried after the witch, rolling her single suitcase behind her.

James turned to say something to Shay, only to find her back turned and her hand near her face.

"Problem, Shay?"

She snorted and turned back around, eyes slightly red. "Just the pollen in these Virginian trees."

James decided not to press her on her obvious tears. He wasn't about to cry, but he also felt how much it hurt to see Alison walking away.

"C'mon, Brownstone. We still have a flight back to LA to catch, and you don't want Alison to think you're being stalky about possible boys."

They took several steps toward the SUV.

"What boys?" James spun around, surveying the nearby students with an angry glare. "There were boys looking at her?"

Shay was annoyed that she'd almost cried in front of Brownstone. The last thing she needed was for him to have any sort of emotional leverage over her.

Still, she couldn't help it.

Darkness had choked her life for so long, and seeing Brownstone doing his best to be a good dad—to try to give a shit—had just snuck past her defenses.

Am I going soft spending time around Brownstone? The guy's not exactly touchy-feely.

They were halfway back to the airport before he spoke again, which made things easier for her.

"What's with the case?" Brownstone rumbled.

"Huh?"

"That silver case." He jerked a thumb over his shoulder. "The one in the back."

"Oh, that? Just something I picked up on a quick day job. Just need to keep it with me until I can hand it to the client. Don't worry, it's not a bomb or an Inca zombie rod or anything." She chuckled. "You should have just asked me, if you were curious. I figure we have that kind of relationship now. I watch your stupid barbecue shows, and you ask me if I'm carrying cursed explosive bones."

He slid his eyes to her. "*Are* you carrying cursed explosive bones?"

Shay laughed and shook her head. "Nope, just some stupid boner magic shit."

"Boner magic?"

"You know, like Viagra, except magical. That kind of shit is serious cash nowadays. Never underestimate how much a man will pay to make sure he can get it up."

James snorted. "Okay. Anyway, figured you'd tell me if I needed to know. I…" He shrugged. "I half-ass trust you."

"Fair enough."

He exhaled slowly. "Speaking of jobs, I kind of need your help."

"Oh?" Shay shot him an annoyingly familiar seductive smile. "Finally decided to give into the truth?"

James grunted. "No."

"Closet case," she muttered, and rolled her eyes.

"I'm not fucking gay," James growled.

"Whatever. Just keep telling yourself that."

"I don't have to!"

Shay didn't know what she believed, other than she couldn't figure out why Brownstone didn't seem to be into her. He'd at least acknowledged that he thought she was attractive, but even with all the time they'd spent together, he hadn't tried to make a single move.

It wasn't that she wanted him that way. He was just a partner. Sure, a partner with a body that looked like it'd been carved by some master sculptor, but still just a partner.

"Tell me about the job, Brownstone."

James glared at the road for a few seconds before talking. "I'm trying to get an Oriceran artifact from the Professor and he's agreed to help me, but he needs a favor in turn."

"Quid pro quo makes the world go around. What's this have to do with me?"

"The Professor said he needs both of us."

"Not to be a total bitch, but let me make it clear that my heart didn't grow three sizes just because we killed a bunch of scumbags together. That was partially self-preservation." Shay sighed. "Or does this have something to do with Alison?"

A thoughtful look crossed James' face. "If you're trying to work up a motivation, the Professor said he'd pay you."

Shay grinned. "Oh. Well, if someone is paying me, of course I'd be glad to help."

James side-eyed her for a second with a faint smirk on his face. "I never doubted it."

6

Father O'Banion needed to be much drunker.
Maybe if he were, the presence of two obvious
spies in the Leanan Sídhe wouldn't have bothered
him so much. The damned men weren't even trying to be
subtle as they continually searched the crowd with their
suspicious little eyes.

Their too-slick hair and too-perfect suits didn't fit the
atmosphere of the Irish pub. Worse, they were barely
touching their drinks. Spending an hour in the pub and
drinking only a quarter of a beer was ridiculous. Not only
were they draining the joy out of Father O'Banion's
wonderful buzz, they were all but stealing from him by not
pounding down beers.

Very few people knew that he owned the Leanan Sídhe.
He found that a useful convenience. Surprise, he'd found
through the fifty-two years of his life, was a wonderful
weapon against the arrogant and the impatient.

Father O'Banion wondered if James might have figured

out the truth, but if the bounty hunter had, he'd never bothered to mention it.

A huge man at the bar raised his glass. "To the best damn bar in all of Los Angeles."

"To the best damn bar in all of Los Angeles," everyone else shouted.

No. Almost everyone, not the two slick-hairs.

Idiots.

The best way to spy on people was to blend in with the local environment. That was Intelligence Gathering 101.

Father O'Banion's irritation grew when the crowd erupted into a rowdy drinking song and the two interlopers didn't even fake interest.

Lazy fucking bastards. I hope they aren't getting paid well. Time to rattle their cage a bit.

With a sigh, the man rose from his table in the back and made his way to the bar. The bartender had a mug ready for him before he arrived. He grabbed the drink and offered the man an exaggerated bow.

His circuitous return path took him near the spies' table. The men whispered while the loud singing continued around them. The chaos provided an almost perfect cover for anyone who hadn't already attracted attention.

Of course, they had no reason to suspect the ruddy-faced drunk stumbling past them of being anything more than three sheets to the wind.

Father O'Banion couldn't make out much, but he made out one syllable, which was more than enough: brown.

A feigned stumble ended with his mug on the two men's table.

"Oh, sorry, lads. I guess I wasn't paying attention to where I was going." He swished the beer in his mug with a grin. "But at least I didn't lose anything important."

"What the hell, man?" one of the slick-hairs snapped, glaring at him. "Fucking be careful. You could have stained my suit."

"I've only had four drinks tonight," Father O'Banion replied. "And so I still care, lad. That's why I'm here."

"Get out of here, you old drunk. I don't give a shit about any idiot crap you spew."

Father O'Banion lifted his mug, keeping the smile on his face. "I'll give you one fair warning."

The other man pulled his suit jacket back to reveal a holstered gun. "And I'm giving you one warning, you drunken piece of shit. You don't know who you're messing with, and you're pissing me off."

"Aye, I don't know who I'm messing with, lad, and so that's why I'm giving you the warning. You don't want to be here when he arrives, because I will tell Brownstone you are looking for him. This is my happy place, you see. The place I come to relax, and I won't have people causing trouble—especially men flashing guns."

The other man's face twitched. "I have no idea what the fuck you're talking about, old man. Get out of my face before you regret it."

Father O'Banion shrugged. "I've done my due diligence. Enjoy your beer, you cheap bastards."

Idiotic pieces of shit. You'd think these fuckers would learn.

"Feels good to be in a real vehicle," James said, flexing his fingers on the steering wheel of his F-350.

Shay laughed. "I love my Spider, but not enough to marry it—unlike you and this fucking antique truck." She gestured with a flourish. "I now pronounce you man and truck."

"Quality never goes out of style, Shay."

James' phone beeped inside the console. He pulled it out and frowned.

"What?" Shay said.

"The Professor says he got our message, but he doesn't want to meet tonight. He says you should call him, though, for some background info."

"Sounds simple enough."

James' frown lingered on his face.

"What's wrong, Brownstone?"

"Nothing. Just it's not like the Professor to cancel a meeting. I wonder if something happened."

Shay shrugged. "Maybe he had a bad burrito and is worried about having to run to the bathroom. It happens, Brownstone."

"If you say so."

"I'll let you know if he tells me anything useful when I call him."

James nodded.

Maybe it was nothing, after all.

Shay settled on her couch before calling Dr. Smite-Williams. She didn't know if he'd had a special reason to cancel the meeting, but the atmosphere at the Leanan Sídhe grated on her nerves. She wasn't sad to have an excuse to avoid the pub after a day of traveling.

She dialed and waited for Smite-Williams to answer.

"Good evening, Miz Carson."

"Brownstone said you wanted me to call you directly, and I assume he wasn't bullshitting me when he mentioned that you're willing to pay for my help."

Smite-Williams chuckled. "No one does anything unless they get something out of it. Some might be satisfied with just a warm and fuzzy feeling, but I assume you'd prefer money."

"Yes, preferably shitloads."

"Given what I'm asking, I might have to provide just that."

"I'm listening."

"Have you heard of the Green Dragon Crescent Blade?"

Shay whistled. "The weapon of the legendary ancient Chinese general Guan Yu—a man who could probably take a dragon or two. What the fuck are you hunting that needs that kind of ass-kicking ability?"

"It's not the blade I'm interested in, it's the enchanted jade in the base that legend says powers it. My information suggests it might be somewhere relatively close."

She hesitated for a moment, wondering if she should give away any information for free, then decided it was a test. There was no way Smite-Williams didn't already know the basic history of the weapon.

"Legend says," Shay began, "that Taoist priests sailing in the treasure fleet of Admiral Zheng had the weapon with them. They were worried about encountering demons on their travels that might be beyond the ability of their magic to handle."

"Aye, I've heard that as well."

"According to at least some recent translations of the Lost Navigation Records of Admiral Zheng He, a small group of his men were detached in 1421, with the priests in tow, to continue on when the rest of the fleet turned around because he had some sort of vision. They allegedly reached what we now call Mexico, though that's debatable because they were never heard from again."

Smite-Williams clapped. "Congratulations, Miz Carson. You're very well-informed."

"So that's what you want me to get? That blade, or the jade?"

"Aye, and soon. Within the next few weeks."

Shay frowned. "Why the hurry?"

"I have my reasons. You don't need to know them."

"And in exchange, I'll get paid my standard fee and Brownstone will get the shit he wants?"

"Because of the pressing nature of my request, I'm willing to pay you twenty percent above your normal fee. I think you'll find I'm fair."

Shay snorted. "Yeah, I know you *say* you are always fair with people—and Brownstone says the same thing—but I'm going to have to see it several times before I believe it. No offense."

"Trust but verify, Miz Carson. It's a good policy to live by. Talk to you later, hopefully soon."

The treasure hunter sighed as the called ended. More than a few of her kind had gone looking for the Green Dragon Crescent Blade, and none had ever come back alive. Some claimed the blade would destroy anyone who lacked the spiritual strength to wield it.

Shay sighed and headed up to the bedroom where she kept her bookshelves and computer and grabbed *Ancient Chinese Legends Reevaluated in Light of Post-Oriceran Contact*. In a world of returned magic, a stray piece of information might be the difference between an artifact destroying a person and that person controlling it.

She opened her browser and clicked on her favorite bookmarks, Archaeology Plus and Archaeology Source. Each was a massive database of academic articles on archaeology and related fields. She also opened a database of articles on historical and applied extra-dimensional engineering.

The field archaeologist couldn't help but chuckle at the convoluted name every time she saw it. She didn't understand why so many researchers didn't want to admit they were studying magical artifacts. Whatever it took to keep some people from freaking out over how the world had changed so much in the last couple decades, she supposed.

A lot of people might think Shay was using the title "field archaeologist" flippantly, but the truth was a good tomb raid required a lot of academic leg work ahead of time. The main difference was that unlike academics, she also had a variety of more colorful contacts.

First, though, a lot of reading awaited her. She needed to know the right questions to ask before calling anyone.

"Let's see what people have to say about you, Guan Yu."

James moved the painting of Saint Jerome hanging in his living room aside, revealing his biometrically-sealed weapons locker. He placed his palm on the sensor to unlock it, then started placing his various death-dealing implements inside.

That night he had only a light load: a single .45 handgun and a K-Bar.

The bounty hunter sighed at the silence of his home. Only the tick of clocks broke up the choking lack of noise.

He'd gotten used to having Alison around, and before that, having Leeroy rush up to him barking and demanding to be walked.

Now he had no one.

James shook his head. The school was the best place for Alison—he didn't doubt that. Not only did he know nothing about raising kids, he wasn't a wizard.

Using a few magic items was totally different than wielding innate magic power and casting spells. He couldn't help Alison learn what she needed to know to control her powers.

After hanging up his coat, James dropped into the black leather recliner in his living room and picked up his remote. Worrying wouldn't solve shit. He'd just have to throw himself into work to try to take his mind off things.

The Professor must have moved their meeting for a reason, and it kept gnawing at the edge of the bounty hunter's mind. Maybe if he hadn't so desperately needed Smite-Williams' help he wouldn't have cared as much.

You better come through on that item, he thought.

James turned on his television. It was the near the end of an episode of *Barbecue Wars: New Generation.* The season finale was coming up, and even people who didn't care about barbecue had taken an interest because of the presence of an elf competitor who consistently earned high marks from the judges.

He shook his head. Unicorn and Kirin roamed Virginia, and elves were cooking barbecue. He'd been young when the truth of Oriceran came out, but it'd still taken years for the influence of the magical world to truly affect things.

Everything that had happened in recent weeks made him wonder. He wasn't from Oriceran, but he also couldn't deny his strength went well beyond that of a normal man. The strange amulet necklace he kept at the warehouse, the reason for his Granite Ghost nickname, was obviously magical. The necklace had been found with him when he was a young child wandering alone by himself and unable to speak.

He'd thought about the different possibilities. Maybe he had an Oriceran relative, or his family had died protecting him from an Oriceran.

James snorted.

I should stop thinking about shit I won't ever know.

He forced his attention to the show.

"It's really not that complicated," Henry, one of the judges, was saying. "A good rule of thumb is thick meat, low and slow. Thin meat, high and fast. But, that's just a generalization. At this point in the competition, especially with the protein we used today, you have to be thinking about combinations of temperatures, otherwise you're not going to get maximum quality—like the failure you had with the bark there. Remember, we're evaluating all aspects of the meat during judging. But to be totally honest, there was a noticeable quality difference in the flavor between what you gave us and what the other three contestants provided, and I'm actually shocked to see that from you this late in the competition."

Sam, the portly gray-haired contestant being critiqued, shook his head. "I had some time issues because of the nature of the challenge. I wasn't as familiar with this meat, so I relied on what I knew."

Another judge, Cassie, gestured to the other three contestants, who were standing in a row behind Sam. "Everyone has the same amount of time to cook." She pointed to the elf contestant. "Nadina has had far fewer years of experience with any of these ingredients, let alone a cultural or national history with this cooking style, and both her plates were spot-on. She didn't even use any Oriceran spices this time."

The light-haired elf blushed, and the color spread all the way up her pointed ears. She looked down at the ground as the camera lingered on her.

Sam ran a hand through his thinning hair. "We all make mistakes, you know."

The third judge, Larry, furrowed his brow. "My issue is less with the first plate than the second plate. We clearly stated that the challenge for the second plate was about perfect bark. You obviously lacked temperature and smoke control. Do you think you smoked it long enough?"

"I think... Uh, like I said, there were time constraints."

"And like Henry said, everyone had the same time constraints."

"I had some problem with my wood."

Larry narrowed his eyes. "Everyone had the same materials available. And I'll be honest—even if you'd managed the temperature and smoke well, I'm still confused by some of the choices you made for your rub. Did you really think such a minimal rub was a good choice for a bark challenge?"

James let out a sigh of contentment. Maybe he couldn't control a lot of things in his life, but at least he'd always have barbecue.

7

The next morning, James opened his eyes and stared at popcorn ceiling. He'd always thought about replacing it since he didn't like the look, but it always seemed like more trouble than it was worth.

Sometimes the simplest path was the one of least resistance.

The funk from Alison's departure still hung over him, but that didn't mean he could rot in bed like some bitch-ass emo teenager. He rolled out of bed and stood up.

James cracked his knuckles, ready for his morning routine. Paying money to go work out was a sucker's choice. On top of that, it messed with his desire to live his life as simply as possible.

Keep it simple, stupid. When things got complicated it was at best annoying, but more often than not someone end up suffering—or in his line of work, dead.

Gyms made exercise complicated. All the bounty hunter needed was a good space for his movements.

Quickly dropping to the ground, he put himself into push-up position and started his reps.

The minutes passed as he dipped and rose.

"998...999...1000."

James finished off his push-up reps and rolled to his back. It was time for some sit-ups.

An hour later, after pounding out a variety of additional exercises, the sweat-soaked bounty hunter headed into the shower.

Now fully dressed, James made his way downstairs. The morning's exercises were intense enough to give him good cardio, but he still liked to hit the neighborhood for a little run. If anything, it helped keep him aware of who was wandering the streets near his house.

"Hey, Leeroy, get ready for some exercise—"

He stared down at the empty space where Leeroy's food and water bowls had been. It'd been a week since he'd last forgotten that his dog was dead.

James ran most days, and he'd made sure to run with his dog a few times a week. The black lab had loved it.

"Fucking Harriken," he growled. "I wish I could kill another fifty of you fuckers."

The anger drained away, and James sighed. With Alison gone, it might be time to consider another pet.

Animals were simple. A man didn't have to play word games or worry about their loyalty. If he treated them well they'd have his back, just like Leeroy.

He shook his head. Never again. James didn't want another poor animal to get killed because of who he was.

"Dogs love me," he muttered. "But they can't fight those I fight."

Running didn't seem all that appealing anymore. It wouldn't hurt to skip it.

Pulling out his phone, James headed to his couch. If he wanted a real work-out, he'd go after a bounty. It'd also help him work out some frustration—and get paid for it.

The bounty hunter tapped on his phone to connect to the LAPD Bounty Hunter Outreach Department app. Maybe there were some good local bounties he could pick up. Money, exercise, and stress-relief all in one—efficient and simple.

"Jordan Adams," James read aloud, "aka 'King Pyro?'" He snorted. The douchebags who gave themselves nicknames like that always caused more trouble. It was like they were compensating for small dicks or something.

From what James skimmed, King Pyro had been a run-of-the-mill bank robber until two years prior, when he'd gotten his grubby paws on the distilled essence of a fire spirit in a potion. Fortunately for the king he didn't spontaneously combust when he drank the potion, which suggested at least some latent magical potential. Unfortunately for everyone else, the potion gave the man the power to control and manipulate fire.

James didn't really give a shit about the details of how the man had gotten his powers. All he cared about was taking him down. He skimmed farther down to get better insight into the man.

King Pyro was nothing more than a violent thug,

according to the reports. That would make him easier to find, since among other things, it meant the sonofabitch wouldn't be as good at hiding his trail.

The man's level-four bounty would be worth a nice chunk of change, and suggested he was dangerous enough to warrant James' time. There were plenty of other bounty hunters to take care of the small fries.

James' gaze drifted to the painting of Saint Jerome concealing his weapons locker. Anything level three or lower he could handle with ease, but going up to level four meant that he might have to consider the necklace. It made him nearly invulnerable, and enhanced his normally weak telekinesis ability. That would require a trip to the warehouse.

No. Don't want to use that thing unless I have to.

Even though the artifact had saved his life more than a few times, James knew there had to be some sort of hidden cost. The revelation of Oriceran had changed a lot of things and put magic back into the world next to science, but that didn't change the fundamental rule of the universe.

There was no such thing as a free lunch.

The damn artifact might be sucking his life with each use or changing him in some fundamental way, making him even less human. Maybe that was why he had the strange ridges and mottled patterns on his face along with his strength. They'd found the artifact with him as a child, so maybe it'd already worked its terrible magic by then.

One day James might wake up a monster. He was half-convinced the necklace was cursed.

He shook his head. He'd avoid the necklace for now,

saving it for when he had to fight a real monster. Or clear an entire house filled with ruthless criminals, but he doubted that'd happen a third time in a couple of months.

When did my life get so fucking complicated?

James stared down at his phone. "Yeah, King Pyro, you'll do for now. I'm gonna enjoy kicking your ass."

It was time to get armed and even more dangerous.

An hour later the bounty hunter pushed into a dingy bar in Westlake called the Black Sun. Dim lighting helped the place live up to its name. The cracked tables and barred windows didn't add a lot to its charm. One passed-out gang member sat at a corner table, the idiot's gun clearly on display. James was half-tempted to take the man's gun and throw it in the trash just so the fool would panic when he woke up.

He suppressed a snort. The Leanan Sídhe was inviting and full of life. This place made him feel like he'd need another shower after leaving.

It didn't matter. He hadn't come there to drink the piss they called beer. He marched up to the bar and took a seat.

The tall, pale bartender looked up from polishing a glass and frowned.

"James Brownstone." The bartender sighed, putting up the now-shiny glass and grabbing another. "I haven't seen you around for a while."

"That's probably good for you then, Tyler." James gestured. "I see this place is as shitty as ever. Hell, even shittier. Congratulations. I hope you won your award for 'Most Appealing to Roaches.'"

"We all enjoy a different ambience. People come here to disappear into their drinks. They don't much care about the look of the place."

"Yeah, that much is obvious."

Tyler put down the glass and the rag. "Do you want something to drink, Brownstone? If not, well, you know what the sign over there says." He gestured toward the door. "Management reserves the right to deny service to any customer for any reason."

"I'd like to see you try and kick me out." James chuckled. "And we both know this place is just a shitty front so you can deal in information, so spare me the hurt feelings bullshit."

Tyler shrugged. "I'm a bartender. People like to talk to me. Sometimes they like to give me a little extra money, and I pass on useful tidbits in exchange. I'm not hurting anyone, so I don't understand where all the attitude's coming from.

The bounty hunter's nostrils flared. "*Attitude?* You work with scumbags; complete pieces of shit. You look the other way when people ask you stuff, and they go out and use that info to become even bigger pieces of shit."

"Don't kid yourself, Brownstone. You're not exactly royalty." The man put his elbow on the bar and leaned forward. "And you've benefited from those useful tidbits yourself, so again the attitude is crap. If you want my help, I suggest you stop talking shit to me. Understand?"

James locked eyes with Tyler. If it came to blows, the other man wouldn't last one second. He must have been convinced that his usefulness as an information broker made him safe.

"Whatever." The bounty hunter shrugged. "I just need fucking information, and I'm willing to pay for it. If you play along, we both benefit."

"Okay, I'm listening. Information about what?"

"A level-four bounty I'm tracking named Jordan Adams. He goes by the name 'King Pyro.'"

Tyler shook his head. "We've talked about this, Brownstone. Within reason, I will give you info on level threes and lower, but not level fours. If I started pissing too much in my own water bowl, where would I be? Everyone knows that if they reach a certain level of...respect, I give them extra respect. Sorry."

"That could be a problem for you, but it's not like I fucking care." James leaned forward. He was reaching the limits of his patience. "Maybe you *should* care if you want to be able to keep polishing your glasses."

Tyler smirked. "No bounties on me, Brownstone, and I've got cameras all over this place. You beat me down," he nodded to a nearby camera. "even those bitch cops will have to do something, not to mention my lawyer. Oh, I'd love to sue your ass, because it'd be funny to drag you into court and watch you squirm in a suit. I bet you have all sorts of money I could sue you for, Brownstone. You running an LLC? You know how to protect your assets?"

The bounty hunter's hands curled into fists, and he weighed the risks versus the satisfaction of punching Tyler before deciding on a different tack. The fucker must have *some* small sliver of humanity left in him.

"This isn't some garden-variety asshole. This guy killed

a whole family, including little kids, when he blasted away like a fucking maniac during his last bank job."

Tyler shrugged. "Accidents happen. You so sure everyone you've killed had it coming, Brownstone?"

"Yes, and fuck you, you piece of shit. I've never killed a kid."

"Yet."

James grunted. "It's not an accident when you use an explosion to rob a bank. This Pyro fucker doesn't care who he hurts, and I'm going to bring him down. You should help me so you get my thanks rather than pissing me off."

Tyler rolled his eyes. "This is becoming boring, Brownstone. Even if I knew anything about King Pyro, and I'm not saying I do, I couldn't tell you. I've made that policy clear in the past."

"Fuck your policies." James stood and pointed at the man. "If I find out you've seen this guy and you don't tell me, this neutrality shit we have," he waved a finger between the two of them, "goes away."

"Until I have a bounty on my head," Tyler picked up his rag and glass once more, "you can't touch me."

James spun and stormed off toward the door.

"Next time buy a drink, you cheap bastard," the man called after him.

James was halfway to another contact when his phone beeped. The Professor. He put the call on speakerphone.

"Hey, Professor."

"Good morning, lad. Sorry about having to cancel the

other day. Something came up, but I'd like to meet with you later today. I've got an extra lecture at the college until 7:00, but right after that I want to meet you at the pub."

"And this is about the deal for the item?"

"Aye. Miz Carson will be joining us. I think we'll all benefit from this."

James grunted. "Just as long as you hold up your end."

"Have I ever not?"

There was a first time for everything.

8

King Pyro pushed into the Black Sun. The huge man inhaled deeply, loving the stale smell permeating the place. A dozen other men were scattered around the bar. Most hunched over their drinks; only a few chatted together.

What a bunch of sad pieces of shit. It's not even worth kicking their fucking asses.

It'd been a couple days since he'd last beaten someone down, and he craved the rush. Plus, if he took someone down in this place, the right people in Los Angeles would know not to fuck with him.

The robber strutted to the bar, wanting everyone to see him. Fear was for pussies. King Pyro was the king of fire, maybe even a god. He sat down at the bar, chuckling to himself about changing his nickname.

The bartender set a beer in front of him. "On the house."

King Pyro smirked. "Nice. What's your name, bar bitch?"

The other man's face twitched for a moment. "I'm Tyler. I own the place."

"You're just the bitch I'm looking for. You know who I am?"

"Jordan Adams. They say you go by 'King Pyro.'"

"That's right. I'm the damn king, and you must bow before royalty." The criminal gave the other man a feral grin. "Word is that you're the man to see when someone needs to buy or sell information."

"That's true, but I have a special offer for you today…in addition to your drink." Tyler glanced around the bar for a moment. "Free information."

King Pyro slammed his hand on the bar. "*That's* what I like to hear."

Tyler narrowed his eyes. "You better get your ass out of town."

"Yeah, that's… What?" King Pyro frowned; he hadn't expected such a blunt statement. The man in front of him might need to be made into an example. "If you know who I am, then you know, you do not disrespect me, bitch."

Tyler pointed to the drink. "It's because I respect you that I'm telling you this. You don't understand. Earlier today, Brownstone showed up looking for you. That's not the kind of heat you need, king of fire or not."

"Who the fuck is Brownstone? I don't know any bitch named Brownstone, so why should I care?"

The bartender shook his head. "He's a bounty hunter, and you don't *want* to know him. If you want to stay free—or alive for that matter—get the fuck out of town while you can."

"You think some bitch-ass bounty hunter's gonna take

down King Pyro?" The man barked a harsh laugh. "I'm not some punk-ass criminal. I'm almost... No, I *am* a god. I'm the God of Fire, and I burn what I want when I want." He hopped out of his seat. "You think I'm gonna leave town without doing what I need because of a *bounty hunter*? You know how many cops I've killed? How many bounty hunters? I'm a level-fucking-four. I'm worth a lot of money, and I'm gonna force them to make me level-five." He spread his hands to his sides and yelled, "Hey, bitches!"

Every man in the bar looked his way.

"Did you hear? I've got a huge bounty on me. Any of you want to take a shot at King Pyro? You could drag my ass in for a lot of cash." He glared around the bar. "But none of you have the balls to face a god."

A man in a worn suit stood and whipped out a Glock. "Bet you're not bulletproof, asshole."

"Gentleman, please don't do this in here," Tyler said with a weary sigh, pinching the bridge of his nose. "This is neutral ground. You know the rules. You cause trouble, you can't ever come back to the Black Sun."

"Sorry, Tyler. This guy's worth a lot of money, and he's getting on my fucking nerves. He thinks he's big shit because of some magic? Who gives a shit? A gun is the real magic."

"I hope the money's worth it," Tyler muttered. "Because assuming you survive the next few minutes, you'll never be allowed back here again."

King Pyro shook out his arms. "You think you can take down royalty, bitch? I rule through strength. I'm beyond human now."

"You face is certainly ugly enough," the man with the gun agreed.

The fire master sneered. "We'll see how your face looks after I burn it off."

"Let's just take a walk down to the nearest station," the suited man suggested, motioning with his gun. "I'm in deep with my bookie. Sorry, pal—just not your lucky day."

King Pyro turned his back to the other man. He didn't fear the gun, but he didn't want to show all his cards yet. For all his bluster, he understood that a powerful ruler should be both strong and intelligent. He held his hand in front of him with a grin. Flame grew above it over the course of several seconds, and then he spun and blasted an orange-white fireball at the other man's hand.

The sizzle of burning flesh filled the air. The other man screamed and stumbled backward, his hand cracked and charred. The half-melted gun fell to ground, hissing on contact with the floor.

"Fuck," Tyler muttered. "This was not what I needed tonight."

The suited man collapsed to his knees, still groaning. "My hand... My damned *HAND*!"

King Pyro stalked toward the man and kicked him in the stomach. "I'm feeling generous, so you don't die, fuck. You can tell this Brownstone bitch that he will burn. He can kiss my ass. I hope this Brownstone *does* show up to try and take me in. I'll enjoy killing him and showing everyone in this town who they should really be afraid of." He grinned at Tyler. "Give me another drink, bar bitch. I'm not leaving Los Angeles until I've killed James Brownstone."

Tyler sighed and shrugged. "Your funeral."

———————

James stepped into the Leanan Sídhe. He stopped for a moment and chuckled, thinking how the rowdy and bright bar contrasted with the Black Sun. Not only was it a more inviting place, but customers swarmed it.

He spotted the Professor sitting in a booth in the back, and the man waved merrily at him. As James closed on the man, he wondered if Father O'Banion had already come out. There were two empty glasses and a half-filled glass of beer in front of the red-faced man. O'Banion usually waited to come out until after their business was finished, but not always.

The bounty hunter slid into the booth. "Hey."

"Good evening, lad. Miz Carson informed me that she'll be here soon." The Professor glanced toward the door, then smiled at James. "So, you delivered the girl to her school without trouble?"

James nodded. "Yeah. Weird place."

"You're a man who recently killed three blood warlocks, and you're letting some junior wizard and witch school concern you?"

"There was a ferret that walked around on two feet and wore a top hat. A fucking *top hat!*" James griped. "When do rodents walk on two feet? That shit isn't right."

The Professor laughed. "What's wrong with being fashionable?"

"It at least could have worn a... I don't know, a fedora or a ball cap or something. Not a damn top hat."

"I'll tell that to the next fashionable ferret I run into." The Professor gulped down some beer before continuing. "It is a school of magic. A man should expect a few oddities when they set foot on the grounds. Besides, given who Alison is, it's probably the best place for her...and the safest."

James let out a low grunt. "Not saying I disagree, but still feels kind of strange dropping off a kid at a place with top-hat-wearing ferrets and Kirin."

"They have a Kirin there?" His eyebrows rose. "Impressive. As for the getting used to the girl being there, these things take time." The Professor picked up his half-full glass and took a sip. "Before Miz Carson shows up, I wanted to make you aware of something."

"What?" James asked.

"There were two undesirables loitering here the other day. I'm fairly certain they were looking for you. I couldn't hear everything they said, but they said at least part of your name, and I find too coincidental to believe it has nothing to do with you?"

"Assassins?"

"For sure they weren't nice men, but they didn't have that air about them. They didn't seem dangerous enough."

James grinned. "Most assassins aren't dangerous to me."

The Professor shook his head. "I'm saying I don't think they'd be dangerous to *me*. I assume they were just interested in keeping tabs on you."

"I kind of assume *everyone* wants to keep tabs on me. I keep blowing shit up and killing people."

That elicited a chuckle from the older man. "I'm only telling you so I can drink with a clear conscience tonight.

What you do with that information is up to you. Ignore it, or go on a path of bloody vengeance—that's on you."

"Thanks, Professor. I'll keep that in mind."

A broad grin spread across the Professor's face as he looked past James. "And here is Miz Carson now."

James glanced behind him and spotted Shay maneuvering through the crowd. He kept waiting for her to lay out somebody who dared brush against her, but she made her way to the table and slid in next to the Professor without a single glare, punch, or kick.

"How is my favorite happy drunk doing?" the field archaeologist asked.

The Professor laughed. "Why am I your favorite?"

"Because you give me jobs that make me a lot of money." She shrugged. "And you don't make passes at me."

James frowned, but the Professor chuckled.

"Young lady, that is not because I'm smart enough to avoid your wrath, but merely because if you accepted my advances, I'm too old to actually do anything useful about it. I'd be dead from strenuous activity by morning." He patted the slight bulge around his middle. "It'd be a glorious way to die, for sure."

Shay shrugged. "Either way works for me."

They shared a laugh.

"What about the job?" James interjected. The last thing he wanted to do was sit there while Smite-Williams flirted with Shay.

"Due to Miz Carson's efforts, we're ready to move on this even faster than I had anticipated. I talked to her about it the other day, and she did some research and passed it my way. I in turn was able to ask some of my other contacts about it discreetly."

"And?"

"I believe we have a location for the Green Dragon Crescent Blade, and I want you to support Miz Carson in its recovery."

"Green Dragon Crescent Blade? Isn't that the weapon of a character from *Romance of the Three Kingdoms*?"

The Professor and Shay exchanged glances, and James smirked.

Everyone underestimated him when it came to areas other than barbeque and ass-kicking, but with a photographic memory, even the occasional out-of-the-box read was useful.

"That book is a fictionalized account of a real war," Smite-Williams began, "and Guan Yu was a real man, but yes, you're correct. As I explained to your partner, I need the enchanted jade in the base more than the rest, but the whole blade would be fine."

James frowned. "I don't really feel like going to China. I don't have any contacts there, and I don't speak the language. They aren't all that fond of bounty hunters, either, except in Hong Kong, and I'm guessing this thing isn't buried in the middle of Hong Kong."

The Professor waved a hand dismissively. "Fortunately for you it's in Mexico—Baja California Sur. Much closer than even your last little errand for me."

"Some ancient Chinese weapon is in Mexico?"

"There's a story that goes with that," Shay began.

"Don't really care, to be honest." The bounty hunter

shrugged. "Okay, whatever. It's magic shit, so it doesn't have to make sense. But why am I involved, then? I get that I'm gonna get the item I want, but why do you even need me?"

The Professor nodded at Shay. "I'd prefer that she have at least some backup. Just in case."

"Yeah, the place is not exactly peaceful, drug war and all," Shay explained. "Plenty of bounties down there too if you want to earn a little bonus cash, though you'd need to be careful not to piss off the cartel controlling the territory where I'll find the Green Dragon Crescent Blade. I have some contacts down there, and I'd like to be able to use them."

James decided not to press Shay on why she had contacts among a cartel-controlled state. Given her previous vocational specialty of death dealing, it wasn't surprising.

"As long as I get one level-four or -five it'll be worth my time, even before the Professor's payment."

The Professor chuckled. "Tons of bounties down there, lad. Chaos reigns. You can either get money locally or bring your quarry back to Los Angeles for a greater payout, if you can arrange it."

James turned to Shay. "You don't think these cartel guys will mind you running around stealing treasure from under their noses?"

Shay shook her head. "The trick is to lie to them and just pretend I'm there for boring, normal archaeologist stuff, plus pay them a few bribes. We'll be flying into Cabo San Lucas. They can't handle supersonic flights at their airport, but this won't be a repeat of our Peru odyssey. It's only about two and half hours down there even by normal plane."

"The less time on planes, the better. Already flew too many times this week."

The Professor clapped his hands together. "Wonderful. Now, if you'll excuse me, I need to get back to drinking."

James gestured to the glasses. "Aren't you already drinking?"

"No, this is drinking to prepare myself to drink. Care to join me in the real thing?"

"I'm looking into some other shit tonight," James told him, "so I can't get drunk."

"Don't work yourself too hard, Brownstone." Shay winked. "I don't want you to be too tired tomorrow to have...fun with me."

The bounty hunter rose, his face set in stone. "I'll keep that in mind."

Shay rolled her eyes. "Man, are *you* boring!"

He looked at her, confused. "Boring is simple, and simple is good."

She stood. "I have a few things to handle myself. Sorry, Professor."

The older man smiled. "It's all right. Some other time."

Shay turned back toward James. "See you in the morning at LAX, Brownstone. I'll text you the flight information." She headed toward the door.

James also started making his way to the exit, the crowd parting in front of him, then stopped. If the job took a while, it'd be easy enough to swing through Las Vegas on his way back when he went to the parents' weekend. That meant on his way to see Alison he'd have a chance to hit up Jessie Rae's.

In the rush to get the girl to the School of Necessary Magic, he'd not even thought about trying to visit Vegas. He could almost taste the God Sauce already. It'd been far too long. No place in LA could hope to match Jessie Rae's.

James stepped into darkness outside, dreaming of the best barbecue on the planet. His phone beeped, pulling him out of the delicious fantasy.

"Damn it."

It was a text from an unknown number. He really hoped someone hadn't sent it to threaten him.

Brownstone, your boy is holding court at my bar.

The bounty hunter smirked. All that preening, and Tyler had caved. He couldn't resist a little poke.

Thought you said you couldn't tell me if he showed up.

The asshole caused trouble in my place. Respect is a two-way street, and he's disrespected me far more than you have.

James cracked his knuckles. "Looks like I'm gonna have a fun time before Mexico."

9

S hay pulled her Fiat Spider into her garage. Her head slumped against the steering wheel, and she let out a long sigh.

"I shouldn't care so much," she muttered to herself. "I am *pathetic*."

She'd told herself that exact thing countless times the last few weeks, but it didn't help. One very important fact kept annoying her, and each time she saw Brownstone her irritation grew.

The man hadn't hit on her yet.

Hadn't even hinted at something approaching a pass. At this point she would have taken a leer. Even Smite-Williams wasn't immune to her charms, and he was old enough to be her father.

Shay had initially thought Brownstone was just clueless about women so she had started flirting with him more, but he still didn't seem interested.

She bounced back and forth on whether she thought he

was gay. Brownstone's protests did little to convince her he wasn't. That had to be the only explanation for why he wasn't into her.

Maybe he was gay, but didn't know it. He was so far in the closet that he didn't know he was in the closet. What was that called? Being in the deep closet?

Shay was the complete package. Nice dark hair, and toned athletic body. Witty with a sharp tongue. Damn sexy femme fatale. She'd be the first one to tell you.

All men wanted her. At least all straight men did, but Brownstone didn't. Hadn't even hinted at wanting her.

She shouldn't care. Brownstone should remain nothing more than a professional partner, but the idea that he didn't even want to take a quick roll in the sack with her hurt more than she expected.

"Are you just fucking with me, Brownstone?" Shay muttered. "Is this some sort of mind game?"

He didn't really seem like the type, but she couldn't be sure. Brownstone had a lot of secrets, and the man didn't like to say much unless it was to blather on about barbecue or taunt bounties.

Shay's phone chimed and she snatched it out of her pocket, ready to deliver a verbal beat-down to Brownstone.

The fire seeped out of her when she looked at the caller ID and she lifted the phone to her ear.

"Hey, Bella!"

Her girlfriend was quick to reply. "I haven't seen you in ages, Shay. I joked the other day to Kara that someone had dragged you off to South America to dig up some moldy mummy or something."

Shay snickered. Close.

"Sorry."

"The university keeping you busy?"

Lying to people you called friends wasn't the best strategy for building long-lasting relationships, but sometimes Shay just wanted to have fun without worrying about her past or the dangerous world of tomb raiding for magical artifacts. Sometimes a touch of normalcy could keep a person sane, even if it was built on a lie. Or a whole pile of lies.

In this case, a little white lie about how she worked for a local college didn't rate in the same league as lying about her deadly past or the way she'd helped Brownstone take down the Harriken.

"Yeah, just had to go out on some digs, that sort of thing," Shay mumbled. "Sorry. It's been keeping me really busy. What's up?"

"Sounds tough, which makes me think it's even more important that you relax. You're going to go gray early if you're too stressed out."

Shay winced. The idea of her friend trying to help her relax freaked her out far more than going up against the Harriken.

"Relax?" she replied. "How?"

"How about going dancing with me and Kara and Janelle tonight?"

"Dancing?" Shay deflected. "I don't know. I'm supposed to fly out tomorrow for a job. I can't be partying all night."

"Oh, come on, girl," Bella whined. "Work hard and play hard, and all that. Remember the gray hair."

"Don't beg. Have some dignity." Shay wasn't sure if she

was talking to Bella or herself. "I guess it'll be okay, but I have to leave by midnight...and no drinking."

"Yay! Okay, Cinderella, you can leave before you turn into a pumpkin. Text me when you're ready."

"Talk to you later." Shay ended the call.

I wonder if Brownstone likes dancing.

She burst out laughing at the image of Brownstone's stiff ass trying to move to a beat.

James pulled his F-350 into the parking lot adjacent to the Black Sun, making sure to stay on the side farthest from the building but positioning his vehicle so he had a clear view of the entrance.

The bar's lack of windows made it easy to watch the door without being spotted, even from the other end of the parking lot. There was no reason for King Pyro to sneak out the back if he didn't even know James was coming for him.

"Safety first," he murmured.

The bounty hunter could handle King Pyro taking a few shots at him, but he didn't want to risk his truck being blown into a melted pile of slag.

Just because he could take down the bounty didn't mean he could accomplish it without collateral damage. He loved his truck almost as much as he had loved his dog, and he'd killed dozens of people to avenge his dog.

James pulled out his phone and texted Tyler.

He still in there?

Yes.

This might get messy.

Take it outside. Otherwise I'll have to get the real authorities involved. I'm doing this because he disrespected me, but if you bust up my bar you're disrespecting me as well.

James lowered his phone to his pocket, then stopped, realizing he'd forgotten something important. Something far more important than kicking King Pyro's ass.

Shit, I should make sure Alison's okay.

He dialed her number and waited, each unanswered ring forcing his heart faster.

I'll fucking kill every unicorn and fucking top-hat-wearing ferret with my bare hands in that school if something's happened to her.

"Mr. Brownstone... I mean James?" Alison answered sleepily.

James bristled. They were working the girl so hard that she was exhausted. He'd need to have a loud talk with the headmistresses, and he didn't give a crap if she threatened to turn him into a toad.

The anger drained out of him after he glanced at his dashboard clock. Alison wasn't in California; she was in Virginia.

"Oh shi— I mean, I forgot about the time zone difference." James sighed. "Guess they don't have some sort of spell that makes whoever's calling you always match your time?" He gave a weak laugh.

Alison didn't laugh at his lame joke. She yawned. Appropriate.

"Sorry, kid," James told her. "I just wanted to check in with you and see how you're doing at magic wand school and all."

"Only been doing orientation, but I like it so far," Alison said, her voice barely above a whisper. "My roommate Aya is really nice, though she's kind of quiet. I thought she was creepy at first, but I think it was just because she was quiet...and she has weird dolls. I mean, the girl down the hall told me it was like straight out of a J-horror movie, long hair and all. She chuckled softly.

"Wait, *what* weird dolls? Horror movies? What the hell is going on there?"

"Oh, it's nothing bad. Aya has this magic where she can make stuff move. It's not very powerful yet, and she said something about dolls being easier. Even then she can't control them that long. When I first stepped into our room there were a couple of dolls moving around her, and she was standing there in this white dress and staring straight ahead of her, bangs over her eyes—or at least that was what Vannie from down the hall told me."

James' brain took a few seconds to catch up. Despite the fact he used magic in his job and hunted people who used it too, it was still strange to hear the girl discussing her roommate having unusual powers as if it weren't a big deal and everyone had them. Of course, at the School of Necessary Magic that was true.

Fuck, was this what it meant to grow up when this stuff was always around? You didn't give a shit? Or was Alison just that way because she was special to begin with?

James shook his head. He needed to focus on the conversation at hand. "But you say she's okay?"

"Yeah. She's cool once you get her to open up a little. Her soul told me she would be." Alison let out another long yawn. "She's taking me to breakfast tomorrow before the next part of my orientation."

James frowned. "What time is it there?"

"Right now? One sec. Um...it's 10:45."

"Okay, I should let you go. I promise I won't call so late next time, but I'll be busy for a while on a job."

"When are you going to call?" There was a faint hint of desperation in Alison's voice.

"Three days maximum, I promise."

"Okay. Talk to you then, James."

"Talk to you then, kid."

James ended the call and slipped his phone into his pocket. No one had entered or exited the Black Sun since his arrival, which meant King Pyro was still inside. This would be the easiest and most satisfying money he'd made in a while.

"Time for a little revolution against the crown," he muttered.

The bounty hunter weighed his options. If he waited he'd be able to take on the man in a larger area, something that would let him take advantage of his strength and speed. The main issue with that was, he had no idea how long it'd take King Pyro to get bored and wander out, and for all James' strength and abilities he still needed to sleep. He had to travel the next morning.

Why didn't anyone stick their magic artifacts in the LA sewer? They might smell like shit, but at least he wouldn't have to travel. Or hell, bury them under the Hollywood sign.

"Fuck it," he muttered. "Let's just get this shit over with."

James reached into his glove compartment to pull out leather gloves. It was probably the first time in a long time it had actually lived up to its name. He wanted to make sure he could land punches without burning himself too badly.

After slipping the gloves on he stepped out of the truck, checked his weapons, and marched toward the Black Sun. Ass-kicking was at the forefront of his mind.

The bounty hunter had the advantage. He knew King Pyro was there, but the criminal didn't know he was coming.

When James threw open the door to the bar, several people shot nervous glances his way. The place was more crowded than it'd been during his last visit, but still nowhere nearly as crowded as the Leanan Sídhe. That might complicate things even more, not that taking down a level four was ever that simple.

Tyler nodded to James as he entered, but didn't say anything. James understood. The man might not have a problem turning King Pyro over to a bounty hunter, but he didn't want to announce it to every piece of shit in the place either.

The bounty hunter scanned the room. A dark scorch marred the floor not that far from the bar. King Pyro had been busy.

His eyes narrowed when he spotted his bounty, a huge brown-haired man in a tight white T-shirt, black jeans, and boots.

The sheer banality of the outfit made James chuckle. With a pretentious title like "King Pyro," he'd expected Adams to strut around in a costume or something. Maybe even a purple cape.

King Pyro stood in front of a table where three men sat laughing.

The robber gesticulated with his arms. "So, that's when I said, 'Who ordered the extra-crispy cop?' You should have heard the guy. He's all screaming like a little girl just because he's on fire. What a cockbite."

All four men burst into hearty laughter.

James strode toward the criminal.

I'm gonna really enjoy this.

A few minutes earlier King Pyro had stood at a table, enjoying the newer crowd. The bar had bored him before, except for burning the man's hand, but now some real men had shown up rather than a bunch of wimps afraid of some boogieman bounty hunter.

He didn't know the names of the three men sitting at the table, but they'd offered him a drink when they entered and saw the wounded man being helped outside. At least a few people in the City of Angels could recognize their king on sight and show some proper respect.

"My last bank job was great. Blew right into a vault." King Pyro waved a hand. "If I concentrate I can make some real fire, but even without trying that hard I can throw football-size fireballs." He held up a hand, and a fiery aura formed around it. "I can get this hot enough to turn some poor bitch's bones into ash."

The three men watched with rapt attention, like children being told some wonderful bedtime story. James shook his head, disgusted.

"What about guns?" one of the men asked. "Cops got guns."

The king's fire vanished and he sneered. "I control the power of a god. Now, it's not like I'm bulletproof, but I've been shot both before and after, and it hurts less now. If I really get going, go full-on human torch and all that, I can melt 'em out of my body, even. I heal real quick-like, too. Don't know why. Don't really give a shit either."

"Damn, man! You're a one-man army."

King Pyro snickered. "You're damn right I am." He pointed at Tyler. "But that pussy bartender told me to get out of town. That I should run because of some asshole named Brownstone who was looking for me. I'm fucking King Pyro, and I don't run from any bounty hunter."

All three men's eyes grew wide.

"Brownstone?" one of his fans asked quietly. "The Granite Ghost wants you?"

"'Granite Ghost?' What kind of bullshit is that? I hate when these bounty hunters have stupid-ass names like that. They are always bitches who think they are the shit, but they start screaming once the fire comes out." King Pyro laughed. "Fuck the Granite Ghost. Everything turns to ash in the end."

One man started trembling. He yanked out his wallet and slapped some cash on the table before standing and slowly backing away.

"What the hell has gotten into you?" King Pyro asked. He noticed that the other two men were looking not at him, but past him. He snorted. "Brownstone's behind me, isn't he?"

The men nodded.

10

L oud techno shook the walls and floors, along with Shay's bones. She loved every second as she shimmied and bounced to the rhythm. It'd been a long time since she'd felt so free. There were no Harriken or strange magical artifacts or traps to worry about, just a fun release.

The DJ bobbed in time with the music, one hand on his equipment and the other in a fist in the air. Small semi-translucent orbs pulsed different colors in time to the music above the dancers. They were some sort of magical creature from what Shay could tell, but she had no clue what they might be. Even Oricerans spirits should be able to hit the club.

The song ended, and Shay wiped the sweat from her forehead. She'd forgotten how good a workout dancing could be.

With the music gone her normal instincts returned, and she quickly scanned the nearby crowd to make sure there were no obvious threats. It was hard to totally let her guard down, even around her friends.

She'd killed a lot of people, and could never be sure that someone wasn't watching her and waiting for their chance to take her out in a revenge attack she probably had coming.

A new song started up, blasting most of the concern out of her head.

Bella leaned close to Shay's ear. "I think I need a break."

Shay nodded her agreement. A little break and some water would work for her.

Her friend grabbed her hand and pulled her to a table in the corner. Their friends Janelle and Kara were already sitting there drinking cocktails.

Shay eyed the cocktails lovingly, but reminded herself that she would be getting up in less than seven hours to drive to the airport. Even with the short flight time, she wanted to keep her wits. Once they hit rural Baja, they'd be dealing with an unstable area drowning in violence.

The addition of newer Oriceran-linked drugs like Dust and Aurora had only exacerbated the existing problems. In addition, there were more than a few acolytes of Santa Muerte who now, unlike their predecessors, could call on magic to defend their cartel masters.

"Thanks, Bella." Shay took a seat. "I'm glad you made me come. This is great, and it's a lot more fun than what I've been doing lately."

The other woman brushed a few blond strands out her eyes. "Yeah, digging up broken pots or mummies...I can imagine." She made a face and shook her head.

Shay chuckled. Pots or Inca zombie rods, same difference. That, and gunning down gangsters and hitmen.

After a final glance at a cocktail and imagining the wonderful salty taste of a margarita on her tongue, she took a sip of her waiting glass of water. There was no way she'd risk not having the clearest head possible the following morning.

Kara smiled at them all. "I have a little surprise."

The other women focused on her.

Kara bit her lip. "I *guess* I should tell you, since it's been a while since we've all been together." She let out a little laugh.

"What?" Shay asked. She liked Kara, but *damn* the woman liked to play games at times.

"I've got a new guy," the redhead caroled.

"Ooohhhh," the other women—except Shay—cooed in near unison. She gave a little golf clap instead.

"When did this happen?" Bella asked.

"A few weeks ago," Kara replied. "He works at my company, although not in my department. I met him in the cafeteria."

Shay chuckled. "Work romance, huh?"

Kara smiled. "Yeah. I know it can be risky, but come on…we're all busy women. If we're not going after the great guys we see all the time, we're shooting ourselves in the foot."

A flash of Brownstone's tight jeans-clad ass entered Shay's mind, and she had to stop herself from frowning.

Fucking Brownstone. Stay out of my head, you damn tease.

"We're playing it light and breezy right now," Kara continued, "but we'll see where this goes."

Bella patted her friend on the hand. "I met my ex-boyfriend at work. I think it's going to go well for you."

"Telling me about your ex-boyfriend isn't filling me with confidence."

Bella shrugged. "He's my ex only because we got bored. We still hang out sometimes and have sex."

Kara looked at her. "I don't really know if that makes him your *ex*-boyfriend then."

"Labels are so restrictive," Bella argued.

Janelle sighed and shook her head. "I didn't want to bring y'all down, but I kicked my man to the curb yesterday."

"What happened?" Shay asked.

"Darius cheated on me." Janelle pasted on a fake smile. "And he tried to convince me he was just visiting his sister all those times. Stupid sonofabitch. I told him I better not ever see his face again if he wants to keep it."

"What a scumbag!" Kara exclaimed.

Bella nodded. "You're better off without him. I never liked him."

Shay leaned closer and lowered her voice, her eyes piercing. "I could go kick his ass. And I'm sure Lil' Miss Tramp-stamp won't be any harder to take down." She slammed her fist into her palm to emphasize her message.

This was the problem with men.

Letting yourself get involved in a true relationship meant putting yourself at risk by linking yourself to another flawed person. Shay could barely keep her shit in check; the last thing she needed to worry about were someone else's problems.

Brownstone probably had so many problems it'd take a fucking army of headshrinkers to deal with him.

Janelle laughed. "Oh, girl, you're too much sometimes. Imagine little ol' you going after Darius?"

The other girls joined in the laughter.

Shay opened her mouth to make it clear she was serious about delivering the pain, but she hesitated and laughed instead as she leaned back. "Just sayin'!"

All her time around Brownstone and Smite-Williams lately had made her almost forget that most people didn't know what sort of work she was involved in. The more random men she went around beating up, the more likely she'd attract the wrong sort of attention. The lethal kind.

She was just about to add another comment when two handsome guys in their mid-twenties strolled up to their table. Their tight short-sleeve shirts showed off their toned arms and chests, but they didn't have Brownstone's muscle, even though they were a few inches taller than him.

Stop it. Stop thinking about him that way. Fucking traitor mind. Brownstone is just a job partner, nothing more. Well, a friend. But just that.

I think.

"Hey, ladies!" The first man flashed a smile so bright it had to be the result of either tooth whitening or magic. "I'm Jason," he pointed to his friend, "and this is Patrick. We saw you lovely angels over here, and thought we'd ask if anyone was interested in dancing?"

Shay resisted a snarky rejoinder. Just because she wasn't interested in the guys didn't mean Janelle or Bella might not want to have fun. She hoped those smooth operators understood they'd better keep their hands off her ass if they didn't want their own handed to them.

All the women at the table exchanged glances, but Bella was the one who finally responded.

"Sorry, guys. We're having some girl talk."

Jason shrugged. "No problem, ladies. We'll be here another couple of hours if you change your minds." He and his friend both nodded and headed back into the massive throng clogging the dance floor.

Shay watched them walk away, trying to push down her suspicions.

Guys were supposed to approach women in clubs, and they were a good-looking group of girls.

Kara took a sip of her drink and peered at Shay.

"Why are you looking at me like that?" She thought she'd kept her face in check, but maybe some of her suspicion had leaked through.

"We've all been talking about our men," Kara explained, "but what about you, Shay? Hmm? Anyone special we should know about? A new boyfriend? You never talk about your love life. You can't be so busy digging up the past that you can't find yourself a future."

Damn it.

The smart play would have been to make up a fictional boyfriend—only to conveniently break up before she had to introduce him to any of her friends— but Shay wasn't creative enough to come up with a decent lie about a man on the spot.

Lying about herself was easy. Lying about made-up boyfriends was not.

Shay shifted in her seat. Now she wished she'd drunk

some booze. "I... I don't have a new boyfriend or anything, just a new guy friend." She winced.

She'd not intended to say anything about Brownstone, but the damn man had set up shop in her head. Maybe it was inevitable.

A hunter's gleam appeared in Kara's eyes. "So, what... you're saying he's not a boy?"

"He's a boy. Well, a man. Maybe too much of a man." Shay laughed.

Kara exchanged glances with the other women. "What do you mean by that?"

"He's just not into me, or, as far as I can tell, women. He's an interesting guy, and, uh, we've worked together a few times. I've never seen him around any women, or much interested in women. I asked him if he was gay, and he said he wasn't, but I'm pretty sure he's in the closet and just doesn't know it...or something." She rubbed the back of her neck, wondering if it was okay that she was sharing Brownstone's personal business, even if it overlapped with hers.

Kara laughed. "Oh, girlfriend, that's perfect." She had a huge grin on her face.

Shay blinked. "Perfect? How is it perfect that the guy's gay and not into me?" She waved her hands. "Not saying I'm into him or anything, just that, you know, if I were, it wouldn't be perfect that he was gay. I'm hot, but I'm not so conceited that I think I can turn a gay man straight."

"You're not thinking of the side benefits." Kara shrugged. "Seriously."

"'Side benefits?' Like what?"

"All the delicious eye candy without any of the pawing.

Hell, I had a gay guy friend back in college, and we'd cuddle up and watch romcoms together. I've never been able to get any of my boyfriends to do that." Kara nodded, wearing a satisfied smile on her face.

A harsh laugh erupted from Shay. "There are no romcoms in this guy's movie list, trust me. I think he'd explode if he had to watch a romcom. He's more into barbecue, action movies, and kicking ass."

"Definitely a closet case," Janelle declared, and Bella and Kara nodded in agreement.

"You haven't even met him!" Shay was confused about why she felt the need to defend Brownstone's sexuality. "I think he is, but maybe I'm wrong. Shouldn't you all be talking me down?"

"Does he clean?" Kara asked.

She nodded. "Yeah, he's a neat freak, and OCD about organization. It was a bit intimidating."

"He's gay," her friends chorused.

"You think so?" Shay asked doubtfully, unsure if their confirmation made her feel better or worse about the situation with Brownstone.

Bella raised an eyebrow. "Yep. He's overcompensating with all that barbecue and action-movie stuff. Let me ask you one question: has the guy ever hit on you? At all?"

Shay shook her head.

"You're hot, Shay. If the guy's not hitting on you and he's doing all that other stuff, he's gay. I'm like ninety-ninety percent certain."

"I thought so," she mumbled. "Good to hear someone tell me I'm not crazy."

"Sorry." Bella glanced into the crowd. "Don't mean to

confirm your fears and run, but do you mind if I go dance with those guys? They were nice on the eyes."

"I wanted to take a shot too," Janelle said. "I need to get back in the saddle after that crap with Darius."

Shay pulled out her phone to check the time. "Sure. I have an early day tomorrow anyway. I'd better get going." She turned toward Kara. "Are you going to be all right by yourself?"

She grinned. "I'll just go dancing with them and the guys."

Shay pulled each of her friends in for a hug. "Thanks for the fun, girls. It's been too long, and it's nice to not deal with so much testosterone."

"Archaeologists are really that brotastic?" Kara wondered.

Shay stopped herself from grimacing. She'd slipped up. This was one of the reasons why she wanted to spend time with friends, but not *too* much time. They would never understand her world.

"Yeah, you know…men. They always find a way to beat their chests." She did her best imitation of a Brownstone grunt. "Me archaeologist. Me find more bones than you."

The girls all laughed.

A good lie always went down smoother with some humor.

"Don't let those bastards at the university work you too hard," Bella suggested with a wink.

"I won't."

Shay's playtime was over. Tomorrow she needed to start her search for the Green Dragon Crescent Blade.

The police cruiser barreled down the streets, lights flashing but siren silent. Dispatch had just reported a 415 followed by a possible 240: disturbance and possible assault with a deadly weapon at a bar near their patrol route.

Officer Santos, the driver, shook his head. "What's the report say again? That address sounds like the Black Sun."

His partner Johansen peered at the dispatch report on the cruiser's central display. "That's because it *is* the Black Sun."

Santos grimaced. "Shit. Maybe we should slow down."

"Why?"

"It's the fucking Black Sun. Why the hell are we going to stop them? Anyone in there is an asshole criminal, and they can all kill each other for all I care. They won't even *want* our help, so we're going to risk our lives so some scumbags can shoot us in the back?"

Johansen tapped the screen to bring up more information. "Nope, you're wrong."

"*Nope?*" Santos spared a glance his partner's way. "How am I wrong?"

"The call was from the owner. He specifically said he wanted the fight broken up by the police."

"Since when does that scumbag wants cops to help him? What else does the dispatch report say?"

Johansen laughed. "I can't believe this shit. Listen to this… 'Additional information: Class Six bounty hunter onsite: Brownstone, James. Jordan Adams, aka 'King Pyro,' level-four bounty onsite."

"Oh, shit. Damn it!" Santos sucked in a deep breath. "I can't believe this."

"What's wrong?"

"The Granite Ghost is taking on King Pyro? I wish I had some popcorn."

They closed on the bar just in time to see the front door explode in a shower of burning wooden fragments.

"What the hell?" Santos yelled.

A body flew through the burning hole.

11

J ames stepped into the Black Sun and glanced over his shoulder at the bar. Tyler stood there with a scowl on his face and his arms crossed.

"Fucking Brownstone!" the bartender yelled. "Don't tear up my place. Doors aren't cheap."

"I'll pay for the door," the bounty hunter said. "At least now the fight's outside, right?" He shrugged and offered a playful grin. "Unless you want me to bring him back in here?"

"Just keep it away from here." Tyler watched Brownstone step out before mumbling, "Fucking prick."

King Pyro hopped up and dusted off his shoulders. "You got in a good hit, Brownstone, I'll give you that." He slapped a hand over his chest. "But I'm still moving. You see, the only chance you had of winning was knocking my ass out with your first hit. Now you're going to die, and I'm going to enjoy killing you."

"You're only still moving because I didn't hit you all that

hard. I can't risk killing you, since I want the money. This isn't for fun."

The other man snorted. "You think you're all that, Brownstone? You think you're big shit?"

"I know I'm bigger shit than you. You're nothing more than a pathetic thief who thinks he's special because he's a living lighter."

"No," King Pyro shouted, thrusting his hands into the air. "I'm the motherfucking *KING* of Los Angeles now. I'm a god, and I'm going to kill you to make a point to all the other people strutting around thinking they are badasses. You mess with the king," he jerked a thumb at himself, "you burn."

A police cruiser screeched to a halt in the street and two cops hopped out, guns drawn, but stayed behind their doors.

James couldn't blame them for not rushing in. Two street cops wouldn't last thirty seconds against a level-four bounty. An AET team was probably already on its way.

Anti-Enhanced Threat teams might still be not all that common, but for the fortunate cities and departments that could afford them, the members had the training and the gear to handle some of the deadlier magical threats that had popped up in the last two decades.

The clock was ticking. If James wanted his money, he needed to take down King Pyro before the AET team showed up. Otherwise he'd just be a guy who had to pay for an asshole's door.

James charged toward the bounty and a football-sized fireball erupted from the man's left hand, narrowly missing the bounty hunter's head. He closed the distance and launched a left hook, sending King Pyro stumbling back with a grunt.

"Congrats on not getting knocked out already, asshole." The bounty hunter shook out his hand. King Pyro was a lot stronger than he looked—and he looked pretty damn strong. Not that James was worried. He'd expected a level four to be a little challenging. It'd just make things more fun.

"You know what I've figured out?" James asked, keeping his attention on the man's hands as he circled the flame master.

King Pyro grinned. "What, that you're going to die screaming? That you're going to shit yourself while you're begging me to finish you off and end the pain?"

"Nope. That it takes you too damn long to really get the heat going." James sprinted forward, slamming his shoulder into his opponent's chest and sending the criminal reeling backward.

King Pyro threw two more fireballs as he fell. One missed James entirely, instead slamming into the door of some poor sucker's Kia and scorching it, and the other clipped the bounty hunter's shoulder.

James pivoted to take cover behind a car, pulling off his leather jacket, which now sported a new hole. His skin stung a little, but his jacket and shirt seemed to have taken most of the damage. He still didn't regret not bringing the necklace.

I can handle this dick without that messed-up magical shit.

"I really liked that jacket, asshole," James ground out.

"Guess I'll have to use your bounty to buy a new one. Gonna have to dish out a little payback, though."

A football-sized fireball nearly winged him as it zoomed past and exploded against a nearby chain-link fence, reducing the metal to dripping molten liquid.

James risked a glance around the corner and saw that the man had another fireball ready.

"They told me all these stories about how badass you are," King Pyro shouted. "But you're just another bitch in the end, aren't you, Brownstone? Hiding because you know you can't handle royalty. A royal god, yeah!"

What a fucking dipshit. I knew a guy with a nickname like that was going to be a fucking idiot.

James resisted pulling his gun. He needed the man alive to collect the bounty, after all.

He sprinted away from his hiding place, but not directly toward King Pyro. Two more fireballs zipped past him, exploding against the ground and sending out waves of heat. An abrupt change of direction sent him barreling toward the criminal.

King Pyro raised his flame-covered hands. James threw a quick, low punch into the man's stomach, then followed up with another to his mouth. The other man grunted under the blows and fell back, but he still managed to sweep out with a burning hand.

Pain spiked from the bounty hunter's arm. The smell of his sizzling flesh filled the air, which was just enough to distract him.

His enemy hopped off the ground and wiped some blood from his mouth. "Bet that hurts, doesn't it? I've got a lot more coming. Ever wanted to see a cremation up close and personal? Once you see it, it's kind of a rush. Like a fucking drug, bitch. Better than heroin or dust, that's for sure."

"I've had worse." James shrugged. "You know, the reports all got your powers wrong."

"Why do you say that?"

"Your real power is boring people to death with your bullshit speeches."

King Pyro laughed. "You don't even get it. I'm just playing with you. You're going to burn, Brownstone, and then you know what I'm going to do? I'm going to track down everyone you love and burn them to ash. Got a kid, Brownstone? Got a woman? They'll die in fire screaming your name. Fuck, I'll ash all the plants in your house just to make an example out of you."

Get ready to say hi to the Devil for me, asshole.

The criminal was still laughing when James charged again. The bounty hunter's pulse pounded in his ears as he slammed his fist into Pyro's face again, this time at full strength. The other man soared into the air.

James tackled him before he landed. Pyro's entire body burst into flames, but the bounty hunter ignored the heat and stinging pain. He slammed the man's head several times against the concrete, then hammered away with both fists. The flames died out.

The bounty hunter barely could see the man in front of him as he continued pulverizing him. Instead, James could only see Leeroy whimpering and Alison screaming. An image of Shay lying dead, burned beyond recognition, passed through his head.

"I'll fucking kill you, you piece of shit," James roared. He slammed another fist into the barely conscious criminal. "You're dead."

"Brownstone, stand down," a distant voice yelled.

The bounty hunter stood and then slammed his foot into King Pyro, sending the man into the windshield of a truck. He growled and stomped toward the bounty.

"Brownstone, stand down," the voice yelled again.

James realized it wasn't that distant. He spun, his pulse still deafening. He was ready to kick more ass. If King Pyro had brought friends, they were going down too.

The two street cops from before had closed on him. They didn't have their guns out.

In the sky, four LAPD-marked tactical drones armed with stun cannons whirred overhead, and an armored van was parked down the street.

Six figures clad in heavy black armor rushed toward him, a couple with stun guns and the others with assault rifles. Twelve red circles glowed in the darkness from the tactical lenses of the men. The rest of their faces remained covered by their helmets. LA AET was emblazoned across their chest in huge white letters.

James took a deep breath and stepped away from the groaning King Pyro. If the man had been normal, he'd have already been dead—which was about where the bounty hunter wanted him after the asshole's threat.

"I want the fucking credit. I took him down before AET showed up." He glanced at King Pyro and the smashed window. "And I'll pay for the window out of my bounty."

One of the street cops nodded, holding up his hands in a placating manner like Brownstone was some vicious dog about to attack. "Yeah, yeah. I'll call it in, Brownstone. Let AET secure him from here."

The bounty hunter took a single step toward King Pyro and the drones pivoted, aiming their stun cannons at him.

"You even think about touching anyone I love," James warned, his voice full of lethal intent, "and I will find you, no matter where you are or what fucking rock you're hiding under. You could run to fucking Oriceran, and I'd go there. And I'd find you and wait until you were sleeping and rip your head off and shit down your throat."

King Pyro could only manage a weak groan in response. Blood covered his swollen face and jaw.

James shrugged and turned around. The AET team still had their weapons trained on him, but he wasn't going to threaten or attack cops. They were on the same side as him, in the end.

"I'm done here." James spat on the ground and stomped toward his truck. "Should have brought some fucking burn cream," he muttered.

As Shay made her way toward the club's exit through the still thick crowd, a huge musclebound man sauntered toward her. His face suggested he was young; probably in his early twenties at the oldest. She ignored him and continued toward the front door.

Captain Muscles fell in behind her, and she gritted her teeth. A few seconds later he pinched her ass.

Shay spun around and slapped his hand. "Keep your hands to yourself, asshole."

Captain Muscles grinned. "Hey, babe, don't get so upset. It's a compliment, you know. You're hot." His words came out slow and slurred as he turned left, then right as he spoke. "You don't see me touching any ugly chick's ass."

Several other men rushed over. Shay tensed, but then noticed the apologetic looks on their faces.

"You're an idiot, Xander," one of the new arrivals told the kid. "Remember what coach said about getting in trouble?" He turned to Shay. "I'm sorry. He's just had one too many tonight. Please, we'll take him and sit him down. It doesn't have to be a big thing."

Shay considered if she wanted to make it a big thing or not, despite Mr. Reasonable seeming embarrassed over his friend. The size of all the men suggested athletes, as did the reference to their coach. Judging by the ages and builds, she suspected they were college football players.

That didn't make them dangerous, at least not to her. They were trained in a very stylized and sanitized form of violence, one with rules and restraint.

I don't need this shit right before heading to Mexico. Guess it's your lucky day, asshole.

"Whatever," Shay muttered, and turned to leave.

"Probably a fucking lesbian anyway," Captain Muscles snarled. "What she needs is a serious deep dicking, so she knows what a real man feels like."

Shay spun on her heel. She didn't look at Captain Muscles. Instead, she shot a murderous glare at his friends.

They all moved to the side. They could sense the true predator in the room.

"You're on your own, man," Mr. Reasonable told Xander, his hands in front of him.

"What?" Captain Muscles sneered. "You think this little bitch is gonna do anything about it?"

"I think she's gonna kick your ass, and I think you have it coming."

A little admiration flowed through Shay for the other men. Recognizing lethal potential was a rare skill. They might have made good killers or bounty hunters.

Captain Muscles laughed. "Just because I'm a little drunk doesn't mean I'm scared of some little w—"

After a loud crunch, his head snapped back. Shay's roundhouse had been so fast it took the other men a few seconds to realize what had happened.

Captain Muscles fell to the floor moaning, and Shay grabbed his arm and prepared to bend it backward.

"Don't do it!" Mr. Reasonable yelled.

Shay narrowed her eyes. "Give me one good fucking reason."

"Because he's our star quarterback, and we have a good shot this season. The rest of us shouldn't suffer because of him." Mr. Reasonable scrubbed a hand over his face. "I know he's a douchebag, but you're already taught him a lesson, right? Shit, if you want, I'll promise to tell everyone he got beat down by a woman half his size. It'll humiliate him, but he'll still be able to play."

Shay glared at the downed football player in disgust before leaning in to speak to him. "You're lucky Brownstone isn't here." She waited for a few seconds, then yanked on his arm, dislocating it.

Captain Muscles screamed.

"Damn!" the other players yelled in unison.

Shay stood and dusted her hands on her pants. "You can

pop it right back in. He'll still be able to play for the rest of the season."

She stormed toward the exit. A bouncer walked toward her, then looked between her and the moaning football player and stepped out of the way.

Officer Santos watched as paramedics loaded King Pyro onto a stretcher. The AET had fitted him with a stun collar, but given the state he was in, a meter maid could probably handle him.

He went over to the stretcher and leaned over the moaning man. "You're one lucky motherfucker, Adams."

King Pyro turned his head toward the officer. His battered face and swollen eyes made it hard to tell if he even knew who was talking to him. He mumbled something, but with his broken jaw it was hard to understand.

"Brownstone is not the kind of heat you want to bring down on yourself. Ask the local Harriken. We used to have a lot of them. Now we don't. You know why? Rumor is that they killed Brownstone's dog to make a point, so he killed all of *them* to make a point back."

A groan escaped the wounded criminal's mouth. It sounded like something approaching the word "family."

"What's that?" Officer Santos asked. He furrowed his brow trying to figure out what the other man was getting at. "Oh no, I don't think Brownstone has a family, really. But the guy could have a fucking Barbie doll, and I'd leave the doll alone if I wanted to keep breathing." He shook his head and waved a hand. "Just keep this in mind, Adams—if LAPD hadn't been here, your ass would be dead. Never say cops didn't do something for you."

King Pyro moaned some more.

1 2

The world around James blurred at the edges. Buildings stood too far away or close compared to where he knew they should.

This shit wasn't real.

It was fake reality; a dream, nothing more than an expression of his own mind. Even though James knew that, he still couldn't seem to control himself. His body moved of its own accord.

James raised the necklace over his head and slid it over his neck. Burning pain shot from the point of contact and spread. The sizzle of his flesh reached his ears and nostrils, and he clenched his teeth as the pain burrowed through his body until he could have sworn every cell was on fire.

Something whispered in the recesses of his mind: cold, distant, inhuman, but all too familiar. He didn't understand what it was trying to say, but there was intelligence behind the communication.

The bounty hunter's eyes snapped open and he jerked upright in his bed, his heart pounding. He shouldn't care.

It was just another damned dream.

James scrubbed his face with his hand. Problem was, the dream was a reflection of his memories. When he wore the necklace, something whispered to him. He'd tried to ignore it, thinking he was just psyching himself out, but there was no denying that whatever was calling him to him was getting stronger. The whispers had been louder, especially this last year.

His free ride with the necklace was coming to an end, and whatever dark magic powered it would want its due sooner rather than later.

Could something good come from something evil? He was pretty sure that necklace was evil.

Still, the bounty hunter was about to go to a place embroiled in a conflict that was one small step down from a civil war; a foreign country where he didn't have the contacts and reputation he did in Los Angeles. He couldn't be sure someone or something more powerful than him didn't lurk in Baja California Sur waiting to tear his head off.

James didn't fear death, not really. He feared letting some monstrous piece of shit get away because he wasn't strong enough; scum like King Pyro or bastards like the Harriken who were ready to torture a woman to death.

Darkness threatened to swallow the world. Maybe his efforts were pointless, only delaying the inevitable, but he wanted to at least try.

Father McCartney had always told him that he was meant to be a force for good; a soldier serving God. James often wondered if he was some sort of demon who had been kicked out of Hell and just had his memories wiped.

That might explain the necklace.

Whatever its source, the power of the necklace could make sure James was the guy breathing at the end of the day. He'd handled the power for years, so maybe one more job wouldn't be too much. He'd packed plenty of weapons, but he hadn't grabbed the necklace from the warehouse the night before when he'd visited.

"No." James shook his head. "Can't keep relying on that thing."

Stopping an addiction had to start somewhere, and the current job was as good a place as any. If the necklace truly was evil, then every use threatened something much more important than his life. He didn't want to be seduced by the power and end up being the asshole murdering a family someday.

"King Ghost," he muttered, then snickered.

What bullshit.

The bounty hunter had taken down a level-four bounty without using the necklace. A few scorch marks here and there weren't a big thing. He could handle a few arrogant *sicarios* in Mexico. If he stayed away from level-six bounties, he shouldn't have much trouble.

On top of that, Shay was supposed to have contacts that would keep him from having too much trouble with the cartel hitmen and soldiers anyway. It wasn't like he was going to Mexico to mess with them.

James slid out of bed, now more comfortable. It was time to clean up and head out for the airport.

Fuck the necklace. Fuck whatever curse or demon or ghost of a top-hat-wearing ferret that lives inside it. *Fuck the past.*

Shay eyed Brownstone as he lugged his two huge cases. One of them was obviously a go-case filled with weapons and other dangerous implements of his trade. She'd made her own arrangements to get her equipment past security and customs, and it didn't involve strolling to the front desk with contraband.

She couldn't decide if that meant Brownstone was brave or stupid. Given everything she knew about him, she figured it was a little Column A and some Column B.

Their last flight in and out of country had been on chartered planes so it hadn't been as big of an issue, but this time the idiot was going to get them arrested before they even left the country.

She couldn't risk a fight in an airport.

Shay frowned. For that matter, that sort of risk didn't seem like Brownstone. The guy might be cavalier about his own safety, but she'd never seen him put innocent people in danger. She was missing something, and that realization only irritated her more.

Brownstone nodded to the woman working the desk and placed his hand on the palm scanner on the counter.

She looked down at her computer and up at him. "Hello, Mr. Brownstone. I'm sorry to have to ask you to do this, but I'm going to need you to show me additional proof of your level-six status. Federal regulations, you know." She gave him a sheepish smile, as if she expected him to explode.

"No problem."

The bounty hunter reached into his jacket and pulled

out a chip-embedded card with his picture on it, which he handed to the woman. She quickly typed something into the computer in front of her and slid the card into a reader to the side of her computer.

James' movement revealed a shoulder holster, so he likely had a case filled with guns—several of which probably weren't legal—and was getting ready to march through airport security with a loaded weapon.

Fuck, Brownstone. How about a little more subtlety? Did you hit your head last night? Are you drunk?

The woman glanced to her side. A police officer pulled away from the corner and headed their way.

Shay swallowed and her gaze shot around the room, seeking exits not near any obvious police.

The cop neither went for his gun or Taser nor pulled out his radio to request backup. Instead, he walked to the wrong desk and placed his hand on the palm scanner.

"Please give the verbal verification for the record," the woman requested.

"Officer Tom Johns," the cop said. "Verifying special transport exceptions for James Brownstone." He rattled off the time and date, then nodded to the bounty hunter. "You going for work or pleasure?"

"Work, though I do take a lot of pleasure in my work."

The cop chuckled. "Be careful down there, then. You get away from the cities and things can get real dicey."

"Thanks. I'll keep that in mind."

Brownstone nodded, and the cop strolled away.

Another airline employee, a large man, came over to grab Brownstone's suitcases. Rather than placing them on the conveyor running behind the desk, he opened a door and pulled them into a back room.

"Well, don't they treat you special?" Shay muttered under her breath.

She shook her head at the spectacle and stepped up to the counter to finish checking in herself.

And here I am just smuggling things the old-fashioned way.

As they walked toward their boarding gate twenty minutes later, Shay's curiosity finally won its battle against her desire not to show any weakness in front of Brownstone—especially since he'd basically been allowed to walk through the later security checkpoint without even going through the metal detector.

"What was all that about?" Shay asked. "They just let you bring all that stuff on, no questions asked? Not to mention…" She gestured toward the general location of his now-concealed holster.

James shrugged. "You've been on the other side for too long. You forget it doesn't have to be that way."

"Huh?"

"The other side of the law. When you're on the right side, a lot of allowances and exceptions are made to help you take out bad guys easier, especially when you've got an established track record. It also helps that we have a bunch of law enforcement treaties with Mexico, which is one of the reasons I like to stick close to home and not go wandering off to places like China where the rules are tighter."

Shay sighed. "I think I'll stay with my own methods. I don't want to be too far up cop butts. I'm a shady character, you know." She grinned.

"Suit yourself, but nothing you've been doing lately has helped the bad guys."

"Nor was it always strictly legal."

Brownstone chuckled. "Yeah, guess so."

They closed on their gate, and Shay took a deep breath. This job wouldn't be like Peru. She'd have to deal with a lot of dangerous people before she got anywhere near the Green Dragon Crescent Blade.

She glanced at Brownstone, unsure if he'd be an asset or a liability in the end. If she needed to kill every single asshole in Baja California Sur that was one thing, but the bounty hunter also had a way of attracting a lot of undue attention.

Shay also didn't like the idea of becoming too reliant on him. That path led to sloppiness. She'd spent years working without a partner; it made things less compli- cated. In the last few weeks, she'd involved herself in a lot of things she probably shouldn't have.

"Yeah!" a man shouted, jerking Shay out of her reflections.

A group of college dude-bros in rather garish t-shirts that announced in pictorial form their preferences in women lingered near the gate. From the sound of it, the men were already drunk.

"Cabo, bro!" yelled one of them. "Fuck, yeah!"

"Yeah, dude," another agreed, slapping him on the back. "This is gonna be so badass."

The gate attendant rolled her eyes, as did Shay. Just what Mexico needed: imported dude-bros.

After grabbing their luggage, Shay and James picked up their rental truck and headed to their hotel, a nice if low-key place Shay had stayed at before. The pair exchanged few words until they stood in her hotel room.

"Yours is across the way," Shay told him, handing him a keycard. She then fished a small silver cylinder from her luggage.

"Frequency scanner?"

"Yeah."

James eyed the room. "Had trouble here with bugs?"

Shay shook her head. "Nope, but never hurts to be too careful, especially with all the friends I might have made recently helping you out." She winked.

James slapped one of this suitcases on the bed and opened it. He pulled a shabby coat out of his luggage, a long ugly brown puffy-sleeved mess.

"Where did you buy that?" Shay asked, eyeing the coat with disdain. "The thrift store?"

"Yeah, actually. Got a good deal on it."

Shay sighed. "And here I thought you had good fashion sense, though I guess with what I've seen you wear before, I shouldn't have been surprised at this point."

The bounty hunter stared at her for a moment. "Huh?" He shrugged, a bit confused by her weird statement about fashion sense.

James opened the case and started pulling out pistol

and knife holsters, along with several different pistols, with a marked preference for .45-caliber fare.

"You're not gonna do this in your room?" Shay wondered.

"I want to be ready right away."

"And one gun isn't enough?"

James grinned. "No."

The next few minutes involved a lot of clicking and slapping as the bounty hunter loaded magazines into his weapons and slipped them into different holsters, along with extra magazines for his weapons. Knives, both stabbing and throwing, followed.

"That's a lot of guns," Shay exclaimed. "I'm impressed— and not much impresses me about guns—but we're not raiding the cartel, Brownstone. You remember that, right?"

"Yeah, I know."

"Also, these guys might be scum, but they haven't done shit to you as far as I know. I thought you liked to keep it to bounties or revenge."

James nodded. "I do, and they haven't messed with me."

"Then what's with the arsenal?"

"Finding a new gun is more complicated than just pulling a new one off you. Simple enough. And this isn't my home turf, so I want to be prepared."

Shay snickered. "Okay, makes sense, I guess. Just don't go causing unnecessary trouble for me."

"Sure. I won't go causing any unnecessary trouble."

By the time the bounty hunter finished arming up, he carried enough pistols, knives, and ammo to lay waste to hundreds of people if necessary. People said that luck was where opportunity met preparation, and he was ready for some damn good luck.

It wasn't like he was going all-out. He hadn't bothered to bring any grenades, let alone the necklace.

James grabbed a small protected metal case and slid it into one of his magazine slots.

"What's that?" Shay asked.

"Two potions, healing and energy. Just in case."

"Energy?" The field archaeologist's gaze lingered on the case. "Does that make you bulletproof?"

A heavy question lingered in Shay's eyes. She'd seen him take direct shots during the Harriken battle and not get hurt. She'd also seen the necklace bond with him. The woman's sharp mind couldn't have failed to put some of the pieces together.

James appreciated that she hadn't asked too many questions. They'd worked together enough that he trusted her, but that didn't mean he was ready to bare his soul to her. Until he better understood the necklace, he wasn't going to talk to anyone about it.

"No," James admitted. "None of the stuff I brought makes me bulletproof. I'm planning to shoot guys before they shoot me."

"Always a good strategy."

"Do you have any bounties you're interested in yet?"

James shook his head. "Waiting for you to get your shit figured out before I go after anyone."

With his load-out complete, James pulled on the jacket.

Shay laughed. "You look like a complete doofus in that jacket, Brownstone. I think I get your real strategy now. You're going to wait until the other guys fall down laughing, then you'll shoot them." She made a face of mock disgust. "Shooting people while they are laughing, Brownstone? That's cold."

James glanced down at a tear in one of the sleeves and shrugged. "But you can't see any of the holsters, can you?"

She looked him over. "No, I guess I can't."

He pursed his lips and finished with a shrug. "Then looks can be deceiving."

Shay shook her head. "Nope. Just because you're a dangerous doofus doesn't change the fact you look like a doofus."

James grunted.

13

S hay cruised along a worn and cracked road in a
Forerunner. Brownstone sat in the passenger seat,
idly watching the city pass by through the window,
not saying a word.

She wondered what was going through the man's head.
Brownstone didn't seem to get nervous about danger, and
unlike their last job together, they didn't have any reports
that suggested anyone else was closing in on the Green
Dragon Crescent Blade. The whole job should be a nice in-
and-out grab, assuming there were no clever deathtraps or
magical guardians.

Shay could have easily carried out the whole job
without the man, but she'd understood that the Professor
wanted him to come along. She didn't know if that meant
Smite-Williams didn't trust her yet or not, but that didn't
bother her because she didn't fully trust him either.

Her attention returned to James. She didn't want to be
alone with her own thoughts.

"You're a very incurious man, James Brownstone," the field archaeologist remarked. "Surprisingly so."

He looked at her. "What are you talking about?"

"We show up in Mexico, and I grab a truck. Then I take us to get a totally different vehicle, and you don't even ask why."

"That's not being incurious. I'm just not wasting time."

"Oh?"

Brownstone shrugged a single shoulder and returned to looking outside. "I don't bother worrying about unimportant shit that I know other people can handle. We've worked together, both on your job and on mine, if you want to call it that. You're not a dipshit, so I trust you."

Shay shook her head. Brownstone still managed to agitate her even when he was complimenting her. It was like most of her barbs bounced right off the man. That she wasn't in control both disturbed and thrilled her.

"Still no questions?" She just wanted him to play along. "At least give me a little insight into your thought process."

"Why?"

Shay chuckled. "Because I'm trying to figure out what makes you tick, Brownstone."

"I'm guessing you needed this for some rough terrain. It's not exactly a fucking mystery. It's not like you swapped out the truck for an amphibious limo or a motorcycle."

Shay snickered. "Yeah. Anyway, I've got the likely location of the artifact—some hidden caves in a small mountain range up north."

"We're not exactly deep in the Amazon here. How come no one has ever found the artifact before?"

"Glad you asked." Shay did enjoy showing off, mentally

or physically. "The caves were discovered initially during a satellite thermal survey, but weren't there when they tried to image the area again in later surveys. It was chalked up to bad data. Later information suggests the caves are being cloaked with magic, and the satellite just got lucky that one time." She sighed. "And if it gets lucky again, somebody else could end up finding it."

James frowned. "There's magical cloaking? Doesn't that mean someone's still there?"

"Nope. Or probably not. Just means some Taoist priests were very thorough back in the fifteenth century." Shay glanced into her rearview mirror for a second. "Anyway, these are mountain caves, so the terrain might not be all that hospitable—hence the vehicle choice. But before we leave, I need to go hit up a local contact; someone who can put in a good word with us for one of the local gangs."

"Why do we need a good word with the local gang?"

"Because too many damned people around here will kill you for a hundred bucks and a cheeseburger from the crappy McDonalds in Cabo San Lucas." She rolled her eyes. "And the burgers there aren't even that good. Don't ever eat there, trust me. It's like the people have no concept of what a burger's supposed to taste like. Or are sourcing that meat from a strange Ōnıceran cow-like thing."

"So, what...you think these guys might take a shot at us, otherwise?" James grunted, but a hint of a smile appeared.

"Something like that, but throw some money and a few polite words around and a lot of that goes away. As long as you know who to talk to—and I do."

"Not afraid of some local gangs. They want to come at me, they can learn the same lesson the Harriken in LA did."

A vicious grin appeared on his face. "It might be a nice little workout."

"No, no, no." Shay groaned. She wanted to bounce her head off the steering wheel. "We need to keep our eye on the prize, Brownstone. Remember, half the point of this job is to get Smite-Williams to cough up something to you."

She wondered what artifact the Professor might be sending Brownstone's way. The man already had access to enough magic to make him a deadly threat. She had a hard time seeing what else he might need, especially since he was a real hands-on ass-kicker.

"Just sayin'. I can teach them the true meaning of fear," James said, sounding far too enthusiastic about the idea.

"I know you're not afraid of them and all that, Brownstone, but we can't level half this town without it causing trouble for both of us in the future. That makes things complicated…and you like things simple, right?"

"Yes, I guess I do." The bounty hunter rubbed the back of his neck and looked away, like a little boy who'd been caught pissing on his mom's flowers.

"Good. Glad we're on the same page. No blowing up the cartel or gangs while we're here. We're here to get the Green Dragon Crescent Blade and maybe score a bounty for you on the side. We good?"

"Yeah, we're good. Unless they piss me off."

Shay sighed.

They arrived at their location ten minutes later: an old warehouse with dozens of rusted-out cars dotting the area. James spotted at least six armed men, none of whom seemed to know how to smile.

Shay opened her door. "This won't take long."

"You want backup, just in case your guys aren't as polite as last time you dealt with them?"

He understood that they didn't want cartel or gang trouble, but he wasn't going to shy away from a fight if someone else picked it, either.

The woman laughed. "That's nice of you, Brownstone, but I've been doing this without backup for a long time. No way I'm going to let myself get too used to having you around. No offense."

James shrugged. He wasn't offended. He understood the advantages of working alone.

Shay closed the door and walked toward two gang sentries armed with AKs. A short conversation followed, and one of them men gestured with his gun toward a warehouse door. She disappeared inside.

All these assholes think they have strength in numbers. It makes them stupid and easy to take out.

James tried to entertain himself by evaluating the security situation. He'd spotted four more guards roaming the grounds, along with a rooftop sniper.

The warehouse and the surrounding buildings could hide a lot of men, so the small number of gang members outside didn't convince him the group couldn't field a lot more bodies.

His examination convinced him that the rusted-out cars probably weren't left over from better days, when the location had served as a part of the normal economy. The positioning of the wrecks was too careful, and the density was too high. They were really barricades and checkpoints designed to slow down attackers.

"These guys are brighter than I thought," James muttered.

There was nothing worse than clever thugs. They could actually be dangerous.

He grew bored with thinking about how he might lay waste to the warehouse. Instead, he pulled out his phone, wondering if he should give Alison a call. She had sounded like she was fine during their last conversation, but she'd also wanted him to call again soon. He just wasn't sure if the next day was *too* soon.

James frowned, wondering how much a call from Mexico to Virginia might cost. He really needed to get some sort of international plan for his phone if he was going to be spending much time outside the United States. Not that he was short on cash, but international rates were still murder.

Maybe I could set her up with some sort of VOIP app or something. I mean, shit—what if Shay wants to go to Ghana or something next time. How much would that *fucking cost?*

He shook his head, wondering how he'd gotten on this thought track. It was like he thought wandering halfway across the world with Shay would become something common.

James was a bounty hunter, not a field archaeologist. He was in Mexico right now to help Shay out because it'd end with him getting something he needed from the Professor, not because they were partners.

He shouldn't have even been thinking about going off to exotic locales with her in the future. There were more than enough bounties to keep him busy in California, let alone North America if he got bored in the City of Angels for whatever reason.

A soft chuckle escaped his lips when he thought about how quickly things had changed with him in the last few weeks. James had spent years with no one close to him other than Leeroy. The Church was there to save his soul, not be his friend, even though he helped them. He knew how much pain and stress he caused poor Father McCartney. Now he had something approaching a friend in Shay, and with Alison he had something like a family.

Hell, he'd even hung out with the off-duty cops a few times. He was a damn social butterfly at this point.

James still wasn't sure what to make of all this. It felt like a good thing, but at the same time it complicated his previously simple life. Maybe no one who wanted to care about others could in truth have a simple life.

When Shay emerged from the warehouse, he watched her for a few moments, looking for any sign of trouble. No tension lined her features and her movements exuded relaxation, so her conversation must have gone well.

The gang got to exist another day.

He returned his attention to the phone and deciding whether he should call Alison.

The driver-side door opened, and Shay slipped into her seat. "Don't do it."

He looked over. "Don't do what? You just got here."

She gestured toward his phone. "I bet you were going to call Alison, weren't you?"

He looked back. "I just had my phone out."

"Don't call her. You're acting like an overprotective dad. She needs a little space so she can figure out where she fits into that place. If you're on with her every day, even if she wants you to call, she won't be able to transition from her old life into her new one."

James silently put his phone away. He didn't want to lie about what he'd been thinking, but he also didn't want to give Shay the satisfaction of confirming she'd been right.

The woman confused him. Sometimes she seemed to be able to read his thoughts and others, she seemed completely puzzled by something simple and basic he'd said—as if he were some sort of weird Oriceran transplant.

"Let's get going," Shay said, starting the Forerunner back up. "If I hurry and we're lucky, maybe I can find the Blade and we can get back to our rooms before sundown."

James pulled out his phone again, not to call Alison but to check the North American Bounty Hunting Alliance app. It wasn't as up-to-date as the various city department apps when it came to bounties, but it would do for the moment.

First, he tried to limit the bounty area to Mexico and search.

Sorry, too many results. Please add additional criteria and search again.

He almost laughed. Of *course* looking for all the bounties in an entire country would be too much. He had to limit his search parameters just when checking Los Angeles. There were so many scumbags out there.

James limited the search area to Baja California Sur and the level to five and above.

Five records meet your search criteria.

He read through the possibilities. Three out of the five were very far north, and a lot farther than he wanted to drive. The fourth was some sort of revolutionary army leader in exile from Colombia.

James didn't mind pissing people off, but he didn't want to get involved in politics unless he had a good understanding of what was going on. Even though he took people down for money, he wasn't a mercenary. His job used his strength to make the world a better place, and he never wanted to forget that.

He also wanted to be one-hundred-percent sure the target had it coming. He knew that not all bounties were fair or warranted, which is why he chose his carefully. Not pissing off an entire revolutionary army group was high on his list of smart moves.

Having eliminated four out of the five bounties, he looked at the details of the last, hoping for something worth pursuing. The final level-five bounty belonged to a man living in the same mountain range they were already driving toward, one Jose Padilla, who went by the name "Sombra."

James grunted in satisfaction as he skimmed the details. Sombra was the kind of target he'd been born to take down. The man was a necromancer who kidnapped innocent people. Apparently the Mexican government had become so disturbed by his activities at one point, including raising a rather sizeable force of reanimated corpses, they'd sent fighters to bomb the mountains in an attempt to kill him.

"Motherfucking zombies," James muttered. "I hate things that can't be afraid."

"What?" Shay asked.

The bounty hunter glanced at the time. They'd arrived in Mexico early, and Shay's city business hadn't taken that long. If she didn't take all day finding the Green Dragon Crescent Blade, he'd have plenty of time to start tracking down Sombra without even having to sleep first.

"I'd like to take a little detour after your job," James informed her.

"Oh, have some sightseeing you want to do?"

"Nah, want to take down a necromancer."

Shay laughed. "That's fun, too."

150

14

S hay frowned as the rough terrain shook the vehicle. She missed the smooth ride of her Spider on a city street, but at least their target destination would be coming up any minute. Vast canyon walls surrounded them on either side, and mountains rose in the distance.

Light caught Shay's eye, and she slowed the Forerunner before bringing it to a stop. She narrowed her eyes, staring straight ahead.

"Problem?" James asked.

There were caves in the distance, obscured by dust. Finding her destination pleased her, but the faint semi-translucent shimmer in the air worried her as well.

"You see that, Brownstone?" Shay inquired.

"Yeah, I see it. Fucking magic."

Shay slowly exhaled. "That must be the cloaking. From what I've read, you can't actually see the caves unless you're already looking for them and know generally where they are. Neat trick."

James shrugged. "It might also kill you on contact."

"You're barrels of fun, Brownstone."

"I try."

The tomb raider shook her head. Brownstone was right. She couldn't be sure about the secondary effects of the magic field. Dying in the middle of the desert didn't strike her as fun.

"Wait a second," Shay muttered. "See that?"

"The lizard?"

"Yeah."

She narrowed her eyes. An iguana skittered across the parched landscape only a few feet from the field, seemingly oblivious to it.

"Come on, cross it, you lizard sonofabitch. Let's see if it fries you. Take one for history and archaeology."

"That's cold."

"It's not like all that barbecue you eat comes from volunteer animals."

James snickered. "At least they died for a good cause."

Shay smirked at his reply.

The lizard rushed through the field after some tiny prey Shay couldn't make out from a distance and there was no crackle of electricity, no screech, no explosion. The animal kept running. If the magical field had done anything to the creature, it wasn't obvious.

Shay threw open her door. "That's promising."

"Unless the magic turns people into iguanas," James suggested with a grin. "Then it'd make sense it wouldn't affect iguanas."

"Hey, as long as I'm not dead I don't care. I'll pay you if you get me turned back." Shay opened the back door of the Forerunner and pulled out a backpack and a utility belt.

She already had a gun with several magazines. Unlike Brownstone, she didn't expect that she'd be killing any armies anytime soon.

James opened his door. "Finally, something other than sitting around."

"Stop," Shay called.

The bounty hunter turned to look at her.

"From what I've read, this place might have a lot of traps and shit," Shay explained with a sigh. "And I'm not worried about any bad guys inside, so you just stay here. You're great at killing bad guys, Brownstone, I'll give you that, but I think it'd be pretty embarrassing if you died in some six-hundred-year-old trap."

"Seriously?" James grunted. He obviously didn't like being on the bench, but Shay wasn't about to budge on this.

She slipped on the belt. "I'll deal with what's inside. Just make sure that if I come running out, no one pulls a fucking Indiana Jones on me where I run into guns."

"Carlos Rodriguez always uses drones to deal with that sort of thing," James offered.

"Yeah, and I always wondered how he was getting such great signal to his drones when he's deep in some cave." Shay shook her head and finished adjusting her backpack.

"If you can use a movie example, so can I," James told her. "Hey, I wonder if there really *is* some big warehouse where the government keeps ancient magical artifacts."

"Probably." Shay closed the back door and then leaned into the driver's side. "Look, Brownstone, just so you know... This might not be the final site."

"What do you mean?"

"Some of the background research suggests this might only lead me to another place. Just saying there's a good chance this might not end today. I wasn't sure before, because I thought they might have just been speaking metaphorically. That's why I didn't mention it. But now that I see the magic around it, I'm guessing it's a bigger chance."

James shrugged. "Gotta raise the staff at the right time and see where it shines?"

Shay snickered. "Something like that." She gestured behind them into the empty dry wilderness. "Just make sure no one sneaks up on us, Nazis or otherwise."

"Go find your magic Chinese weapon or a map or whatever shit you need," James suggested. "And I'll deal with anyone else."

"Don't kill anyone who doesn't deserve it."

The bounty hunter's only response was a grunt.

The field archaeologist slammed the driver door shut and took a deep breath, which she held until she passed through the magical field. There was no pain or discomfort, and best as she could tell she was still hot as ever and not an iguana.

Shay grinned and waved to Brownstone. He gave her a little salute, and she turned to hurry toward the caves.

They'd parked close enough that the initial hike only took ten minutes, though the vehicle and her backup were mere specks in the distance.

Three different caves confronted her now. If she'd had any doubts about being in the right spot, the faded classical Chinese characters carved above the caves erased them.

Despite the dry climate, the centuries of wind and dust had taken their toll.

Shay reached into a pocket in her backpack and pulled out her augmented-reality interface goggles. Shay hated the things, since they were about as fashionable as Brownstone's coat, but they were still useful. A few quick taps on her phone and they were ready to help earn their cost.

"Let's see how well this translation program works."

The tomb raider might lack Brownstone's photographic memory, but she wasn't a slouch in the foreign language department. Unfortunately, however, she'd never studied *any* Chinese dialect, let alone classical Chinese.

Words overlaid some of the ancient Chinese characters inside the goggles, though most remained unintelligible.

... blade... honorable and strong...

Pass... find... noble...

Stand... speak... Mandate of the Heavens.

"Seems like the right spot, at least," Shay mumbled.

Now she just needed to figure out which cave contained either the treasure or the information she needed for the next leg of her journey.

Shay stepped closer to the caves' mouths.

"Command: adjust lighting filter by ten percent. Command: add contrast overlay."

The characters popped a bit more, but not enough to help with the translation. Something else caught her eye, though; something much smaller.

Shay closed on the first cave mouth and looked up. There were light scratches next to each character; intricate series of lines.

"Command: heighten contrast by ten percent." She waited. "Command: heighten contrast by thirty percent."

They weren't just lines. She recognized the patterns. They were from the *I Ching*. Every Taoist priest worth a damn would have been familiar with the ancient book. The lines formed patterns called hexagrams that were used for divination.

"These have to be here for a reason," Shay murmured, tapping her lips. She tried to think like an ancient Chinese priest, then laughed. "I can barely figure out what modern men are thinking."

The admiral's fleet would have contained both Buddhist and Taoist priests, but all her information suggested the Taoist priests had been responsible for the Green Dragon Crescent Blade.

Shay sucked in a breath. The men had landed in a strange and foreign land, an area they were sure that no one like them had ever visited. They'd gone through the trouble of erecting a powerful concealment barrier, but they couldn't be sure it wouldn't stop locals from stumbling upon the caves if they already knew about them. The priests would have wanted to make sure that they could recover the ancient relic, though...or at least that someone else could. Burying the entire complex would have made that impossible, since they wouldn't have been so deluded as to think a huge imperial force could be sent across the ocean. That suggested traps and magical means of hiding the artifact.

Knowledge. They knew no one native to this part of the world would understand their culture or methods. They'd probably planned to recover it much sooner, not six hundred years later when we had the internet to make it easier.

Shay frowned slightly. The resurgence of magic on Earth meant their mystical defenses might even be stronger than when the priests set them up.

She shook her head. She didn't have time to worry about that. First she had to figure out which cave contained her target.

A careful examination of the hexagrams revealed three sets of twenty-two, for a total of sixty-six. Shay frowned. Something was wrong. There should have been only sixty-four hexagrams. The *I Ching* was far older than the fifteenth century, so she was sure this wasn't an issue of lost hexagrams.

The minutes passed as she painstakingly checked each hexagram with the help of an app on her phone. The hexagrams on the first two caves were normal, but over the right-hand cave, she found duplicates of the patterns for radiance and force.

Either the priests had gotten sloppy, or they had been trying to leave a clue that they thought only an educated Taoist priest could decipher.

Good enough for me, Shay thought, stepping toward the cave on the right. She pulled out a small flashlight and strapped it to her arm.

The tomb raider spared one last glance at the characters above the cave before entering. Her light caught site of a skeleton about thirty feet in, an iron spearhead embedded deep in its skull and a rib. The clothes had long ago rotted, but the poor bastard provided proof that she wasn't the first person to try and recover the treasure.

She grabbed a handful of small but dense weights from her utility belt. Unlike her recent trip to Peru, several of her preliminary readings had suggested the place was likely trapped, meaning she needed to exercise far more caution than she had when collecting the Rod of Supay.

Shay tossed the weights in a wide arc. One landed with a soft *clunk*, as if metal met metal.

Sighing, the archaeologist knelt and pulled off her backpack, then rummaged around before pulling out a tiny drone. A few quick taps sent her drone aloft and interfaced it with her goggles.

"Command: filter one." Shay took a step forward. The drone moved behind her, its buzz sounding like the world's largest mosquito. It transmitted its feed to the corner of her goggles. "Command: filter two."

Not exactly X-ray vision, but the new filter did let her detect density differentials on the ground's surface. There were some sort of metal plates underneath the dirt, and a series of them continued deeper into the cave. Not stepping on them would probably help keep her alive.

"Jeeze, guys, it's like you moldy old assholes were trying to hide some powerful ancient magical weapon or something." She grinned as she made her way deeper into the cave. "Too bad technology is its own kind of magic."

Father O'Banion sighed. The drinks he'd pounded had filled him with whimsy and happiness...and then two assholes had strolled back into his bar and ruined everything. It was the same slick-suit-and-hair crew from

before. He'd hoped his earlier warnings would have fright-
ened them off, but some people obviously needed to be
reminded.

He rose from his table and headed to the bar.

"Give me two Irish Stouts."

Toby, the bartender, laughed. "Now you're going to
start double-fisting it? That's a lot, even for you."

Father O'Banion chuckled. "That's a good idea, lad, but
these aren't for me."

"Okay, one second." The bartender poured the beers
and set them on the bar.

The older man picked them up and headed straight
toward the two men at the table, not even bothering to try
and navigate through the dense crowd. In the Leanan
Sídhe, no regular customer would be party to spilling one
of Father O'Banion's drinks. In a carefully choreographed
dance people cleared out of his way at the last moment,
until finally he arrived at the spies' table with a broad smile
on his face.

The men looked up. Irritation and recognition spread
on their faces.

"What do you want, old man?"

Father O'Banion put the drinks down. "These are for
you, and might I suggest a little reading material?"

"Reading material?"

"Aye, lad. Just look up the local news. King Pyro and
James Brownstone. I think you'll find it most enlightening."

Without another word, Father O'Banion sauntered
toward his own table, not looking back at the men. When
he finally took his seat and looked back the men were
gone, their beers untouched.

"They didn't drink their beers? Now that was just wasteful." He stood again. No reason to let them go to waste.

James slumped against the passenger door, trying to convince himself not to call Alison. Now that they were out of cell range he'd have to use his satellite backup, and he idly wondered how expensive an international satellite call would be.

"I have the money," he mumbled to himself. "And it's not *that* overprotective. It's a weird-ass magic school. It'd be strange *not* to be overprotective. What does she know? Shay doesn't have a kid."

Not that James technically did either, but he was responsible for one.

A flash in the side mirror caught his attention, and when he glanced at the rearview mirror there was plume of dust in the distance. Getting caught in a dust storm wouldn't be great for the vehicle, but it'd survive.

James narrowed his eyes. The plume was far too narrow to be a storm.

The bounty hunter hurried out of the car and pulled out a small pair of binoculars. The people with their fancy AR goggles and drones didn't accept how easily those things could break. A good pair of binoculars would go a lot farther, and couldn't be taken out by a jammer or EMP.

James lifted the binoculars to his eyes and adjusted them. Two vehicles barreled toward his location, old open-bed trucks filled with men. The angry-looking bandana-wearing men with their AKs and pistols obviously weren't there for sightseeing. One bastard even held a rocket-propelled grenade launcher.

"These guys came to play." James grinned. "And here I thought I was going to be bored."

The bounty hunter hopped in the Forerunner and quickly drove behind a nearby rocky outcrop. Leaving it out in the open to get blown to bits was a bad idea. For one thing, Shay would lose her deposit, and he'd probably have to listen to her bitch about it for days.

The dust plume grew closer, and James gave himself a quick pat-down.

"See, Shay?" James mumbled. "You can never be too prepared."

S hay managed to finish her game of ancient deathtrap hopscotch far quicker than she would have ever guessed. Her tech helped; she couldn't see how someone *without* her equipment would have been able to avoid the traps. A couple more skeletons entangled with spearheads provided proof of her hypothesis.

Poor sonsabitches. Wonder if they were locals, or some other guys from the admiral's fleet.

The cave narrowed and split off in two directions. No skeletons or traps were obvious in either, so Shay held her breath and listened. A quiet hum and the faint sound of running water reached her ears from one of the paths and she stalked that way slowly, searching for any sign of traps or angry-Taoist-priest ghosts.

The real trouble was finding the place. I'm already ninety percent to my prize just by being in here and not getting killed by the first trap. I mean, how well could they have fortified this place so far from home?

Shay's smug satisfaction vanished as her path opened

into a large cavern with a huge drop into an inky darkness. The sound of running water had increased, swallowing the earlier hum, so she suspected an underground river lay at the bottom of the cavern.

The barest hints of rotted rope and wood suggested there'd once been a bridge stretching across the cavern to a stalagmite-covered ledge on other side. Maybe if she'd shown up a few centuries earlier, the bridge might have still been around.

How the hell did they even build a bridge in here? It's not like there were a bunch of trees outside to harvest wood from. Some sort of magic?

Worrying about mysterious feats of construction would have to wait, since the answer wouldn't help her get to the other side of the cavern. It was too far to risk jumping.

Shay peered into the darkness as her flashlight beam pierced it. "Dammit, why can't there be a convenient mine cart or giant eagles or something?"

The obstacle was annoying, but not insurmountable.

The field archaeologist sighed and unzipped her backpack. A little feeling around inside netted her a coil of kernmantle rope with a hook already attached. The next couple of minutes passed as she searched for a good place to anchor her hook. Jumping from a ledge without careful planning would just end up with her taking a swim in some pitch-black underground river.

She preferred to aim high rather than going low and climbing up. There was more margin for error with the former than the latter.

Shay considered and discarded the idea that she might be going the wrong way. She saw no reason that someone would build a bridge in a cavern if it led to a dead end, especially when they were not planning for long-term storage of the artifact.

Unless they were trying to trick people like me? Then again, they had the magic and the traps. A misleading bridge seems kind of boring.

Fortune favored Shay, and she selected a good place to aim her hook. Hanging onto one end, she started twirling the rope and attached hook to build up speed, and after a quick release the rope and hook sailed through the air and landed on her rock of choice. The tomb raider pulled on the rope to make sure the hook was secure.

"Nice throw, if I do say so myself."

A big disadvantage of exploring the cave by herself was that Brownstone wasn't there to observe her field archaeology excellence or listen to her loudly extol it. He was probably sitting in the car feeling sad about Alison.

For a tough guy, he sure was a softie inside.

Shay tugged on the rope a few more times and then backed up, the other end of the rope securely clutched in her hands. She darted forward and leapt from her side of the precipice, her momentum carrying her forward and her rope preventing gravity from sending her to her death.

Panic replaced the exhilaration of leaping through the darkened cavern when she spotted a thin, almost invisible line stretched across the space in front of her only a second before she hit it. The line snapped with no effort, and she wasn't surprised when a loud boom shook the cavern a moment later.

"Not good. *So* not good."

Shay glanced behind her, her stomach tightening. Only

her years of training as a killer before being a tomb raider helped her maintain her calm.

A slender gold and red dragon with fire and smoke shooting behind it zipped past. The creature slammed into the wall on the other side and exploded, and debris showered Shay as she landed on a ledge under her target rock. She clutched the rope tighter, worried that the hook had been knocked loose by the explosion. She really didn't want to lose the rope.

Her face stinging, Shay blinked as she stared into the darkness. A strangely familiar acrid smell hung in the air.

"What. The. Fuck?"

She stood there for a good thirty seconds trying to process what had just happened, because it *looked* like she'd hit a tripwire and a small dragon had tried to ambush her, only to explode.

You mad, bro? Just because you didn't kill me?

Her abrupt laugh echoed through the cavern.

No, not a dragon, but an ancient rocket. She wasn't sure if the trap had still worked because of luck, good design, magic, or some combination of all three. She kind of doubted gunpowder and explosives would have lasted that long without a little magic, but she wasn't a chemist. Her expertise with weapons was limited to the pointing, shooting, and stabbing parts.

Shay suspected the trap had originally been designed to kill someone walking along the old bridge, and only the absence of the walkway had saved her from an explosively bad day. For all she knew, an earlier rocket had been responsible for taking the bridge down.

These guys were thorough. I've got to give them that.

Her heart still pounding from the addictive mix of excitement and fear, the woman secured the other end of her rope by tying it around a large rock far from the edge of the ledge, just in case of tremors. It'd still be a little bit of a stunt to get back over.

Shay started into a narrow tunnel leading away from the ledge. She began to realize that even if she'd asked Brownstone to come, he might have had issues with the low roof. The guy wasn't super-tall compared to a lot of men, but he had a few inches on her, and it was already getting tight for her.

Her light highlighted a man's form at the end of the tunnel. She jerked her gun out of its holster, her heart rate kicking up.

"Freeze, asshole. You don't have to die here, but I've had an annoying last few minutes."

The gun was returned to its home a few seconds later when the field archaeologist realized she was looking not a human but at a stylized mural of a huge bearded man in armor wielding a bladed polearm, a *guandao*, which was most likely the Green Dragon Crescent Blade. She'd seen enough representations of Guan Yu to recognize him.

Shay chuckled. "Bet you never thought your weapon would end up so far from home, huh, General? Probably next job, I'll have to pick up some ancient Aztec weapon from Shanghai."

She stepped closer to examine the mural. Something seemed slightly off about the color. She lowered her light to point at the floor and realized the image glowed with a soft green light.

"Yeah, that's not strange at all. Magic painting?"

Shay waited a few seconds for the mural to come to life and attack her, and was pleasantly surprised when it didn't.

Faint drips of water echoed throughout the area, and the underground chill nipped at her skin.

"Should have brought my own ugly jacket," Shay muttered. She saluted the mural. "I'll be off then, General."

The tunnel continued past the mural, curving into the darkness. The path became even rougher, stalagmites littering the ground and long stalactites threatening her head.

"Ow," Shay muttered as one scraped the back of her head.

She stopped at the sight of yet another skeleton when the tunnel dead-ended in a chamber that opened up at the top. Now that she'd moved farther away from the cavern with the ledge, the sound of running water had receded and the hum had returned. This chamber seemed to be its source.

Unlike the skeletons she'd seen before this one still had clothes, even if the outfit was covered with dust. A black and gray robe with a golden fringe enshrouded the bones. The skeleton sat in a cross-legged position with its skull facing down.

Shay tilted her head as she moved closer. A barely discernable blue glow surrounded the robe. She suspected it might be related to the concealment barrier, but she was less interested in finding the truth behind the magic than finding the Green Dragon Crescent Blade and getting the hell out of there.

The bodies and traps all suggested the cave was guarding something of importance, rather than just additional directions or a map. She'd love it if the job turned out to be a simple snatch and grab and she didn't have to go anywhere else.

Shay returned her attention to the skeleton. "You stayed here until you died, huh? I'll give you credit for dedication."

She lifted her flashlight. The cave's ceiling continued off at an angle, and the stalactites were even thicker and denser there. She had no idea how deep underground she was, but she wondered if a few good explosives would reveal sunlight. Absent blowing things up, there was no obvious way to continue or any sign of the Green Dragon Crescent Blade.

"Damn it! Was I wrong after all, or is there something on the body?"

The flashlight's beam caught a glimmer of something on the cave ceiling, but whatever it was vanished as soon as she concentrated on it.

"Hmmm."

Shay pulled a small spherical camera drone from a pouch on her belt, set it on the ground, and pulled out her phone. After entering a few commands, four slots opened in the sphere and the rotor extended. The drone lifted off and an image appeared on her phone screen.

The tomb raider didn't shunt the feed to her goggles. She had something else in mind.

Shay kept glancing between her phone and the ceiling as the tiny drone rose. She guided it toward the location of the vanishing glimmer.

Her video feed revealed a soft green glow that she couldn't see from where she was. She pulled off her goggles, just in case the light was being filtered somehow, but still couldn't spot it.

"Okay, so there's something there."

Some quick navigation commands pulled the drone back so she could get a wider view of the ceiling.

Shay frowned. "Why are there so many stalactites there?"

She pulled the drone farther back and zoomed out with the camera as well.

"You sons of bitches!" She laughed.

Even though she couldn't see it with her eyes, the drone's video feed on the phone clearly depicted two hexagrams carved into the stalactites.

"Didn't plan on some bitch coming with her fancy flying metal demon, did you? What, did you pull a little geomancy there?"

She examined the hexagrams for a moment. One was the pattern for radiance and the other appeared to be force, but there were outlines for single segments in both, whereas the rest of the segments were filled in and surrounded by thick borders.

Using the drone as a guide, she determined that the remains of the priest lay directly under one empty segment. She took a deep breath and moved directly under the other empty segment.

A warm sensation passed through her body, and the hairs on the back of her neck stood up.

"Yeah, this was a bad idea." Shay sat down and crossed her legs. "Probably gonna end up rotting here with you, but what now?"

Her research hadn't given her many clues about the

place other than the location.

"Stand…speak, Mandate of Heaven," Shay murmured, remembering some of the translated words from the front of the cave.

The Mandate of Heaven was the ancient Chinese idea that a proper emperor had the support of the gods and the universe itself.

Mandate of Heaven equals emperor, maybe? Time to stand and speak then.

Shay stood and pulled out her phone. She couldn't pronounce classical Chinese worth a damn, but she did have an app containing information on the Chinese emperors. She swept her finger to highlight a phrase and then tapped so it'd be read aloud.

"Zhu Di, Yongle Huangdi." *Zhu Di, the Perpetual Happiness Emperor.*

The entire cave shook, and the tingle in Shay's body exploded into an inferno of pain. She cried out and fell to the ground.

Fuck. One final trap, huh? Damn it. Guess I should have brought Brownstone after all.

The agony increased, and she screamed.

Then it was gone.

Shay took several deep breaths, flexing her muscles in her arms and legs. No residual discomfort or pain remained. It was like she hadn't been on fire from the inside out seconds before.

She pushed herself up and shook her head. "That sucked." Her eyes widened when she saw what was now lying directly between her and the skeleton.

A long, curved, bladed polearm lay on the ground. It

was clearly a *guandao*.

An ornately carved golden dragon surrounded the joint where the blade and the pole met, its eyes made from carved jade. Another piece of jade had been inlaid into the end.

Shay crept toward the weapon. She wanted to take the whole damn thing. If Brownstone could get his arsenal through Customs, he should be able to get one stupid ancient magical weapon through too.

There was one minor problem that again made her regret not bringing the bounty hunter. Legends claimed the Green Dragon Crescent Blade was heavy as hell. She was strong, but she wasn't barbecue-lover strong.

Shay grasped the weapon, and after taking a deep breath, she jerked up with all her might—whereupon she tripped, fell backward, and slammed her head on the ground.

"Dammit!"

It turned out that the legends were wrong. The Green Dragon Crescent Blade weighed almost nothing.

Shay sat up and rubbed her head. "Okay, this works. I can do this."

A distant crack echoed through the cave system. She frowned, wondering if grabbing the weapon had set off more traps. More cracks and a boom followed.

The noises remained distant, and the cave didn't shake at all.

Shay sighed when she realized what she was hearing.

"Oh, Brownstone, who are you shooting at now?"

16

The two trucks continued to close on his location, so James needed to formulate a plan other than killing every single motherfucker in sight.

He didn't know who the guys were yet, and wasting a man without at least having some clue who he was bordered on being rude—especially when the guy might not have a chance against him.

James rubbed his chin. *Fuck. Wish I had brought a rifle.*

Unfortunately, he didn't like rifles much. When he hunted a man, he wanted to be able to look the guy in the face before kicking his ass or shooting him. Blasting targets from a distance just wasn't his style, even if it occasionally made tactical sense. Unfortunately, his lack of sense sometimes got him in trouble in situations where he couldn't rely on the strength of the necklace and he expected a lot of enemies. Situations like the one in this canyon.

Okay, next time I bring a rifle or two. Just in case. Or a rocket launcher. That might be fun, if a bit messy.

A good shot through their engine blocks would disable the vehicles, at least robbing his enemies of their mobility.

Assuming they were enemies.

James would gladly defend himself, but he didn't want to kill a bunch of men if there'd been some sort of mistake and they'd not come expressly to take him and/or Shay out. Especially if he wasn't going to make any money off it.

He sighed as he watched the vehicles through his binoculars. The number of weapons didn't automatically translate into the men being criminals or killers.

Many militias, large and small, had popped up in Mexico to help deal with both the scourge of the cartels and the chaos of magic-enhanced criminals.

For all his mouthing off to Shay, James understood the importance of not pissing off people without reason.

He looked around, chewing on his thoughts a moment. He needed to get the men in a position where he could question them without any of them throwing too much lead at him or blowing him up.

Otherwise, he risked fucking up things in this area for himself or Shay in the future.

James grunted. A little thinking had drained a lot of the fun out of the fight, but he could still make the encounter interesting. It was time for something that wasn't really his style: stealth.

Time to be a creeper.

The bounty hunter sprinted away from the outcropping hiding the Forerunner. He didn't worry about the men eventually discovering the vehicle; he just didn't want them to blow it to pieces right away. Once he engaged the men, he figured he would keep them busy enough.

Dozens of large rocks dotted the area, along with many other outcroppings along the canyon wall. Perfect cover. If he was smart about tactics, he would be able to close on the enemy without getting a rocket-propelled grenade in his teeth for the trouble.

Man, kicking in front doors was so much more fun than this.

James snickered, wondering what Shay was up to inside the cave. She was probably taking a leisurely stroll and having a relaxing time, while he was preparing to fight off more than a dozen men.

Afterward she would come out and take him to task for not being civilized or something. Worse yet, not dressing appropriately for a firefight. He was surprised she hadn't given him shit for his nails.

The two trucks continued to rumble along the dirt trail. They were now close enough that he could make them out without his binoculars. He rushed between two rocks, ducking behind a large one, and waited for a chance to move again.

A series of protruding stones in the nearby canyon wall formed natural handholds. James looked between the canyon wall and the approaching vehicles. If the men were looking straight ahead and not paying much attention to the sides of the canyon, he could climb up and gain the advantage of high ground. But if he were wrong, it'd leave him vulnerable—and he might get a few bullets for his trouble.

Bullets fucking sucked.

Time was running out, so he needed to make his play and be quick about it. The men might have scoped him out already with their own binoculars or drones.

James surveyed the sky, but didn't spot any drones. They could have been using something smaller and harder to see, but if they were willing to go through that kind of trouble, it didn't seem likely they'd barrel straight down on him in two obvious trucks versus coming in from the air on a helicopter or VTOL craft.

No. These men might have a lot of guns, but they reeked of local disposable muscle, not highly-trained operatives or mercenaries. The only reason the encounter might prove difficult at all was that James didn't want to kill anyone if it wasn't necessary.

He grinned.

Yeah, I think I'll bet on the stupidity of a bunch of local thugs. They think they have the upper hand, but what they don't know will help me.

James jumped to the lowest handhold and then grabbed the next. The man scurried up the side of the canyon like some Oriceran-enhanced goat before finding a nice flat rock outcropping. With a final heave, he pulled himself over the edge and flattened himself on his stomach.

Everyone thought skinny guys were the better rock climbers. It helped, sure—less weight. However, sheer strength in one's hands and arms helped overcome some of the height and weight challenges.

Staging an ambush still didn't sit all that well with James, but he reminded himself that his goal was to kill the enemy's vehicles, not the men. If it came down to taking out all the men, they'd at least know it was coming. Right now he didn't have many other options.

The bounty hunter pulled out his .45 and popped out the magazine. He replaced it with another filled with armor-piercing rounds. Sometimes it paid to be prepared. After slipping the first magazine back into a pouch, he rolled onto his stomach and readied his weapon. The trucks would be passing beneath him soon.

To ensure he took out the engine blocks, he'd have to wait until they were damn near straight under him. He was a good shot, but these vehicles were moving, and he was using a pistol from an odd angle above them.

He smiled. Just made it a bit fairer.

It was almost time: less than thirty seconds until they passed under him, by his estimate. The sun beat down, and sweat beaded on his forehead. He wondered how snipers didn't get bored holding position.

Twenty seconds.

The sweat now tickled the back of his neck. Seriously, how did those fuckers sit still for days?

Of course, if the men were there to kill him, this whole thing would get very messy very quickly.

Ten seconds.

Bad day to be you guys. I hope whoever sent you my way at least gave you some fucking clue who you're dealing with.

The trucks passed right underneath the ledge. The men were looking in every direction except up. Big mistake.

James aimed for a few seconds, then squeezed off three quick rounds into the front of the first truck. The loud report echoed throughout the narrow canyon as the truck screeched to a halt, smoke pouring from the engine. Men shouted in Spanish, their heads darting around as they tried to find their enemy.

Several men complicated their search by firing.

Thank you! he thought. *I appreciate your support.*

Their gunshots layered over the echo from James' weapon, leaving the men clueless about his location.

Concentrating, the bounty hunter fired three rounds into the other truck's engine. His minutes of preparation were over in seconds. The second truck also stopped, thick black smoke pouring from its engine into the blue sky.

Gunfire and Spanish expletives filled the canyon now, but still no one had fired upward. James took his chance and leapt off his ledge, grabbing handholds on the way down and swinging to the ground. He landed with a grunt and a forward roll, then rushed toward a dense patch of large rocks.

One of the men shouted and squeezed off a few rounds at him, but in the chaos no one paid him much attention. Now on the ground with plenty of cover and the enemy's mobility advantage destroyed, James held all the cards.

"Who are you?" James bellowed in heavily-gringo-accented Spanish, and immediately sprinted for another position. Between the men's shouting and the echoes, he was fairly certain they wouldn't zero in on him.

Instead, the dumbasses kept firing random rounds as if they thought they might just get lucky and hit him. The man who'd spotted him earlier was still busy shooting at his old position. A damned ricochet was his biggest risk right now.

"*Soy El Granito Diablo Espiritu,*" James shouted. "You listen," he continued in his broken Spanish. "You not die."

His deep voice echoed around the canyon, and it was

like the rock itself was speaking. Still, it would have been nice if the rock didn't sound like a drunken five-year-old.

He sighed. This was damned embarrassing. Half of being successful in a dangerous situation was talking trash and intimidation, and he couldn't speak Spanish worth a shit.

Sure, he could understand it well enough. His memory, combined with a little study, had helped him with that, but having a great memory didn't automatically translate into verbal ability without practice.

"Need to work on that shit," James mumbled. "Especially if I'm gonna keep traveling south of the border."

The men had managed to stop shooting and shouting at this point. They'd all piled out of their trucks and crouched at the sides of the vehicles.

The bounty hunter chuckled. He understood their instincts. The vehicles at least provided cover, but if he were using any sort of rocket launcher or RPG launcher, he would have made short work of them.

It was their lucky day.

"Who are you?" James shouted in Spanish. He had confidence in *that* phrase, at least. Well, that, and "Please tell me where the bathroom is," along with, "I'd like a beer, please." James only barely resisted shouting that he would like a *cerveza*.

The men murmured quietly amongst themselves, but he couldn't make their words out at this distance.

He'd give the men credit for not blindly charging forward. Even though he was hoping to salvage the situation without killing a bunch of them, *they* didn't know that.

It would have been gloriously brave—if stupid—to charge forward blazing away.

Their caution helped with the bounty hunter's plan. If the men feared for their lives, he might be able to convince them to stand down.

James surveyed the area again, taking note of the exact path he'd have to take to close on them while still maintaining cover. Once he reached ass-kicking range, he could finish this with only a few broken bones.

He cracked his knuckles. It was time for him to move.

Shay's heart thundered as she made her way back through the cave. She skidded to a halt at the sight of skeletons, her eyes flashing open.

"Yeah, that's right. Fucking traps." She sighed and reactivated the filters on her goggles. Rushing out of the cave without being careful would end with her dead and James wondering just how stupid she was.

The field archaeologist took careful technology-aided steps back toward the entrance to the cave, fear creeping into her heart. The initial burst of gunfire had been replaced by stony silence.

Her stomach tightened. Brownstone could already be dead or bleeding out. From what she'd seen he wasn't wearing his creepy necklace, which meant he probably wasn't bulletproof this time. That necklace was the only way she could explain how he'd taken a load of buckshot to the chest and not even flinched. She was still afraid to ask him about it.

She took careful step after careful step. The illumination from the sunlight grew brighter as Shay's mind raced.

They were in the middle of fucking nowhere, and they only had basic first-aid supplies. There was no way she could save Brownstone's life if he'd been seriously injured.

"Damn it, Brownstone," the woman muttered. "If you're dead, I'll travel to the afterlife and fucking kill you again for being such a monumental dumbass."

Shay finally cleared the cave, and she pushed up her goggles. She darted forward, gun in hand, to deliver some sweet, sweet vengeance.

Except, she had no reason to shoot.

She blinked as her eyes adjusted to the sunlight. She couldn't believe what she saw in front of her. She'd been expecting a dying bounty hunter, but instead there were more than a dozen men kneeling on the ground, their fingers laced behind their heads and their faces pale from fear.

The men murmured quietly to themselves in Spanish about the Granite Devil-Ghost.

Brownstone stood next to a man with the most magnificent mustache Shay'd ever seen outside of an Old West saloon, gesticulating wildly to his phone.

"What the fuck?" Shay muttered. She kept her gun up as her gaze cut between the kneeling men and Brownstone and the other man.

"Me hunt death man," Brownstone was saying in mangled Spanish.

The tomb raider winced. Brownstone's Spanish sucked worse than his fashion sense.

The other man shook his head and responded in Spanish. "You don't want to go after this man, Granite Devil. He is a god of death. Even Santa Muerte might bend her knee to Sombra."

"This man monster," James was pointing at the phone, then jerked a finger to himself. "I stop. Save people."

Shay groaned and stomped forward, holstering her weapon. "Jesus, Brownstone. You're fucking killing me with your toddler Spanish!"

The two men looked at her, and Brownstone's conversation partner paled.

He crossed himself. "Santa Muerte, I'm sorry. I did not know Brownstone was your servant."

She stared at him for a second, wondering what the fuck was going through the man's head, then chuckled. She could only imagine what she looked like. She was covered in dust and scratches, her weird goggles were sticking out from her head, and the Green Dragon Crescent Blade was strapped to her back.

"I'm not Santa Muerte," Shay told him in Spanish. She nodded toward Brownstone. "I'm with him."

He looked back at Brownstone, then returned his attention to Shay. "I don't know if that makes me feel better," the man admitted.

Brownstone tapped his phone, then looked at Shay. "I just want him to confirm the area where the fucking necromancer is."

Shay relayed the comment in perfect Spanish.

The other man sighed and shook his head. He pointed to a spot on the map displayed on Brownstone's phone and looked at Brownstone. "Sombra kills by touch, then violates the dead by making them walk. Even *you* can't win."

"Motherfucking zombies," Shay muttered, putting her hand on her pistol.

Brownstone nodded to the man. "Thanks," he offered, this time in English. He waved toward the Forerunner. "I see you got what you needed, so let's get going."

Shay gestured to the gathered men. "And what about these guys? You gonna let them live?"

He turned to the man next to him. "Yeah. They understand the error of their ways now." Brownstone slapped his conversation partner on the shoulder, and the man winced. "Carlos here has a satellite phone. He'll call for a pick up, but we'll be long gone."

Shay cocked her head. "Who the hell are these guys?"

"Local militia," Brownstone replied. "Apparently they thought we were drug runners." He grinned. "Mistakes happen."

Shay shook her head as she waved a hand at the men and headed towards the Forerunner. "It's always fun with you, Brownstone."

17

"That's fucking stupid, Brownstone," Shay said a few minutes later as they drove away from the cave. "Really stupid. Think it through at least once."

"It's not stupid. It makes sense. We're close to the necromancer. It's not a big detour."

"Ok, think it through...twice."

"I have. What's your problem again? Before you didn't seem to mind the idea."

Shay grimaced. "Before I didn't have a magical ancient Chinese weapon in my vehicle." Shay snorted. "I thought I was just going to get a map or clues to somewhere else, but now I've got the damn thing and I don't want to lose it."

Brownstone laughed, waving a hand at the cacti they were passing. "We're in the middle of nowhere, and I'm saying we should go to necromancer territory. It's not like some kid's gonna come and steal it from a parking lot. It'll probably be safer sitting with you than it'd be back in Cabo."

"You don't know that," Shay said. "I would have thought those caves would be safe. Well, the outside at least. Did you expect two truckloads of guys with guns to show up?"

The bounty hunter shrugged. "Kind of."

Shay blinked and glanced over at him. "'Kind of?'"

"Look, trouble follows me around. Maybe I didn't expect those exact guys, but I did kind of wonder if someone might show up. Shit, for all I know, the Brujos Rojos might have guys keeping an eye out for me throughout Latin America."

"Did anyone ever tell you that you have a big ego, Brownstone?"

"Yeah, you've told me that several times."

"Massive ego?" she clarified.

"Yeah, still you, many times," he retorted.

The rough terrain made the Forerunner shake and Shay eased off the gas.

"You don't know if you'll be able to find this guy quickly," she argued, "and do you really want to take him on his home turf when you might get caught out at night?"

"We've still got daylight, and based on what Carlos told me, this guy is pretty close." Brownstone shook his head. "Why waste a bunch of time driving back to Cabo and coming back the next day? You did your job, now let me do mine."

Shay rolled her eyes. "You're serious? You can't wait one day? Plus, we should be securing the Green Dragon Crescent Blade. That was the main reason we both came here, remember? You're getting some special crap from Smite-Williams and all that. I don't like the idea of putting the deal at risk because you're all gung ho about going after this necromancer."

"If I wait, there's too much risk of Sombra hearing that I'm coming."

"How? It's not like the guy hangs out around a lot of people." She clarified, "Who are still breathing."

"Carlos and his men might say something to someone, and it might leak to Sombra. I should do this now, when he won't be expecting me."

"Fine. Whatever. Is this about you making those guys all but wet themselves back there? You believing your own hype about how you're a devil? That shit shouldn't go to your head."

The bounty hunter chuckled. "It doesn't, and it's good that they're spreading my rep. Killing is messy, Shay, and I'd rather people be afraid of me when they know I'm after them. It makes things easier and simpler."

"This Sombra isn't some militia-guy with a twenty-year-old rifle. He's got his own rep, and I don't think he's gonna give much of a shit about yours."

Brownstone looked at her and nodded. "Yeah, I know."

Shay watched the road, blinking twice before asking, "You know?"

"I care about my rep for easier guys. As for this guy..." He shrugged. "Wasn't planning on announcing myself." He grunted. "You should be happy. I'm taking this guy seriously. More seriously than I've taken any bounty in a long time."

Shay groaned. "All the more reason to wait."

"Nope. All the more reason to take him out right away."

Shay slammed a hand on the steering wheel. "Damn it, Brownstone. Could you be any more stubborn?"

A huge grin broke out on the bounty hunter's face. "Yes. Way more."

She huffed. "If we get ambushed and I lose the artifact, I'm telling Smite-Williams it's your fault and making you pay me for the job. And that's assuming I'm not killed."

"And if you're killed?"

"Then I'm haunting your ass."

James pursed his lips. "Fair enough."

With all the Oriceran shit around, she might just be able to do that.

An hour later, they'd reached the area indicated by the militia leader. Shay kept her mouth shut, though James could practically feel the irritation radiating off her.

He didn't want to keep fighting about going after the guy so quickly, but he also didn't want to waste another day. From what he'd read and been told, Sombra killed as often as he could. The guy was a monster, and he needed to be taken down.

Shay might scoff at him for it, but James also suspected that if he made too much noise announcing himself, Sombra might decide to relocate. He couldn't take a chance on losing the guy when he had good information on his location. Early in his career, he'd had trouble landing a level-one bounty because of something similar.

James thought about his career as the Forerunner rumbled along. He didn't much bother with anything below a three anymore. It wasn't out of arrogance, but more because he only had so many hours in the day and wasting them going after bounties that other people could take down meant he was leaving more dangerous men free to threaten innocent people.

Huh. Maybe that is *arrogance. I don't know.*

Despite what his current partner might think, James didn't believe he was unbeatable. He just adjusted his tactics to the relative threat level. King Pyro might have presented more of a challenge if the criminal had been a little smarter.

A sick grin appeared on his face. He didn't regret beating the shit out of that guy. The bastard'd had it coming even before he'd threatened everyone the bounty hunter loved, but the gloves had metaphorically come off when he'd done that.

"I don't even want to ask," Shay began, "but what are you smiling about?"

"Just thinking about assholes getting what they deserve."

Shay smirked. "Be careful, Brownstone. Everybody's an asshole from *someone's* perspective."

"Sure. I'm sure someday I'll get what I deserve, but today it's going to be the necromancer."

For all James' concern about fair play, he didn't give two shits about trying to restrain himself with Sombra. A level-five bounty dangerous enough to warrant a military bombing meant that the bounty hunter didn't have to hold back. For the first time since coming to Mexico, he wondered if he'd made a mistake not bringing the necklace.

James looked down at his phone. "This should be it. Slow down." He gestured out the window to the right. "That's the path Carlos was talking about."

Shay frowned and slowed the Forerunner to a halt. When the car stopped, she looked at him. "Are you absolutely sure about this?"

"Why are you so freaked?"

"I don't know... Maybe almost getting blown up by a dragon rocket today has made me skittish or some shit. I just feel like you're not taking this guy seriously, despite what you've said. Have you looked at everything they say he can do? You being tough might not be enough. This guy literally controls life and death."

James snorted. "You might be a kick-ass field archaeologist, but I'm the bounty hunter. Let me tell you that half the shit you read about bounties is crap they've made up to sound tougher."

"If he's only half as tough as they say, that's still plenty tough."

"If *I* don't bring him in, who will?"

Shay muttered something rude under her breath. "I don't know, maybe some stubborn Mexican bounty hunter who doesn't listen when hot chicks give him good advice."

He looked at her, his eyebrows furrowing. "I'm listening. I just don't agree."

The woman took a deep breath and slowly exhaled, a defeated look settling over her face. "I still think this is idiotically reckless. I want to make it real fucking clear, Brownstone, that I'm not coming on this one. This isn't about revenge or protecting someone. This is just a regular old bounty that you don't have to take on right now. We should be getting back to town and securing the artifact."

James shrugged and opened the door. "I can get back to town on my own."

The tomb raider rolled her eyes in exasperation. "It's not exactly a one-mile stroll."

"I'll figure something out." The bounty hunter grinned and stepped out of the vehicle. "Stay, go…whatever. It doesn't change the fact that Sombra goes down before I go back to town."

Shay crossed her arms and blew some strands of hair out of her face. "If you don't find this guy quickly, I'm leaving. I did *my* job, and I want some damn tacos." Her stomach audibly rumbled.

James chuckled, waved, and jogged away. If he could take out two trucks filled with men and not even have to kill anyone, he could take on one powerful dead-guy focused asshole.

Shay had been right about one thing. James really didn't want to take on Sombra at night, so he needed to find the man and finish him soon. Still, he wasn't very worried.

The more the bounty hunter thought about it, the more he believed that the man's reputation had been exaggerated. Sombra choosing to live out in the wilderness helped with that. Yes, magic could be a pain in the ass to deal with, but he doubted the man couldn't be taken down via good old-fashioned overwhelming force. James hadn't run into a bounty yet where that hadn't been true.

Sure, someday some weird-ass Oriceran dragon or something might end up on the bounty list and James would have a little bit more trouble, but when it came to two-legged human threats James was confident he could win, even if he might end up damaged.

Arrogance or confidence? He knew what Shay would say.

James just needed to find the man. As he strode along the barely-there dirt path, he realized he wouldn't have to put much effort into it.

One crucial fact James had learned through the years as a bounty hunter was that with power came arrogance, King Pyro being a stunning recent example of that.

A man like Sombra, who was living practically as a god and had the military too afraid to take him on, wasn't going to hide. The bastard probably fed off people's fear just as he fed off their lifeforce.

Confidence was a strength. Arrogance was a weakness. Hell, James suspected arrogance might get him killed someday. Not today, he hoped, but someday.

No, he wouldn't have to go looking too hard for Sombra. The asshole necromancer would come to him. If anything, he'd probably already spotted the Forerunner via drone or magic.

Fucking drones.

James glanced around as he jogged farther down the thin dirt path. Signs of recent disturbance were all over. Maybe his bounty had buried mines and he'd underestimated the man's arrogance, after all. He couldn't be sure, so he'd do his best to avoid any suspicious-looking dirt piles and stay on the path for as long as he could manage.

Being killed in a fight was one thing. Being blown up by a landmine because he wasn't being careful would be mortifyingly embarrassing.

The bounty hunter dropped into a crouch as the path faded into the terrain. The density of cacti had increased when the path ended. It was a prickly forest out there.

So, gonna fight with a necromancer in a cactus field that's probably filled with landmines. Yeah, this is smart. I begin to see your point, Shay.

But shit, I'm already here, and I'm not admitting shit *to you at the moment.*

James grunted. The militia ambush had been much more entertaining and less annoying.

He needed better information, so it was time to test one of the dirt piles. Quick searching yielded a small boulder. An explosion would signal that he was there, but he wanted Sombra to come sooner than later anyway.

Straining and grunting, James lifted the medium-heavy rock and carried it toward one of the suspicious dirt piles. He tossed the rock onto the pile and then jumped backward, throwing his arms in front of his face to protect it from shrapnel.

No explosion. No shrapnel. Nothing.

"That was kind of anti-climactic," the bounty hunter murmured to himself.

He ran through the different types of mines Sombra might have buried before deciding most would be far too complicated for a necromancer hiding in the mountainous Mexican wilderness to manage, although there was still the possibility that they were remote controlled.

There also was the sobering reality that James was only seeing the areas where something recently had disturbed the soil. For all he knew, something had been buried in every square foot of the place.

Even if he didn't know what Sombra had buried, he felt more confident that he wouldn't be blown up if he took the wrong step. The more he thought about it, the more that made sense.

A necromancer just didn't strike him as the kind of man who would litter the area with landmines. The mystery of the disturbed soil would have to wait until he caught up with the necromancer so he could ask him.

James crept farther along before dropping to his stomach at the sight of movement in the distance. He crawled along the cacti-infested dirt path. Just because he wanted the necromancer to come to him didn't mean he couldn't take advantage of a little surprise.

That better be you, you arrogant bastard, and not some coyote.

He took a few deep breaths. James suspected a major workout was coming.

Shay drummed her fingers on the steering wheel.

Fucking Brownstone.

He knew she wouldn't leave him in the mountains without a way to get back, so now she had to risk her life and the artifact because Brownstone had a raging hard-on for catching the damn necromancer right away.

"It wasn't like he was going anywhere," she grumbled. "Fuck, he's a necromancer. You probably have all eternity to catch the bastard."

Shay pulled out her phone. It was time for the tomb raider to at least give her employer a little update.

"No signal, of course. Peachy." Frustrated, she tossed the phone on the other seat.

She sighed and scrubbed a hand over her face. She'd need to start carrying a satellite phone or get a phone that could switch between cell and satellite service like Brownstone's. It was always the little inconveniences that really got to a person.

Sure, an ancient rocket trap had nearly blown her apart and almost knocked her into an underground river; that was no big deal. But no cell service?

That was the greatest affront known to mankind.

She looked down the path James had taken. "Hurry up, Brownstone, before I die of boredom and the necromancer has to bring me back."

18

James continued crawling across the rough ground, which was harder than he would have expected if only because of the arsenal he was carrying on his body.

Guess it was a good thing I didn't bring the grenades after all, he mused.

He didn't spot a living soul, human or coyote. Now he wasn't even sure if he'd really seen movement, or if it had just been a trick of the light.

For all he knew, the necromancer might be able to turn invisible. It was true that the average bounty exaggerated their powers, but the smart ones also kept a few trump cards secret in case someone like James showed up looking for them.

"You have come a long way to die, gringo," someone shouted in Spanish, their voice echoing around the canyon. "At least die on your feet like a man and not like a worm."

Well, fuck. There went surprise. This is why I hate trying to do this ninja shit.

With a grunt, James pushed off the ground and started slapping the dirt off his body. A man stood about fifty feet away.

"*No hablo español,*" the bounty hunter shouted back. He saw no reason to let the man know his language capabilities. If he got lucky, maybe the other man would let something slip in his native tongue.

"Only a fool comes to a place like this without knowing the language," the man shouted back, this time in heavily accented English. "I'm going to kill you, mercenary. I am Sombra the Deathbringer, and your life will make me stronger. You think you are the first gringo mercenary who has been sent against me? Here you are nothing but worm food."

The necromancer wasn't exactly dressed like some terrible master of dark magic with his worn blue jeans and a shirt with some Mexican cartoon fox character James didn't recognize.

Something about the casual outfit unnerved James a lot more than if the necromancer had shown up in some ridiculous robe and antlered crown. It suggested Sombra was confident enough in his abilities that he didn't feel the need for fashion-based intimidation.

James glanced down at his coat. He wasn't exactly practicing fashion-based intimidation himself. Then again, he was confident in his abilities.

"Point of fact, I'm not a mercenary," James announced. "I'm a bounty hunter. Jose Padilla, you have a class-five bounty on you, and I'm gonna bring you in. If you surrender, it'll be a lot less annoying for both of us."

Sombra barked a harsh laugh, shaking his head. "I'm not a criminal. I am Death."

James chuckled. No one ever surrendered. He was really having trouble taking the guy in the cartoon fox shirt seriously.

"You find me funny, bounty hunter?" Sombra snarled.

Oh, he wants respect? Thanks for the leverage, asshole.

"I'm just saying... You've got a cartoon fox on your shirt. It's not all that scary."

Sombra chuckled darkly. "I took this off the last man I killed. I go through many shirts because fools like you think guns will work on me." He narrowed his eyes. "Or are you Oriceran?"

"Nope. One hundred percent Earth-born, and all that shit. Still going to kill you, though."

"You are nothing more than a fool who will soon be my lunch." Sombra spread his arms to either side. "I will enjoy killing you, *stupido*. I will drink your soul and use your body as part of my army."

"What army?" James shook his head, twisted around, flung the coat back, and whipped out his .45 before looking at the necromancer again. "I want to thank you."

"For killing you?" Sombra pursed his lips, his voice respectful. "You are not as stupid as you look. You should be honored to die at my hands."

"I won't be dying." James shook his head. "Well, everyone dies in the end, but I'm not gonna die at the fucking hands of a dumb cartoon-fox-shirt-wearing douchebag like you."

The necromancer's face tightened and his voice was harsh. "I will enjoy killing you."

"Yeah, sure. Anyway, I was thanking you for being in a place where I can go all out without worrying about hurting anyone." The bounty hunter pointed his gun directly at Sombra. "Also, thanks for being an asshole in Mexico instead of the United States. You've make this bounty even easier."

Sombra's face scrunched in confusion, and James took more than a little pleasure at disconcerting him.

"You see," James continued, "up north, it's hard to find dead-or-alive bounties. Everyone's very concerned about due process. Down here, though, they are all over the place. If you want to surrender, now's the time. Otherwise, I'm not holding back, and I can't guarantee you'll be breathing at the end of this."

The necromancer laughed. "You shouldn't have told me you weren't Oriceran. Now I know you're nothing to fear."

"I've run into a lot of criminals who said the same thing. And now they are dead or in jail."

Sombra snorted. "I wondered what sort of man would have the courage to face me alone. Now I know you're nothing but a fool…*un tonto*."

James shrugged. "You know, you make King Pyro sound humble—and that's saying something."

"I'll make your death long, slow, and painful."

"I'm more generous than you."

"More generous?" Sombra frowned.

"Yeah, I'm gonna kill you quickly." The bounty hunter rushed forward and squeezed off three quick rounds.

Sombra jerked each time a bullet hit him in the chest. He collapsed to the ground, blood blossoming from his wounds.

"All talk, no walk, huh?" James frowned. The bounty hunter slowed his advance, keeping his weapon trained on the downed man. Too easy. *Way* too easy. No level five went down from a few bullets.

"I am Death," Sombra growled, pushing himself back up. Blood leaked from his mouth. "You can't defeat me. You can only delay your pitiful end."

The bullets had torn into Sombra's fox shirt and chest, splattering blood everywhere. A red-black glow surrounded the man, and his eyes turned solid black. The wounds started sealing themselves.

"Fuck," James spit to the side as his eyes stayed on Sombra. "That's not helpful."

"Your weapons are useless, and when I drink your soul I will be whole again. You can't kill death. You can only succumb to it."

James slapped a hand to his forehead. "Oh, fuck."

"Yes, yes, *now* you know fear."

"Nah, not fear. I just forgot the first rule of hunting zombies. Always go for the headshot."

Sombra ground his teeth. "I am no zombie. I am Death."

"Yeah, you keep saying that. It's starting to piss me off."

Now that James was only about ten yards out, instead of fifty, it was easy enough to snap a round into the other man's head.

Again, Sombra jerked back, but this time he didn't fall to the ground. The glow around him intensified, and the flesh grew back almost instantly.

James grunted. "You're a lot tougher than you or your shirt looks."

The necromancer shook his head, which was still glowing. "Your death comes, mercenary. The army advances."

James muttered, "Bounty hunter, not mercenary. Shit, get that right."

Scratching and crunching echoed through the canyon. The bounty hunter jerked his head around, trying to figure out what the hell was going on.

A rotted hand burst from the ground, followed by another, and then a head. Half the skin was missing, leaving a permanent skeletal half-grin.

"Motherfucking zombies," James snarled through gritted teeth. "So that's what you buried. I think I would have preferred mines."

Bodies erupted from the ground all over the canyon. Men and women, some fresh, some just scraps of flesh barely holding together. More corpses emerged from the ground, these from areas that hadn't looked freshly disturbed before.

The only advantage James could see was that all the corpses had at least some actual skin and muscles move on them. Sombra couldn't apparently make bones move by themselves.

Even the Granite Ghost didn't have a good idea how to take down a skeleton.

None of the zombies moaned. The scratching of their hands in the dirt and the shuffling of their feet in the dust and gravel provided the only noise.

James' skin crawled. Magic bothered him because it made things complicated, but necromancy violated the natural order in a perverse and fucked-up way. Even the stupid top-hat ferret was a living thing.

He grunted. "I'm gonna fuck you up, you piece of shit."

"How do you kill something that is already dead, *idioto*?" Sombra shouted. "I am beyond death. I am beyond life. I am beyond God. I am beyond the Devil."

"No," James replied. "You're beyond my patience, asshole. I hope the Devil's got some real creative punishments ready for you when you get to hell."

About a dozen zombies had surrounded James and were shuffling toward him in jerking movements with their arms outstretched.

Bullets exploded from his gun into four zombies in rapid succession—four perfect head shots. Other than jerking slightly from the impact, the zombies showed no reaction, just kept moving toward him. One turned slightly, revealing that the bullet had blown out the back of its head.

Okay, head shots didn't work. Damn it.

"Well, fuck." James reloaded his gun and then pulled a .50-caliber Desert Eagle from a holster. It was time to go full John Woo. He spun, blasting with both guns, this time going for the legs and knees.

Blowing their lower legs off at the knees slowed the zombies down, but didn't stop them.

Now missing their legs, the animated bodies pulled themselves toward him. James opened up with both guns on the closest zombie, putting hole after hole into the body. It finally stopped moving, but that left him with the rest to deal with. He didn't have enough magazines if it'd take dozens of bullets for each one.

Another wave of zombies closed on him. There was no intelligence in what was left of their faces. James kicked the crawler nearest him, sending it flying several yards away, but several more zombies, both crawlers and upright zombies, came closer. They reached toward him, some with normal hands, others with sharp skeletal fingers.

James kicked, punched, and fired bullets into the bodies trying to drag him down. Several grabbed him from behind, squeezing with surprising force. He slammed his elbows into the zombies behind him, sending them sprawling to the ground. He holstered his ineffective pistols for the moment and charged forward, trying to rush through the thicket of living dead.

Fuck these guys. Chop off the fucking head and the dragon dies.

Zombies grabbed at his jacket, face, and legs. The damn things were slow, but by now hundreds filled the area. His rush toward Sombra brought him only to a group of cacti and more zombies.

"What the fuck?" James exclaimed, jerking his gaze back and forth to find the man in the huge crowd of walking corpses. "Where did you go, you little bitch?"

"Do you realize your mistake now?" Sombra shouted.

In a reversal of the militia encounter, the necromancer's voice echoed throughout the canyon. Combined with the distraction of hundreds of shuffling feet, James couldn't pinpoint his target's location.

Talk about getting what you deserved. The bounty hunter snickered.

"Why don't you stop hiding among these rotters?" James called. "If you're so tough, come after me and prove it."

"You thought it'd be easy, didn't you? I'm sure back in

America you're big shit, gringo, but here, I am Death. I have nothing to prove to you, other than that I can destroy you."

"At least he doesn't call himself *King* Death," James muttered.

The bounty hunter delivered savage punches and kicks to the zombies around him. He held no delusions that he'd be able to take out a zombie by punching it; he was just trying to keep them off him until he could find Sombra.

At this point, so many zombies choked the area that short of the Mexican military blasting away with artillery or an air strike, James couldn't win.

It didn't matter. The asshole had to be in the crowd still, probably somewhere close. He'd want to stay close enough to gloat. James could use that against him.

"If you're Death, why don't you come and take me on man to man? It's hard for me to think you're anything but a chickenshit hiding behind all these rotting skinbags."

"The wolf can howl at the moon all it wants," Sombra shouted, "but that doesn't mean the moon has to listen."

"Fuck. I hope your zombies kill me soon so I don't have to listen to more of that kind of bullshit. It's more painful than getting shot." James shook his head.

The bounty hunter pulled out a knife and stabbed at a closing zombie, but it didn't seem to notice. More kicks and punches followed, but zombies continued to block all his escape routes.

With a roar, the bounty hunter rushed forward, smashing into several zombies and sending them flying, only to run into another thick layer of the beasts.

He yanked out a gun and blasted a corpse point-blank

in the neck. Its head popped off with a surprising lack of blood, and the body collapsed.

James grunted. "Huh. Need to take the heads off? Wish I would have brought a machete. Live and learn."

More dead hands clawed and tore at his clothes, ripping his pants and adding more damage to Shay's not-so-favorite coat. James blasted another zombie in the neck, but the bullet passed clean through, leaving the zombie's head hanging to the side and the creature still active.

The bounty hunter grabbed a zombie by the legs and threw it into several closing on him. They all went down in tangle of limbs.

"Fucking Sombra. If you're supposed to be the Deathbringer, then bring the actual death!"

All the zombies stopped moving. They just silently swayed in place.

James took the opportunity to reload, wondering if he'd finally convinced his quarry to stop running and face him. If he could kill a zombie with enough damage, he could kill a necromancer.

"I win," Sombra whispered from behind him.

James spun just in time to see the necromancer rushing forward, his hand covered in a dark glow. The necromancer's palm landed right over the bounty hunter's heart.

Fuck! I'm sorry, Father McCartney.

A scream filled the air. A few heartbeats passed before James realized it wasn't him screaming, but Sombra the Deathbringer.

The necromancer's eyes flared red as his shrill cry echoed through the canyon. He slowly sank to the ground, shuddering and twitching as his skin shrank in on itself, his eyes blaming James for lying to him.

About what, James didn't know.

"Didn't see that coming," James murmured, scratching his eye as the zombies fell, inanimate, around him.

Shay fidgeted in the car, resisting the urge to open the door and charge toward the gunfire she'd been hearing.

"Not my problem," she muttered. "I made that clear to him. Have to establish some sort of limits."

She took several deep breaths as a new and more insidious enemy attacked: a full bladder.

"Damn it, Brownstone. If we hadn't taken your stupid detour, I could have been back in town using an actual bathroom."

That was the one big disadvantage of her new vocational choice. Men just didn't understand how unpleasant it was to have to pee in bushes. They figured that just because it was easy for them to whip it out, it wasn't a big deal for women.

"Brownstone, if I get sand up my crack, I'm kicking your ass."

———

19

Shay finished her personal business and made her way back to the Forerunner. The entire time, she fought the urge to go check on Brownstone and see if he was still among the living. Tension spread through her neck and shoulders at the lack of recent gunfire.

"That's a good thing," she muttered. "It means he won." A sigh followed. "Or it means he lost and the dumbass got turned into a zombie."

Shay stopped, frowning. If Brownstone were dead, then she needed to go get some vengeance for him. Then again, a monster who could kill the bounty hunter might be too much for her. Knowing her limits was one of the reasons she was still breathing after a lifetime of violence.

"Maybe that idiot got too cocky. I'm not like him. I'm not gonna end up a zombie."

"What about zombies?"

The tomb raider pulled her gun out as she spun. Brownstone stood on the path, bloodied and scratched up, but very much in the land of the living from what she could see. He held something wrapped in a bloody T-shirt decorated with a cartoon fox.

"Don't sneak up on people, Brownstone," Shay muttered, holstering her gun. "Especially when you've just finished hunting a necromancer."

"He's not a problem anymore." The bounty hunter shrugged, then glanced over his shoulder. "What were you doing? I thought you were going to stay in the car."

Shay's face twitched. The last thing she wanted to tell Brownstone was that she had to take a leak. "I got bored, and I'd thought I'd see if you needed help." She shrugged. It wasn't a total lie. She had in fact thought about whether Brownstone needed help, even if she hadn't acted on it.

Brownstone raised the bloodied T-shirt. "Thanks, but I had things under control. I guess you could say Sombra lost his head." He chuckled.

Shay rolled her eyes. "That joke is so bad it should be treated as a weapon of mass destruction."

The fact he held a decapitated head didn't bother her. She'd done far worse when she was a professional killer, even if she didn't always want to remember that.

"Next time I go after a necromancer I'm bringing a machete," Brownstone said. "It'll make a lot of things easier. Or maybe a big-ass sword."

Shay sighed and hurried over to the Forerunner. "Let me get you a bag so you don't get his blood all over the seats. I'd kind of like the deposit back."

James looked around as if the cacti would miraculously cough up something for him before he turned to Shay. "Thanks."

She opened the back and fished a small black cloth bag

out of her supplies. She tossed Brownstone the bag. "So you went through all that trouble just to end up with no bounty? You don't really seem like the trophy type, though, so I guess I'm a little surprised."

"Nope, not a trophy-taker. I'm practical, not psycho." Brownstone assured her, stuffing the bloodied T-shirt, head and all, inside the bag.

The tomb raider stared at the bag, trying to square its presence with what the bounty hunter had just said.

"Uh, Brownstone, I think most people would consider chopping off a guy's head trophy-taking. Or is this part of some sort of weird magic shit?"

The bounty hunter grunted. "I needed the head for identification. And his bounty actually listed him as worth twice as much dead."

Shay blinked. "Huh, really? I thought most of the time they wouldn't take 'em if they were dead. I read all the time about people getting in trouble back home for excessive force during bounty captures."

Brownstone shook his head. "Past the border, sure. Not as much down here, though usually it's not higher, just the same. The Mexican authorities didn't want to have to deal with figuring out how to hold this asshole. Can't blame them after the shit I saw him do."

Shay chuckled. "No wonder this guy had to make his own friends." She started the vehicle once Brownstone had situated himself in the passenger seat. "Let's get back to the hotel before you accidentally run into more armed men. Or the head starts to smell the car up. Roll down your window."

The next day at lunch, Shay lifted a delicious taco to her mouth. It'd been a while since she'd visited El Paisá, but the wonderful flavors in her mouth were the same as she remembered. Ah, the spices, the crunch of the shell, and the mixing of the textures between the lettuce, meat, and cheese. Too damn tasty.

"Flavor this good should be illegal," Shay murmured to herself between bites. Her thoughts drifted back to her call to the Professor the night before.

Smite-Williams seemed delighted, if a bit tipsy, at her recovery of the artifact, and he had alluded to another job he wanted her to do soon.

"Whatever," the field archaeologist mumbled to herself. "I'll worry about that when I get back to the US."

Money was money, and the Professor seemed to have a lot of it to throw around. These successful recoveries also were helping build her reputation, which meant other people would throw work her way.

The tomb raider put down her taco and frowned. There were certain lines she hadn't crossed yet. Smite-Williams seemed like a decent enough man, but she wasn't sure what she'd do if someone dirtier needed her help. The Rod of Supay, for example, would be very dangerous in the wrong hands.

Am I a total mercenary or not? Guess I should figure that out before someone does it for me.

Shay took a deep breath and slowly exhaled. She'd scored an artifact and managed to not get killed, so it had been a good trip. She needed to focus on that, more than some future ethics concerns.

She considered lingering a day or two and relaxing in town. It'd been a long time since she'd been able to enjoy a place like Cabo San Lucas without work hanging over her. The Professor probably didn't need her to immediately leave for the new job.

Brownstone stepped into the taqueria. She was glad he'd dumped that ugly-ass coat, but several customers stepped away from him, eyeing him with visible concern.

Shay frowned, then realized she'd gotten used to his somewhat odd appearance. She even found it attractive, in its own way. Between the muscles, the ridges and birth-marks on Brownstone's face, and his extensive arm tattoos, she could see how a normal person might be afraid that he belonged to some gang like MS-13.

She pushed the thought out of her head, happy to see he wasn't carrying the head around with him anymore. From what he'd told her the night before, they'd sent James away from the local police station, telling him to come back the next day. This was despite the fact he literally had a head in a bag. She couldn't help but wonder how often that exact scenario played out, if the local authorities were so blasé about it.

With both the field archaeologist and the bounty hunter tired from a long day, they had decided to just grab a quick bite to eat and rest at the hotel until the following day.

The bounty hunter had disappeared after breakfast with the necromancer's head, and she'd texted him when

The bounty hunter had disappeared after breakfast with the necromancer's head, and she'd texted him when

213

she'd headed out to let him know she was grabbing lunch at the taqueria.

Brownstone nodded to Shay and headed over to her table to take a seat. He had a slight frown on his face.

"Problem, Brownstone?" Shay asked after swallowing the current bite. "Did you get your bounty, or are they making you wait some more?"

"Nah, they gave it to me, but it was a fucking hassle to get it processed."

"Why? Didn't pay your local bounty dues or some shit? They want bribes?"

The bounty hunter shook his head. "No, they just didn't believe me at first."

Shay leaned forward. "You had a fucking head in bag," she whispered.

"Yeah, but they didn't believe it was him. I'm not the first gringo to show up with a head in a bag and claim it was Sombra the Deathbringer. That was why they made me come back today; so they could inspect the head more carefully."

Shay nodded. "They don't have DNA on file they can run a comparison on?"

"Nope. They don't. I got lucky, though." Brownstone grunted. "I wasn't going to leave this town without them paying me."

"How did you get lucky? You intimidate them into paying you?"

"Nope. They confirmed the identity." He tapped his cheek. "Turns out our boy used to be in a gang and had a unique gang tattoo inside his cheek, so that proved it was him. He was also wanted for the murders of several *Federales* a few years before this more recent shit."

Shay stared at Brownstone. "Wait, some necromancer joined a gang? That's kind of dumb. If the guy can raise an army of zombies, why does he need to bother with a bunch of thugs?"

"That's the fun part. Because he wasn't Sombra the Deathbringer until last year. Before that, he was just Sombra the low-level gang enforcer." Brownstone shook his head. "He stumbled on some sort of Oriceran artifact that changed him, and then he turned into a bigger arrogant prick than before. I'll give him credit; for all his bullshit speeches about how tough he was, he must have understood that if he'd hung out in the city he'd have been taken down sooner rather than later. He wasn't a *total* moron."

"But he still got his head chopped off by a bounty hunter."

"I didn't say he wasn't a moron, just not a *total* moron."

Shay picked up her beer to take a sip. "And he still got enough attention to have a huge bounty on his head. You would have thought he would have kept a lower profile, even out in the countryside."

"That kind of worked to his advantage. From what the authorities told me, locals didn't fuck with him as long as he stayed in his little canyon, and no one came after him. None of the bounty hunters who went after him came back. After he took out a village the government tried to bomb him out, but when they sent in a small squad to confirm his death, those soldiers died, too. After that point, even the government decided to leave him alone." Brownstone shrugged. "They just massively increased the bounty and hoped someone like me would show up and take his ass out."

There was an uneasy expression on the bounty hunter's face. Shay wouldn't call it fear, but it was discomfort at the least. The man had butchered two housefuls of Harriken without showing discomfort.

It was not a good look on him.

Shay couldn't help but wonder if dealing with the zombies had freaked Brownstone out more than he was willing to admit, but since they'd both completed their missions, she saw no reason to bring down the mood by probing at a potential sore spot. She might be able to kick serious ass, but she was far from fearless herself.

"Hey, you hungry?" she said. "These tacos are damn good. Want some?"

The bounty hunter held up five fingers. "*Cinco*."

Shay flagged down a waitress and put in the order. Once the other woman was gone she couldn't help but stare at the bounty hunter, again thinking how he didn't seem like his normal arrogant self.

"What?" The discomfort on Brownstone's face turned to irritation. "Why are you looking at me like that? Got something on my face?"

"Oh, nothing. Just thinking about the bounty money," Shay lied. "I mean, the Mexican government doesn't have enough money for regular law enforcement and military shit, so I was wondering how they can afford big-ass bounties."

Brownstone shrugged. "They don't pay them, mostly."

Shay blinked. "Huh? Then why does anyone bother to go after bounties here?"

"It's not that the bounty hunters don't get paid. It's more who does the payment." He gestured toward the door. "Resort areas in particular have tons of bounties, because the businesses and hotels all pay into a fund. I think they all understand that if the crime situation gets out of control and starts affecting tourists they'll be in trouble."

"So zombie necromancers are fine until they threaten Spring Breakers?" Shay rolled her eyes. "And people say *I'm* ruthless."

Brownstone nodded. "Yeah, imagine if Sombra had bought a fucking clue and kept quiet about converting people. He could have started his own little Mexican zombie apocalypse before anyone knew what was going on. When I fought the guy he had hundreds of zombies, and those fuckers don't go down without removing the entire head. Cops and *Federales* would have had a hard time dealing with them."

"Look, at you, saving the world...or at least Baja California Sur." Shay grinned.

The bounty hunter had opened his mouth to say something else when the waitress appeared with his tacos. She placed his plate down in front of him and offered him a polite nod before leaving.

Shay watched Brownstone expectantly as he lifted a taco to his mouth and took a huge bite. His mouth worked for a moment before he swallowed.

"So, what do you think?"

Brownstone smiled. "These are fucking fantastic."

20

L ater that evening, James knocked on the door to Shay's hotel room. It took a surprisingly long time for her to answer.

He frowned, wondering if she was in trouble. He doubted a fight could break out across the hall without him hearing anything, but he couldn't be sure.

James pounded on the door again. "Shay, you in there?"

The lock clicked in the door, and the bounty hunter stepped back. He didn't want to go down easily if an enemy lurked on the other side.

The open door revealed Shay, not an attacker. Her dark wet hair clung to her face and neck, and she wore nothing but a soft white cotton robe.

"Hey, Brownstone," she murmured, her voice low. "Sorry about the wait. I was just taking a shower. You know how it is when you get in there and there's all that steam and water flowing over your body. It just gets you all relaxed. Makes your mind wander."

"Yeah, I understand how showers work." He shrugged,

confused by where she was going with any of this. "I mostly think about barbecue in the shower."

"Of course you do." Shay rolled her eyes. She leaned against the doorjamb, tilting her head. Her leg moved forward, flashing a little skin. "Wanna come in for a bit?"

"Nope," he stated flatly.

"Huh?" A slight frown appeared on Shay's face.

"Sorry. Just wanted to make sure you didn't need me. I was planning to buy a ticket and head back to LA. From what you said a little while ago, you're good to go without me."

Something James couldn't interpret played in Shay's eyes, but he decided it'd be best to leave it alone. Even though he knew about the woman's dark past, he still couldn't claim he understood her. Sometimes she could be totally ruthless, and sometimes she worried like a soccer mom.

She was complicated, and that unsettled him more than he wanted to admit.

"You're leaving so soon?" Shay sounded almost disappointed.

"No reason for me to stay," James told her. "I got the bounty, and you got the artifact. I'd rather sleep in my own bed, and we have good tacos in LA. Not like we have a shortage of good Mexican cooks there."

"Oh, well…"

"Problem?"

She sighed and shook her head. "Nah, don't worry about it." She smiled. "I think I'm gonna stick around for a day or two. The Professor mentioned some other work, but we're not gonna go over the final details until

I come back to LA, so I think I can manage a couple days off."

"Sounds good."

"Nice working with you, Brownstone." Shay laughed. "I don't know if we can consider this job bloodier or less bloody than last time."

"Last time I killed three guys. This time I only killed one. Those zombies were already dead."

"Fair point." She blew some wet hair out of her face. "I guess I'll see you back in LA then."

James nodded. "See you." He turned to leave.

"Brownstone, just one thing."

He turned back around. "What?"

"Burn that fucking coat when you get back to LA. I don't care how useful it is for concealing shit. It's a crime against fashion, and I can't in good conscience continue to let you wear something like that."

James chuckled. Shay was developing quite the mother complex.

It was too damn late when James found himself standing in front of his house. He didn't care if the flight was short. Something about being that high up for more than a few minutes always left him feeling off and tired. Maybe it had something to do with the air recirculation.

He didn't know.

Yeah, next fucker I'm after will probably hide in an airplane bathroom. It would be just my luck. The Prince of Planes, or whatever shit.

"Fucking cowards," he muttered. "Stay on the damn ground."

James opened the door and stepped inside. It'd only been a couple of days, but it felt like it had been weeks.

Not that there was anything there waiting for him. Leeroy was dead, and Alison was gone.

The bounty hunter pulled out his phone and prepared to call her before sighing and slipping it back into his pocket.

It was late in Los Angeles, so it was super-damn late in Virginia. He scrubbed a hand over his face. He'd taken down a level-four and a level-five bounty in less than a week. It wasn't like he needed to go rushing off to do anything else.

Maybe Shay had the right idea. He'd take it easy for the next couple of days. Everything would look better after a shower and good night's rest.

"I swear by the cumin," said Bill, the host of the *Modern Super BBQ* podcast. "If there's no cumin involved, I might as well go home." He went on to extol the virtues of cumin in barbecue sauce.

James dusted the end table in the living room with a small rag. He didn't quite get how everything had gotten so dusty after him being gone for only a couple of days, but at least it gave him something easy to do.

There was a loud knock on his door.

James paused the podcast with a tap on his phone. He slowly approached the door and looked through the peephole. No way in hell he'd ever open a door without check-ing, especially after everything that had happened recently.

Probably some new douchebag like Emperor Freeze or Caliente, Master of Flame, here to earn some rep points by taking him on.

A skinny young black guy in torn jeans, a leather jacket, and a tight t-shirt stood on the other side with his hands in his pockets. A single bandana on his arm communicated his gang affiliation to people in the know. He looked more bored than anything.

James opened the door. "Hey, Trey."

"Motherfucking Mr. Brownstone!" Trey grinned and stuck out his hand. "It's been a while, motherfucker."

The bounty hunter gave the man's hand a firm shake. "I'm not buying any drugs."

The gang leader laughed and waved. "Nah, man. I know you ain't into that shit." He glanced over his shoulder. "I got some other shit to share with you, but I'd rather do it inside, you know?"

James motioned him inside, and the younger man entered.

Trey stepped forward, glancing around. His eyes narrowed and he shook his head. "It's like... I don't know, man. It's like getting to walk into the motherfucking Batcave. You got some bitch-ass butler hanging out here?"

James snorted. "Not last time I checked."

A confused look settled over Trey's face. "It's... Well, I guess it ain't no Batcave."

The bounty hunter shrugged. "I'm not a billionaire."

Trey held up a hand. "Nah, man. I ain't trying to be disre-spectful. It's just, you're big shit...the Granite Ghost. This is all low-down; no tech dope. I expected this place to be all super-teched up, and not so fucking clean." He grinned. "I get it. You got some sweet-ass maid action coming in?"

"Nope. I just like a clean house." He leveled a stare at the other man. "Are you doing a tour of the houses in the neighborhood, Trey?"

"Nah, man, I just… Look, you know what I like about you, Mr. Brownstone?"

James rubbed his chin, looking Trey over. "That I don't beat your ass?"

Trey laughed and slapped a hand on his thigh. "Yeah, that's the shit, too. Yeah, I appreciate that, but it's something different, you know? You're a man who understands respect."

James eyed the gang member. "Respect?"

"Yeah. If someone shows you proper respect, you show 'em proper respect back. I ain't no fucking dumbass. I know you could lay out every gang in this area and probably still have time to come home and whack off to some porn. But you leave my boys alone, and I appreciate that."

James offered the other man a quick nod. That description wasn't far from the truth, but he didn't want to tell Trey that it wouldn't be worth his time to bother.

Still, there was also more to it. Men like Trey kept things under control. Nature abhorred a vacuum, and a city abhorred a criminal vacuum even more. As long as the low-level criminals stayed under control and mostly messed with each other, James figured they were providing a service of sorts to the local neighborhood.

"What's this about?" James asked.

Trey cleared his throat. "Like I said, it's about showing respect. You show us respect, and we show you respect. I think we both want the same shit in the end."

"I'm a bounty hunter, not a gangbanger. I don't care about territory."

"Nah, man. Yeah, I get that shit, but you care about the neighborhood." Trey nodded. "We do too. You do good shit, you know. Like I heard you took down that bitch-ass King Pyro motherfucker."

James shrugged. "He was a bounty. He was in town."

"I heard that bitch killed some family." Trey sneered. "If one of my boys killed some family in a robbery, I'd get my other boys together and beat their ass to death. Just because we're criminals ain't mean we're animals." He leaned forward. "I heard that bitch also threatened your dog." His eyebrows went up.

"Not exactly," James replied, "but close enough."

"That was a dumbass move." Trey leaned against a wall and crossed his arms. "Also you should know that the word on the street is, the Harriken been asking around about you the last couple of days."

James snorted. "They'll need a recruitment drive before they come after me again."

The gang leader laughed. "Damn, motherfucker. That's cold."

"So, have they been around here?"

Trey shrugged. "Fuck if I know. We ain't been in watch mode. Ain't too much of a neighborhood watch plan around here." He rubbed his neck. "Look, that Harriken shit got a lot of us talking. We don't need outside bitches who don't know when to stop coming in and messing up our hood."

"What are you getting at?"

"Maybe you could help with that shit, Brownstone. I don't just mean the bounty shit. If people know the Granite Ghost will fuck them up if they fuck with the neighborhood, it'll keep 'em in line; maybe keep them out."

James grunted. "So you're saying you want me to make sure that only local criminals have control?"

Trey shrugged. "I'm saying that we don't need bitch-ass dog killers and people going after little girls. I'm saying in the end, motherfucker, we all just want this to be an okay place to live. Not just me and my boys, but a lot of normal working bitches in this neighborhood."

"You deal drugs and pimp women. Don't you think that hurts people in the neighborhood?"

Trey snorted. "We ain't give drugs to no one who can't handle them, and there's none of that bullshit slapping around girls. We give shit to people who want it, and only fuck with people who fuck with us." He waved a hand. "That shit don't matter anyway, because this ain't about my gang, Mr. Brownstone. Like I said, it's about this community. This world is fucked-up, man. You know it, and that's why you do what you do. And all any of us around here trying to do is protect ourselves." He looked down. "It ain't like before this Oriceran crap. You never know what fucking shit's gonna happen now."

James stared at the younger man, not saying anything for a long while. If he'd learned one thing in the last few weeks, it was that he couldn't take on the world alone. Hell, he wasn't sure he even wanted to anymore.

Trey and people like him might be criminals, but at least they gave a small damn about other people around them. That was something to encourage. Ruthless groups like the Harriken shouldn't be able to operate freely, thinking they could kidnap teenage girls and murder dogs with impunity.

James didn't blame the police. They were underfunded, and handcuffed by rules and the harsh reality of the new world. A few AET teams weren't enough to make up for criminals like King Pyro and Sombra. Sometimes he wondered if it was pointless and the world was doomed.

"Getting involved in other people's shit complicates things," James rumbled, breaking his silence. "And I like things simple."

"Shit, yeah, I get that. I'm all about simple, mother-fucker. I'm not saying you need to become shadow mayor or some shit. I'm just saying if people know you're willing to help more on occasion, it'll help everyone. We all respect you, Brownstone."

"You all fear me."

"Same shit." Trey shrugged. "You live here, too, is all I'm sayin'. Maybe we can clean this shit up a little. I got my boys on a tight leash, and I'm thinking that leash can be even tighter if I know I don't have to constantly watch my back. And plenty of other people out there ain't even on the wrong fucking side of the law like me. You the real shit, Mr. Brownstone. I'm just a motherfucker with some friends."

There was something almost desperate in the young man's eyes.

So much for keeping shit simple.

"I'm willing to do something for the community," James offered. "As long as they're willing to do shit for me."

"You gotta spend money to make money. Yeah, I understand that shit." Trey grinned.

"This doesn't mean I'm running around the neighborhood solving everyone's problems. I'm a bounty hunter. I'm just saying that I know how to repay debts." James' gaze flicked to the empty area where Leeroy's bowls used to sit. "And too much trouble in the neighborhood makes my life complicated."

"Exactly, Mr. Brownstone. Exactly." Trey's phone buzzed, and he pulled it out of his pocket. "Well, shit. I gotta get going. I'll let you know if I hear anything, and I think I'll have a few of my boys take turns just keeping an eye on your house. Don't want any Harriken motherfuckers getting the drop on my favorite bounty hunter."

James' face darkened. "It'd be a sad day for them if they did. I only stopped because I ran out of people to kill."

Trey chuckled. "I don't doubt it." He gave James a quick little salute. "Keep it badass, Mr. Brownstone. Keep it badass." He headed for the door.

James watched the gang leader as he left his house. Alison, Shay, and now the people of his neighborhood. The Professor. Zoe. His life was growing more complicated each week.

Father McCartney always told him that he was part of God's plan to fight evil, but he didn't know what he believed. He looked down at his hand, then balled it into a fist.

He wasn't a good man, but at least he wasn't a piece of shit.

21

"I thought you said three days," Alison exclaimed when she answered.

James frowned and started doing calculations in his head. He sighed. Even though he'd thought about calling her many times the last few days, by the time he actually got around to it he'd ended up calling late. He scrubbed a hand across his face.

Yeah, some great father figure he was.

"Um, sorry. There was...sh— Stuff, and, uh. Then Shay said I'd be bothering you, and..."

"Very smooth, Mr. Bro— James." Alison sighed. "It's not a big deal. And I'll never be bothered by you calling. I just didn't know if you were mad at me, is all."

"Why would I be mad at you, kid?"

"Because I'm going to this school. Because I didn't stay with you."

Oh, great. Now he was making some girl upset because he couldn't keep his promises. Smooth. Way to be a douchebag.

James shook his head even though Alison wasn't there to see it. "It's just been a busy week. Sorry, it won't happen again. And don't ever think any mistake I make is your fault. I'm the adult, and I need to damn well act like it."

"Okay," Alison replied, her voice quiet.

I'm not fucking Walt. I'm never gonna make you feel bad for being you.

"How are things going for you, Alison?"

"Well, it's been busy here. I completed orientation and I've started classes, but it's kind of intimidating."

James grunted. He'd gone to Catholic school, so he could semi-relate to the private school experience. "Why?"

"I've always been able to see soul energy, but that's different than doing magic. A lot of kids here know a lot more about magic than I do. I feel stupid, and I'm way behind."

James grunted. "Most people didn't know crap about real magic until not all that long ago. Don't beat yourself up. What about the other kids? Are they talking trash to you?"

His free hand curled into a fist, and he reconsidered the merits of terrorizing some punk teens.

"They're just students, you know? Some are nice, some aren't. I don't know how it compares to normal school, 'cause I never went."

James gritted his teeth. "You tell those little asses they better be nice if they don't want me coming over there and feeding them to a Chupacabra."

Alison laughed. "I don't think we have a Chupacabra on campus. It's okay, you know. I've made some friends, and I'm getting to know more people." She sighed.

"If it's okay, then why are you sighing?"

"It's just… Okay, I'm scared. I lived at home my entire life, and now I'm over here. Mom's gone, and… It's a lot to deal with."

James took a deep breath. "You need to do what's best for you, but always keep in mind that if you want to leave I've got your back. I have a room here for you."

"Thanks, James. I…think I'm gonna be okay. One sec." A scratching noise came next, followed by some muffled talking. James assumed she was talking to someone else. "I have to go now. Sorry."

"Everything okay?"

James couldn't help but imagine some rabid top-hatted ferret flying around and blasting the school with fireballs.

"Yeah. Just more orientation stuff. They are showing me some of the special creatures, and it's a big scheduled thing, so I can't miss it."

"You do what you have to do, and call me if you need anything."

"Thanks. Talk to you later. Tell Shay I said hi."

"Talk to you later, and I will."

The line went dead.

James stared at the phone for a long moment, still wondering if he'd done the right thing by sending Alison to the School of Necessary Magic.

He shook his head. There was no doubt that the half-Drow girl would benefit from learning to control her powers. He couldn't be a bitch about it just because he felt a little lonely.

"Fuck," the bounty hunter muttered. "Isn't there some-one's ass I can kick to take my mind off things?"

James grinned at a sudden idea. There *was* someone he could potentially take out his anger on. He dialed Stephen.

I hope for your sake, you didn't fuck this up, Broker Boy.

The broker picked up on the first ring. "Hey, Brownstone."

"Hey, Stephen. I wanted to follow up on my little investment deal."

"Yeah, about that."

James didn't like the man's tone. He frowned and pulled back to glare at this phone, even though he knew it wouldn't do any good. If the stockbroker had screwed him over, the bounty hunter would have to reconsider his decision not to bring him in.

"So, yeah," Stephan began, an amused undercurrent to his voice, "your plan worked well. The stock ended up doubling and then some, but then it went down like a cheap hooker."

"What the fuck? Doubling and going down? I wanted to help the church, not throw my money away."

James took a deep breath and slowly let it out. Even though he wanted to be pissy with the man and take out some frustration on him, the stockbroker had gone out of his way to warn him of the risks. Punishing people for his mistakes wasn't James' style. He gritted his teeth.

"You okay, Brownstone?"

"It's all good. I'm hoping my church friend knew when to sell." He rubbed the back of his neck. "So what am I down?"

"Oh, you're really not understanding this, are you?" Stephen laughed. "You're not, Brownstone. You're up."

"Huh? What about the hooker dive?"

Stephen snickered. "This is why it's good you came to a professional instead of trying this shit yourself, Brownstone. You might be good at kicking ass, but you wouldn't last three seconds day-trading." His voice dripped with contempt. "I started pushing your stock, but I'd barely bought much of anything when it took off like a rocket on its own. Somebody sold ten thousand shares all at once when it was already well over double."

Relief washed through him. At least Father McCartney hadn't taken a hit. The small number of outstanding shares associated with the company at least suggested such.

"That'll probably be my church friend," James said.

"Well, I guess all that praying paid off, because he knew just when to exit. Once he sold, it started a sell-off. Like I told you before, Brownstone, these microcaps are volatile."

"So how am I not down, then?"

Stephen chuckled. "It never fell below the original price. You're up on the deal, and your church buddy now has a lot more money to spend on candles and incense. It's almost like God really is on your side."

"Or the Devil."

"Yeah, love of money and all that crap. Hey, whoever delivers the profits in the end, right? You didn't lose any money, and your friend made a lot. Everyone walks away happy."

James blinked several times, both surprised and happy. "Thanks, Stephen. You've actually done something worthwhile with your life."

"Damn, Brownstone. Now you sound like my wife."

James slipped out of his F-350 and headed uneasily into the church. He should have been happy. He'd taken out some bad people in the last week, and his stock plan had helped Father McCartney and the orphanage out of their financial hole.

At least he assumed as much. That was one thing he needed to confirm.

He didn't even bother to look around before heading straight into the confessional booth. Even if he'd done what he considered good works the last week, that didn't change the fact that he'd killed a man and beaten another half to death.

Once inside the booth, he slid the door closed. The shadow of Father McCartney crossed the grate.

"Bless me, Father, for I have sinned. This week, among other things, I beat a man half to death."

"I see," the priest said, not a hint of surprise in his voice. "God asks us to control our wrath. And what did this man do?"

"Threatened to kill everyone I loved."

A pained sigh escaped Father McCartney's mouth. "I would hope that after a while that these people would learn their lesson. And what else, my child?"

"I killed a man. I'll be honest. I'm not sad because he's dead. He was a necromancer. He killed innocent people and fuc— He defiled their bodies and made them into the walking dead."

The priest sucked in a tight breath. "While the Church is still clarifying what types of magic are sinful, from the beginning there has been no ambiguity about necromancy. To defile a body in such a way is among the gravest of sins."

"Like I said, don't feel bad. The thing is, I killed him, but I don't know how. That's not sitting well with me."

"You don't remember?"

James sighed. "I remember. I just don't understand it. I was neck-deep in zombies, and he snuck up on me. He has some sort of death touch–at least that's what they told me —but when he touched me, he just fell to the ground with his eyes glowing, twitched, and died." He ran a hand over his head. "Magic. Can't trust it, I guess. Crazy sh— Crazy stuff."

"Hmmm. You sound as if you don't believe it."

"I believe it. I was there. It's… I don't know."

"Just try and explain slowly what's going through your head," Father McCartney requested.

"What kind of monster am I, that a necromancer dies when he touches me?" James asked.

"You're not a monster."

James looked at the grate; the priest was barely discernible on the other side. "Then how do you explain it?"

"Do you know how many saints have faced demons or deadly animals and survived? Do you know how many faithful have called upon their intercession to survive evil?" Excitement filtered into the priest's voice, heightening his Jersey accent. "What you're describing, James, isn't being a monster. It's divine intervention. It's a miracle."

James barked out a laugh. "A miracle?"

"This isn't like before Oriceran. Science can't claim a monopoly on knowledge and truth. Magic is real, so there's no reason to doubt the power of divine miracles. This necromancer, this dark servant of Satan, found that his dark power had limits when challenging a servant of the Lord. Whatever troubles you about your work, you shouldn't worry that an evil man has been sent to enjoy his time with his master."

James grunted. "What if it's just some weird magic backfire?"

"A miracle of timing is still a miracle. You lived. He died. There's nothing to be concerned over."

James pondered that for a few moments. He wasn't convinced, but he couldn't dismiss the explanation out of hand. Father McCartney was right about how miracles weren't so easy to ignore in an age of open magic.

The priest was one of the few men James dared showed weakness in front of, so he decided to unload all his concerns.

"I got kind of freaked out by the whole thing. I ended up using my health potion. I don't know why. Maybe I thought I'd die right after or something. Right then and there, it was hard to believe."

James had made a point of not telling Shay that little detail. Even though they'd grown closer, he still didn't think she needed to know everything that had happened—especially when he didn't understand the events himself.

"It doesn't hurt to be safe," Father McCartney assured him.

"Yeah, but now that I used that potion, I'm gonna have to go back to Zoe and get a new one."

The priest chuckled. They'd discussed the lush witch on more than a few occasions.

"I'll pray for your willpower," Father McCartney told him. "Oh, and the confessional isn't always the best place to talk about this sort of thing, but I know you find it more comfortable than my office. There's something I needed to tell you."

James' stomach tightened. "What?"

"I sold that stock you gave me. I don't know what happened; the price kept increasing and increasing until it more than doubled. I didn't want to be greedy, so I sold it."

James grinned, happy to have it verified that the ten-thousand-share movement was from Father McCartney.

"Maybe it's another miracle," the bounty hunter suggested.

"You think you're being funny, but you may be right. Both the church and the orphanage are in good shape for at least six months, and that includes many upgrades to the facilities. Your tithe has saved that orphanage."

James nodded to himself, all his concern about Sombra's death vanishing. He still didn't buy into the idea that a miracle had saved him from the necromancer, but for that brief moment, happiness consumed all the heaviness weighing down his soul.

22

Four hours for some barbecue might seem extreme to a lot of people, but James knew his little jaunt to Las Vegas would be worth it. The drive from Los Angeles to Las Vegas had gone smoothly enough, and it'd given him an excuse to take the F-350 to his mechanic for some overdue maintenance. A little loving care for his truck, and it'd continue to serve him well.

James pulled his Ford into the small parking lot outside Jessie Rae's. One wouldn't discern the meaty treasure within from the unassuming exterior. Even the landscaping was low-key; a few small palm trees here and there, none of the gaudy flair you saw elsewhere in Vegas.

The typical ignorant tourist would hit up a place like the nearby Mandalay Bay, not realizing how close the fancy building was to a place that offered pure barbecue perfection.

The most glorious sign James had seen in the last few weeks sat in the window: YES, WE'RE OPEN.

A few steps through the parking lot brought James into

the restaurant and its small two-room dining area. It had only eight tables, four in each room. From what Mike Ross had told him, the majority of his business came from pick-up and delivery.

There was a modestly-sized TV in the corner and the menu was on the wall, its content detailing mouth-watering barbeque and sides.

The simplicity of the restaurant stood as a testament to the fundamental quality of the product. Jessie Rae's didn't do well because of some fake-ass ambience, or by filling the walls with a bunch of random pictures and knick-knacks.

Instead, it ruled Las Vegas barbeque by providing a delicious and unbeatable product.

Near the cups and the drink machine, trophies and plaques stood on shelves connected to the walls. An inspection would reveal all the barbecue contests won by the small restaurant. One of the earliest dated back to 2015, and the place had upheld its success in contests in the following years. James wouldn't be surprised if that streak kept up for as long as the place continued to exist.

A woman finished paying for a large bag of ribs and eyed James with suspicion as she stepped past him. The bounty hunter didn't do anything more than offer her a tight smile. The last thing he'd ever do was stir up trouble in Jessie Rae's.

"Well, here's a man I haven't seen in a while," called a man standing near the cash register. It was Michael, the owner.

James shrugged. "What can I say? I got a hankering for ribs, so I hopped in the truck and drove to Vegas."

"From Los Angeles?" Mike asked.

James shrugged. "Yeah. Not like I had anything better to do today."

Michael chuckled and pointed to a table. "Take a seat. I'll bring out some food. Lucky you. You missed the lunch rush."

Fifteen minutes later the two men sat across from each other devouring the best damn barbecue on the planet. The glorious flavors played across James' tongue, and the tender ribs melted in his mouth.

Father McCartney had spoken of miracles and divine intervention. As far as James was concerned, the existence of the restaurant proved there *was* a loving God. There was even a God Sauce at Jessie Rae's.

The bounty hunter chuckled at the thought as he took another bite.

"Did you watch *Barbecue Wars: New Generation* this season?" Michael asked.

James swallowed before answering. "Yeah. I just watched the final episode the other day. I was out of the country for a few days, so I missed it on the first run." He shook his head. "It's... Damn! I never saw that coming."

Michael chuckled. "Freaked out that an elf won?"

"Not freaked out. I just didn't know if they were being easy on her because they wanted an elf for the ratings. Then she *won* it. I mean, those guys have their reputations, so I don't think they'd give her the win unless that shit tasted great."

"Yeah. Times are changing, man. That's not always a bad thing."

James finished off his rib and picked up a new one. "Not saying it is. It's just, I like things simple, and it's hard wrapping my mind around an elf winning a barbecue competition. I mean, yeah, all this magic and shit's been around for a while, but before it was like us and them. Things were separate. Now we got Oriceran barbecue, and humans are running around tossing magic all over the place."

"It's more than that." Michael shot him a grin. "It's not even Oriceran barbecue, you know."

"Huh?"

"Nadina's style; think about it. It's Oriceran-Carolina fusion, you know? And it's not like there's such a thing as even just American barbecue. That elf brought her game from her home, but think about all the different regions. Think about all the intelligent critters they have over there. Some talking elk-man might be making your barbecue in the future." He shrugged. "Elves are going to seem pretty freaking normal by then."

"Doesn't that bother you?" James grabbed one of the waffle fries with the white sauce and tossed it in his mouth. "All the change?"

"Whole world's changed in a lot bigger ways than just barbecue. Just got to go with the flow."

James grunted. "Don't I know it, but maybe some things shouldn't change." He shrugged. "I don't know."

"Got to think long-term." Michael swallowed a bite of his food. "I've got my preferences, but barbecue's always grown. Every once in a while I get some dumbass who comes in here and says some garbage about how my Las Vegas Style is crap, and there's only one real style, which is whatever random thing they grew up with. Small minds. Small taste buds."

James gestured to one of the larger trophies. "I think that proves whose style is crap and whose is good."

"Yeah, everything's been going great, but I don't do this for the trophies." A broad grin broke out on his face. "But the trophies don't hurt."

The men shared a laugh.

Michael slapped a hand on a table. "You know what, James? I don't know a man who isn't in the industry who is as much into barbecue as you. You should come to a competition sometime. You should try out. Got several coming up soon. You'd love it."

"Nah. I'm happy being a civilian in the barbecue war. I figure I'll leave it to the experts."

"You *are* an expert, James. Even if you don't want to cook, you can still come and taste. Even if a bunch of Mr. Memphises and Mrs. Lexingtons are talking trash, that doesn't change the fact there'll be a lot of quality flavors from all over. And now with that elf girl having won that show, you're going to see a lot more experimentation with the Oriceran stuff, too. Brave new world. Try it out. You might like it."

James stared at the trophies and plaques. "Maybe I *will* come. Might even have someone join me. Someone I'm trying to get to understand barbecue more."

The other man shook his head, his eyes wide like he'd seen a ghost. "Oh? Someone else, as in a woman?"

"Maybe. Everyone should love barbecue, man or woman."

Michael gave a rueful chuckle. "Never thought you would succumb, man. There's nothing more complicated than a woman, and I know how much you like the simple life. You think Oriceran barbecue is going to blow your mind? Just wait until you're trying to keep a woman happy. That's the single most complicated thing a man can do."

James was spared having to immediately respond by the timely arrival of another tray. Little meat remained on the massacred remnants of the original one. He'd devoured the majority of it himself, only barely aware of how much he was eating.

Not that he was satisfied. Not yet.

As James ripped into some brisket, he thought about why he'd even hinted at bringing Shay to a competition. They weren't together; not in that way. He didn't even know how he really felt about her, other than the fact that he trusted her. His response to Michael had almost been reflex, which maybe spoke to a hidden truth he wasn't ready to face.

Shit. Michael's right. That woman's making even my barbecue trip complicated. Need to get this conversation away from breasts...chicken, and back to ribs.

"Lot of people on the barbeque podcasts thought the *Barbecue War* judges were too biased this year," James offered. "Even ignoring Nadina, there were some weird calls."

"Hard to say since we weren't eating it, but I know what you mean. Sometimes the judges totally went against what the diners were saying." Michael set his rib down and furrowed his brow in concentration. "I don't know. Can see it both ways, and I think that was more about Cassie. That woman's way too obsessed with white sauce. She's the reason they kept pushing Sam through. That guy just didn't want to leave behind those Alabama roots."

"Got to be honest. You know I'm not much on the mayonnaise sauces."

"Lot of people love my Bama Slama. It's not God Sauce, but it's at least demigod sauce."

James snorted. "I want barbecue sauce, not potato salad. That's why I always order shit like the Pig Sweat or the God Sauce."

Michael pointed his beer bottle at the other man. "Next you're going to give me some big speech about the constant superiority of low and slow vs. fast and hot. Got to be flexible and mix techniques, otherwise you'll miss out on a lot of good stuff." He tapped his forehead. "I've kept an open mind and experimented with my own types of fusion, which is why I've been tearing it up for years now."

"I'm flexible," James muttered. "I just got my favorites, is all."

"If I had too many customers who got stuck on only eating one style, I might have some trouble."

"I just drove four hours to eat some of your damn barbecue. I don't think I'm too stuck."

"True enough." Michael finished his beer. "How long are you in town?"

"Just the day and the night. Wanted to clear my head and get some good barbecue. You should be honored."

Michael shook his head and pointed at James. "*You* should be honored to eat my food."

Both men chuckled.

James thought about his recent travels. He'd had some of the best tacos ever in Cabo, and now he was eating the best barbecue. It'd been a good week for both bounty hunting and eating.

"Heading back home tomorrow morning." James added, "Though I'm taking five pounds of your ribs with me to the hotel tonight."

"Keep in mind what I said about the competitions."

"I'll think about it, but things have a way of getting complicated when I least expect it so it's hard for me to plan for that sort of thing."

"What?" Michael asked. "Like you're worried some random truck full of guys with guns will show up when you're on your way to a competition?"

James laughed darkly. "You'd be surprised how often that shit happens to me."

23

James already missed the distinctive Jessie Rae's flavor by the time he turned onto his street. He didn't regret taking the road trip, and speaking with Michael had been relaxing in a way he'd not felt in a long time. The idea of going to a barbecue competition was appealing, even if he didn't think he could fit it into his lifestyle. And the less he thought about taking Shay to a competition, the simpler his life would be.

Probably a bunch of fucking Harriken would attack me if I went to a competition. People shouldn't get close to me. It's a good thing Alison is in Virginia with a bunch of fucking wizards and witches protecting her.

A rough-looking teen waved to him from the street, and James slowed. He didn't recognize the kid, but he did recognize his colors. He was one of Trey's boys.

The F-350 pulled to a stop and the bounty hunter rolled down the window. He gave the gangbanger a fist-bump.

"Welcome back, Mr. Brownstone," the gangbanger said.

"Trey be telling us that if we saw weird shit around your house we need be telling you about said weird shit." He slapped a hand over his chest. "So here I am, ready to deliver the motherfucking weird-shit news."

James grunted. So much for his relaxing mini-vacation. At least he'd gotten his barbecue.

"And what weird shit did you see?"

"Nothin' until earlier today." The gangbanger leaned forward and lowered his voice. "That's when this black SUV with tinted windows rolled into the hood. I ain't ever seen that piece of shit around here before." He gestured up the street. "They been three blocks up from your crib since fucking lunch, man."

A patient enemy was a dangerous enemy. James was getting sick of people fucking with his home or his neighborhood. Trey had a decent point about keeping outside influence on the neighborhood to a minimum.

James could accomplish that through the not-so-careful application of copious amounts of violence, but he needed to know who to beat down first. That would require a little investigation.

"I know you don't recognize the car," the bounty hunter began, "but do you have any idea who it is?"

"Nope." The gang member looked up and down the street. "You think it's some of them Harriken bitches? Trey says we're supposed to keep an eye out for those sword bitches, whether they around your crib or not."

James' gaze flicked up the street. The car was too far away to see from where he was. "Maybe. They've got enough of a beef with me."

"It's more like you got a major beef with them. Those

bitches have a death wish." The gangbanger snorted. "Stupid motherfuckers should learn to leave well enough alone."

James chuckled. He couldn't disagree with the kid's evaluation of the Harriken. They were the dictionary definition of stupid motherfuckers.

"You can head on out," the bounty hunter told him. "I'll handle whoever it is, and it's best if they don't see you around me."

The gang member turned to leave.

"I've got a message for Trey," the bounty hunter added.

"What, Mr. Brownstone?"

"You tell him the community just did me a favor, and I don't forget people who do me favors."

Delroy leaned back in the seat of the SUV. "Are you a complete fucking moron, Greg? I can't believe you're saying that shit."

"Kiss my ass, Delroy," the man in the driver's seat shot back. "You're just mad because your boys can't hit worth a damn. If they ever want to see a World Series again they better start learning some magic, because that's the only way they'll get better." He chuckled. "Maybe they should let some Oricerans on the team."

Greg glanced at the display screen in the center of the dashboard. It was divided into two halves, both providing feeds from their surveillance drones.

"Shit, the aerial feed isn't that clear," Greg complained. "Why don't we drop its altitude?"

Delroy shrugged. "Because it'll be too fucking obvious if it's hovering at twenty feet."

Greg pointed toward the lower screen, which provided a low but wide-angle view of the driveway. "The problem with these insect drone models is that damn camera angle. Is this fucker ever going to come home?"

"I don't know. We haven't been able to tag him in town. It's like he disappeared."

"You think he knows we're watching his place? What if that old drunk told him?"

Delroy slammed his fist into a palm. "If Brownstone knew we were watching he'd come after us. He's not the kind of guy who runs off with his tail between his legs. Just ask the Harriken."

"We don't have solid proof he did that," Greg argued. "Official word is, it was a gang fight. Isn't that half the reason we're looking into this shit?"

"Proof? Everybody in fucking town knows he did it."

A loud clink against the side windows made both men look that way.

James Brownstone stood there with a .45 in his hand, but not pointed at them. Faint smile in place, he gestured for them to roll down the window.

"Shit," Delroy hissed. "What do we do, drive off?"

"We'll be dead before we make it ten feet. If he wanted us dead, he would have already shot us. Let's just hear what he has to say." Greg pressed a button and the window lowered with a whir.

The bounty hunter's smile grew into a grin. He didn't point the gun at the men but neither did he holster the weapon. Both men inside realized that if they tried to draw they'd be dead before they got their guns out of their holsters, and that was assuming bullets would even work. Both had heard a lot of strange rumors about the so-called Granite Ghost.

"Just want to talk, assholes," Brownstone rumbled. "No one has to die unless they do something stupid."

The men in the SUV frowned, but didn't say anything.

"See, my life is about keeping things simple. I tell myself that all the time: keep things simple, stupid. You know what's *not* simple?"

Greg and Delroy exchanged looks, then shrugged.

"Dead bodies without bounties aren't simple," James explained. "So I'm really hoping that you two assholes can explain why you're spying on my house, and that this doesn't end with me killing you." His expression darkened. "You're obviously not Harriken, but that doesn't mean you aren't doing their dirty work for them. I know they are fucking looking for me."

"Whoa, whoa, slow down, cowboy," Delroy exclaimed, waving his hands in front of him. "We're cops."

"Why the fuck should I believe that?" Brownstone growled.

"I don't know, maybe because it's the damn truth?" Delroy snapped back. He didn't like the fact that they were having to kiss the civilian's ass. Brownstone might bring in a lot of bounties, but he wasn't a cop.

"I'm going to reach into my jacket nice and slow and pull out a badge," the man said. "So don't kill me, okay?"

Brownstone raised his gun. "Okay, do it. Nice and slow."

Delroy pulled out a badge and held it out. "See? We're LAPD, Brownstone."

The bounty hunter's eyes narrowed. After a few seconds, he holstered his weapon and crossed his arms. The cops let out a sigh of relief.

"I'm a licensed class-six bounty hunter," Brownstone said. "So fuck off if this is about the family of some scumbag whining about me knocking around little Johnny Scumsalot."

"We don't give a shit about your bounties," Delroy told him. "We're part of an interagency anti-gang task force, and ever since the incident with the Harriken, there's been a lot of strange movement among the local gangs. We're worried about a gang war breaking out. And your name pops up every time we talk to an informant."

James snorted. "So, what...you think I'm the local kingpin or something?"

The cop shrugged. "Just saying your name pops up, and dead bodies pile up around you."

"Show me someone who didn't have it coming, and maybe I'll give a shit."

Delroy stared at the bounty hunter. "We're not here to hassle you, Brownstone. We just want to stop a gang war."

The bounty hunter grunted. "I don't know shit about gang warfare."

"How do I know you're not blowing smoke up my ass?"

"If it's not a bounty," Brownstone said, "I don't give a shit."

The cop smirked. "Unless it's personal."

James eyed the man, his eyes narrowing. "That's different. And plenty of cops can vouch for me." Brownstone shook his head. "Fuck this. You know what? I bet you don't even have a warrant."

Delroy tried not to wince. A few people mentioning the bounty hunter's name might have been enough to arouse the department's suspicion, but it hadn't been enough to convince a judge that the man should be a surveillance target.

Watching for Brownstone at the bar had been simple enough. It was a public place. Using drones and doing continual surveillance of his home would be harder to justify if too many people started asking questions.

Bending the rules a little in defense of the public didn't bother the cop, but he didn't like getting called on it, either. He'd hoped that if he didn't say anything, Brownstone would just assume they'd followed all the proper procedures.

"We're allowed to do basic surveillance in public places." Greg withered under Delroy's angry glare.

"Last time I checked, my house isn't a fucking public place," the bounty hunter snapped. "Anyway, thanks for confirming this is all bullshit."

"We're just doing our jobs, Brownstone," Delroy replied. "You can go around kicking bounty ass all day, but that doesn't mean regular crime goes away."

Brownstone inhaled deeply. "Look, like I said, I like my shit simple. As far as I've heard, the gangs in this area are trying to keep things light, not gearing up for war. But if you want to talk to me and not spy on me, we can meet later. You guys might not always like my methods, but we're on the same side."

Some of the tension left the cops. If they could just get a

tighter rein on the bounty hunter, this might work out well enough for them in the future.

"Fair enough," Delroy said. "We'll be in touch."

Brownstone pulled out his phone.

"We don't need your number," the cop told him. "We already have it."

"This isn't for that," Brownstone replied. "It's for something else. My way of making a point." He smirked and tapped through a few menus on his phone.

SIGNAL ONE AND TWO LOST appeared on the console's display screen.

"How high did you have the first one?" Brownstone asked. "Because your standard issue drone isn't that sturdy. Unless it was real low, it's smashed to pieces now. You gonna clean that up?"

"Oh, shit!" Greg yelled.

"Damn it, Brownstone," Delroy snarled. "That shit was expensive."

"Next time get a warrant." Brownstone shrugged. "Can't help it if shit's in my property's airspace. Sucks to be you guys." He put his phone back in his pocket. "I'll let you go pick up the other one. From the looks of the screen before, I'm guessing it's one of those stick-bug models. I fucking hate those things. Creepy as hell."

The central display buzzed, and both cops looked at it. Greg tapped a few options on the screen and text flooded it.

"What's going on?" Brownstone asked, trying to tilt his head to read the screen.

"Fucking sonofabitch," Delroy said. He didn't want to give the bounty hunter another reason to think he was big shit, but he could be useful. He slowly turned to look at the bounty hunter. "It's an APB."

"For who?"

"Jordan Adams."

"King-fucking-Pyro?" Brownstone's face darkened. "How the hell did *he* get out?"

"Don't know. Just says he's escaped, and he took out a couple of cops during his exit." Delroy gritted his teeth. "Damn it."

"There a bounty out on that asshat yet?" Brownstone's voice was practically a growl.

The bounty hunter's hatred poured off him like deadly radiation. Delroy's stomach tightened.

"You know how it works, Brownstone," the cop responded. "You already got paid for bringing him in, so they'll have to do the processing to set up a new one—and that's if they even decide they want one."

"Tell someone to get on that shit," Brownstone suggested. He pulled out his phone and tapped away, his eyes blazing in anger. "I've just submitted a donation to the Los Angeles County Citizen's Bounty Fund requesting a bounty issuance against that fucker. That should help things along."

Greg and Delroy looked at each other in confusion.

"You're going to take a bounty that you're funding yourself?" Delroy asked. "What's the point?"

"He's level four and a cop-killer," Brownstone said. "That combo should almost automatically result in a dead-or-alive flag."

The cops stared at the man. He'd already brought down King Pyro once, and the only reason he hadn't killed the man is because the police on site had stopped him. Now the criminal had added several LAPD officers to his victim list. About the last thing either Greg or Delroy wanted to do was protect the asshole.

When a monster showed up, throw another monster at him.

"I'll see about expediting things," Delroy offered. "I know some people who work in Bounty Processing."

Brownstone nodded and turned to leave. "Remember to pick up your drone before you leave."

Greg rolled the window back up once the bounty hunter was out of earshot. "You think that's kosher? I mean, he practically told us he's paying into that fund to go kill a guy and get away with it."

"Nah, he's paying money to take out a murderous sono-fabitch who killed a bunch of cops. I'm not gonna cry for King Pyro. That fucker is about to reap what he's sown."

H alf an hour later James stood in front of the shelving unit behind the false wall in his hidden room in Angel Long-Term Storage, his so-called "warehouse." He peered down at a safe near the wall.

I beat Pyro last time without the necklace. I shouldn't use that shit. Maybe next time I put it on, I'll listen to the whispers and start ranting about how I'm King Ghost.

The bounty hunter sighed and shook his head. He didn't understand how King Pyro had escaped so quickly. He'd beaten the man down and broken more than a few bones. Even if the maniac had healed quickly, he should have been out of commission longer.

What did you hide, asshole?

James chuckled darkly to himself. It was just like he'd thought when dealing with Sombra: the smart bastards always held back one last trick, just in case. The LAPD and the bounty hunter had underestimated King Pyro, and now several cops were dead because of it.

No. The bounty hunter needed to go all-out before

more people died. Besides, dealing with the bastard had stopped being about a bounty the second Pyro had issued his threat.

This was now personal.

A personal vendetta that would end with a piece of shit being removed from the streets. Sounded like win-win to James. Father McCartney might disagree, but the bounty hunter would leave it to the priest to save his sinner's soul.

James knelt in front of the safe and placed this thumb on the DNA reader. A burning sensation spread over this thumb. Thirty seconds later the safe popped open, revealing the interior safe with its keypad and required sixty-digit code. He started the long, laborious process of entering the code.

The smaller safe clicked open, revealing the artifact he both feared and needed: a circular gold and silver amulet connected to a necklace. The familiar three crystals colored azure, crimson, and jade lay inside the amulet without even a speck of dust on them.

James frowned. His heart thumped with fear at the idea of having to use the cursed artifact, but he couldn't get past the fact that King Pyro was rampaging again.

Both Adams and Padilla were nothing—just weak-ass pieces of shit who found something and got stronger. What did that say about him?

His rough fingers slid under the necklace, and he pulled it out. James wondered if he was any better than King Pyro or Sombra the Deathbringer. No one could see the bounty hunter in action without realizing he was stronger and tougher than a normal man, even without the necklace.

One sick thought kept returning: he'd been found with the necklace as a child.

What kind of monsters would Adams and Padilla have been if they'd grown up already influenced by magic like that?

James lifted his arm, ready to throw the necklace to the ground in disgust, but instead he slowly lowered the artifact and shook his head.

"Maybe I'll die in ten years at the hands of an AET team," he muttered to himself. "But before then, I'm gonna do what I can to stop the bastards who've already crossed the fucking line."

James set the necklace on an empty spot on the shelf, then searched the safe for a small gray box. He found the object of his search and pulled it from the shelf.

It wasn't anything special or lethal, just small metal squares and plastic strips with adhesive backing. A man never knew what he might need during a bounty hunt.

The bounty hunter pulled off the paper covering the adhesive pad on one of the metal squares and then affixed it to the back of the amulet portion of the necklace. He couldn't be sure if the bonding process wouldn't start if the amulet portion didn't touch, but he hoped so. In battle, he wanted to be able to just tug off the backing to quickly gain the necklace's power.

James took a deep breath and slipped the necklace over his head and under his shirt. The cool metal square touched his chest, but no pain or burning spiked his nerves. He'd been right. More importantly, the amulet necklace wasn't whispering to him.

Good. If I need it, I can use it. If not, no harm, no foul. And no creepy whispers.

The bounty hunter pulled a go-case filled with weapons from the other side. He still needed to clean his equipment from the Mexico trip, but that could wait until after he'd dealt with King Pyro. Fortunately he always kept a few cases ready, just in case he had to kick a lot of ass in rapid succession.

It'd been a busy week.

James grabbed a duster from the shelf. It provided plenty of concealment for weapons, and the last time he'd worn one, Shay hadn't bitched so much about his fashion choices.

What the fuck? Why was he worried about what that woman would think? She wasn't involved in this shit.

He grunted and pushed the thoughts of the dark-haired tomb raider out of his mind. Michael had been right. Women were complications, and James still wasn't sure if he needed more of those in this life.

A loud groan escaped his mouth a moment later.

James might not have to worry about Shay, but before he dealt with King Pyro he'd have to negotiate with another difficult woman.

How did I end up with so many women in my life?

James steeled his nerves as he hopped out of his F-350 and marched toward Zoe's front door. He'd wasted her last healing potion, but he didn't want to risk taking on the out-of-control King Pyro without a new one. The last encounter had made it clear that the pyromancer was right in one sense—even the bounty hunter had burned in the end.

The front door swung open before James even knocked.

"Hello, James," Zoe purred, her breath stinking of wine. Unlike their last visit, this time the woman at least had on a dress—even if the hunter-green sundress was a bit on skimpy side. "I was delighted when I got your call." She motioned him inside, then took several unsteady steps.

James wasn't sure how much of Zoe's drinking was because she was an alcoholic, or because she followed the alcohol-intensive Dionysian Way of magic. Probably like most things in life, it was a little of both. He couldn't argue with the results, though, and he didn't know her well enough to question her life choices.

The bounty hunter followed the potions witch into her kitchen, having to duck to avoid some of the plants hanging from the ceiling and shift to the side to avoid pots on the floor. Every time he came to Zoe's house, he was convinced that it was slowly changing from a home into a mystical arboretum. He couldn't spot any actual furniture in her living room.

Snapping and rustling caught his attention when he stepped into the kitchen. A bright orange plant sat in the corner; it was several feet tall, and its top was adorned with a single huge orange-red flower. Twitching razor-tipped tendrils surrounded the flower, and an angry fanged maw snapped in the center.

"What the fuck is that?" James said, pointing to the monstrosity.

"Oh, I don't know what they call it. The Wood Elf who sold it to me told me I wouldn't be able to pronounce the name anyway. I just call it Audrey II. It's very hard to raise, though. It can only be fed small creatures already infused with magic." Zoe shook her head, trying to focus her bloodshot gray eyes. "And they've been cracking down on invasive alien species lately." She rolled her eyes and blew a few rogue strands of dark hair out of her face. "Those bureaucrats in Sacramento; always standing in the way of an honest woman's work."

"Why do I think I'm gonna end up having to kill that thing for you?" James mumbled.

Zoe giggled and sashayed over to the bounty hunter. "I'll make it worth your while if you do."

He frowned, not wanting to go through another round of her attempts to seduce him.

The witch raised a slender finger and tapped him on the chest. "I can see it in your face, you know."

"See what?"

"The irritation."

"It helps when people aren't trying to piss me off." James shrugged. "And I've never claimed not to be an asshole."

Zoe laughed, swaying slightly. "No, you haven't." She ran a hand down James' chest.

He grabbed her wrist and pushed her hand back. "No, Zoe. I don't have time for this shit."

The witch sighed and stepped away. "I know." She took a deep breath. "I'm like a bug; you know, attracted to the light. Do you even understand that light in you, James?"

He stared at her for a second, wondering what the

woman was getting at. Alison had made it clear that she saw something special in his soul, but he'd never heard Zoe talk about being able to see souls. Knowing the woman, the whole speech was probably just a new seduction strategy.

"What the hell are you talking about?" James asked.

Zoe sighed and shook a finger. "No need to be rude, lover. I can look, but not touch."

"But you *did* just touch."

"You have me there." The humor fled her face. "Like I said, it's like a bug being attracted to the light, but I realized something important recently and it's made me a little sad."

"You realized you drink too much?"

Zoe snorted. "No. If anything, I don't drink enough." She gestured to the ceiling light fixture. "Let's just say a bug might see a friend playing with a light and get fried, and then they realize that maybe playing with the light is dangerous and you should avoid it."

James nodded slowly.

The witch looked him up and down. "If only the light wasn't so damned yummy." She gestured to her kitchen table, where a rack containing several vials sat on top. Her slender fingers picked out a small vial filled with red liquid. "You know why I want you, James?"

"Because you're drunk most of the time?" James replied. "You can't see the ugliness?"

"You have character, even if you're not totally my type."

"I'll probably regret asking, but what's your type?"

Zoe chuckled and shook her head. "I don't like boytoys; those men with perfect hairless bodies and unblemished skin. Give me some handles to hold on to when the bucking gets violent; that's what makes a night memorable." She tilted her head as her gaze roamed his body. "You've got some of that, especially a face with character, but not all of it. Maybe I just want you so badly because you keep saying no."

"Well, if I find someone who matches that description looking for a wild alcoholic woman, I'll send him your way."

The witch shrugged and held out her hand, palm up, with the potion. "You're lucky I had an extra one of these sitting around, but it won't be cheap."

James pulled out a one-carat diamond out of a pocket in his duster and held it out. "How about this? I figured you could use it in your potions or some shit. Sell it, for all I care."

Zoe dropped the potion into his hand and snatched up the diamond. She eyed the gemstone. "There's a lot of things I could do with this. Some delightful things."

"We have a deal then?"

"Oh, yes."

"I should get going." James turned to leave.

"Before you go, I've heard something whispered among those in the magical community you might find of interest."

The bounty hunter turned around. "What?"

"The kemana down south has been reporting sightings of new elves; dark ones."

"And?"

Zoe licked her full lips. "If that doesn't concern you, don't worry about it. But you do have a bad habit of pissing people off, and your name comes up more often than you might think." She sighed. "Just...don't get killed, James."

He offered her a quick nod. "Thanks for the information and the potion."

Zoe watched as the F-350 pulled out of her driveway into the street, then closed her front door.

She shook her head. "James, you're a clueless idiot, and I'm a dumbass fool." She lifted the diamond and stared at it. "Well, it's not exactly a ring, but I'll keep it, James." A grin spread across her face. "I've got the perfect use for this little gem."

"Huh, the new door looks better," James said as he stepped toward the Black Sun. Nice polished metal with no scratches. Shit, it didn't even stink of urine.

He didn't regret paying for the door now. He also didn't know if Tyler would be happy to see him, but he suspected the man would be far more concerned about King Pyro coming back and causing trouble. At least James had paid for the damage he'd caused.

The bounty hunter slipped on leather gloves and threw open the door. Six lowlifes sat around the bar, and only spared him the briefest of glances. Tyler gave him a nod and turned toward a TV in the corner.

"As you can see," blared a reporter on the TV, "our news chopper has been following the notorious Jordan Adams, who goes by the name King Pyro. According to a voice mail he left with authorities, this is the beginning of a reign of terror in which he, and I quote, 'Will burn Los Angeles until only ashes remain.'"

A motorcycle barreled along hundreds of feet below the helicopter. Every few seconds a fireball blasted from the rider, smashing into a nearby car or building. King Pyro certainly didn't do subtle.

The motorcycle jerked to the side, heading southbound on the 110. He pulled off at an exit and disappeared, hidden by the buildings.

"We've received reports that the LAPD AET has been dispatched to the area," the reporter continued. "Authorities are asking that everyone keep clear of the area. Police want to remind everyone that Adams is a level-four threat." The reporter tilted his head, looking to the side and listening to his earbud before looking straight into the camera. "We've just been informed that a new bounty has been issued on Jordan Adams, and in a rare turn of events, it's an official dead-or-alive tag. Again, authorities advise all citizens to avoid engaging this man unless you're a licensed class-four bounty hunter or higher."

James narrowed his eyes, wondering why the hell King Pyro was being so obvious. Sure, the guy was tough, but he'd recently received a beat-down that proved he wouldn't always win. Even ignoring the bounty and the other bounty hunters it might bring, he was asking AET to show up—and that could end in a missile or railgun being used.

Something didn't smell right about the whole thing. James pulled his phone out and started searching a map of the area where the news chopper had lost King Pyro.

You're not the dumbass I thought you were, Adams. I'll give you that. But you were dumb enough not to leave town when you had the chance.

"Like the new door, Tyler," James called, and turned to leave.

The other man raised his middle finger. "Fuck you, Brownstone."

James barreled down the road in his F-350, blaring his horn and cutting off other drivers. He hit the 110 and headed north. He'd convinced himself that King Pyro was trying to get the entire LAPD going in the wrong direction. For all the man's pretentions and arrogance, in the end he specialized in a very old-fashioned crime: bank robbery.

If AET were busy searching an area miles away from the man, Pyro could rush into a bank, grab what he needed, and escape before the cops even knew what was going on. There was a bank just off the 110 a few miles up the road from the criminal's last known location.

It was a halfway-decent plan.

James made a twenty-minute trip in ten with his aggressive driving. With all the traffic drones flying around the city he was sure a large ticket was already on its way, but at least no cops stopped him. His truck roared off the exit toward the bank. He squealed to a stop in the parking lot, not even bothering to park.

After a quick check of his weapons, he threw open the door and rushed toward the bank.

Shit. I better be careful about this. Don't want anyone to think I'm robbing the bank.

James kept his pistol holstered as he opened the glass door leading into the bank lobby and stepped inside.

Light instrumental K-Pop played over the speakers. Two long lines of bored-looking customers waited to talk to the tellers. A single security guard with a revolver sat in a chair, eyeing James with suspicion.

The bounty hunter tore his gaze away from the security guard to look around the bank, but he didn't spot King Pyro.

"Shit," he muttered. "Was I wrong?"

James stepped farther into the bank, past the lines toward several desks in the back. The security guard rose, his hand on the grip of his revolver.

Not your time to shine, idiot. Just sit down.

"Excuse me, sir," the security guard said. "You'll need to wait in line."

James ignored him. Annoyance shot through the bounty hunter. He'd thought he'd figured everything out, but King Pyro obviously wasn't there. Somehow the other man had outsmarted him after all.

"Damn it," the bounty hunter muttered. He needed to get back on the road and figure out where King Pyro was really going.

The security guard cleared his throat. "Sir, do you even have busi—"

The front door exploded in a shower of glass and flame.

Screams filled the lobby, and the customers fled to either side of the bank. The security guard ducked behind a desk, and James pivoted behind one of four cement pillars rising to the ceiling.

"Guess you're not smarter than me after all," James muttered. "It ends this time, asshole."

He reached under his shirt and yanked the metal square

off the back of the amulet. The cool touch of the metal and crystals against his skin was replaced by an inferno of discomfort, and tendrils of pain shot from the point of contact through the rest of his body until every part of him was in agony.

James gritted his teeth as the necklace sank into his skin.

In the back of his mind, a low and hollow voice whispered in a strange language he couldn't begin to understand. He hadn't heard anything like it...yet.

Guess you can't tell me to kill everyone I love if I can't even fucking understand you, Mr. Cursed Amulet.

Several long seconds passed before the pain began to ebb. James took several deep breaths, his limbs feeling slightly heavier. The whispers continued in the back of his mind, along with the faintest of hums. The Granite Ghost had awoken.

Cloaked in flame, King Pyro strolled into the lobby, sneering at the cowering people against the walls. "Tell me where the vault is in the next thirty seconds or you'll all burn."

The security guard popped up and squeezed off a round. The robber jerked from the hit, but didn't fall. He turned, narrowing his eyes on the guard.

"You would kill your king?" Pyro growled. "You're nothing to me, and now you die."

Five more shots followed. The king didn't go down, but James could see several bullet wounds through the flames surrounding his body.

So you're not bulletproof, asshole. Guess what, right now I am.

"Run!" James shouted to the guard. "You can't beat him."

King Pyro raised both hands and shot a column of flame from them that consumed the guard. His agonized screams filled the air for several seconds as the flames charred him. The bullet wounds closed on his killer.

"What the fuck?" James exclaimed, stepping away from the pillar.

"Brownstone," King Pyro shouted, and pointed at him. He cackled. "This is fucking perfect. This is fucking *DESTINY!*"

"Why aren't you in a hospital somewhere with a broken jaw?"

He pointed to the charred black ruin that used to be a security guard. "I have to thank you. You pushed me to my limits, and now I truly am a god. I can take the life from others to make me stronger."

James groaned and shook his head. "Last guy who said that to me ended up dead."

King Pyro's face contorted in rage. "You're fucking dead, Brownstone." The flames surrounding his body flared into a white-blue flame. "I will melt you where you stand." Two fireballs burst from his hands.

The bounty hunter rolled to the side and opened up with the .45, but the bullets melted before reaching the other man's body.

"Okay, that's a problem," James muttered. "Now he *is* bulletproof."

King Pyro laughed. "I am beyond pathetic bitches like you, Brownstone. I am a *GOD!*"

The bounty hunter sent a throwing knife sailing toward his enemy. He hoped it'd have enough metal to get through, but the flames consumed the knife just as eagerly as they had the bullets.

James shoved his hands out, grabbing two monitors with his now-strengthened telekinesis and tossing them at the other man. Pyro batted them out of the air, and the smell of burnt plastic filled the bank.

"Run, you idiots," the bounty hunter yelled to the cowering crowd. "Get the fuck out of here while I've got him distracted." He punctuated the sentence by emptying his magazine into Pyro, to no better effect than the first time.

King Pyro stalked forward, ignoring the scurrying people. He raised a hand, and an orb of white-hot flame grew in his palm. "If you get on your knees and beg your king to forgive you, I'll kill you quickly," he snarled. "Otherwise I'll make you suffer until you beg me to die, bitch."

He tossed the ball toward James, and the bounty hunter leapt out of the way. The desk behind him exploded, shooting out burning wood fragments and red-hot metal.

James holstered his empty .45. With the crowd now gone, he could go to Plan B. He yanked out a frag grenade and pulled the pin. "Suck on this, asshole."

King Pyro grunted as the force of the explosion knocked him back. The bounty hunter followed up by yanking another gun out and tossing lead toward the center of the flaming mass, but the bullets couldn't penetrate the flame shield.

The other man pushed himself off the ground. He had no wounds on his face; the shrapnel from the grenade hadn't even managed to scratch him.

"What level do you think I am now, you little bitch?"

King Pyro shouted. "Five? Six? Maybe I'll be the first level-seven. For I am the king, and I rule over all you fuckers!"

"This is America, asshole. We don't do kings." As James sprinted for the column, a bolt of flame struck him in the shoulder and another on the thigh. The smell of his burning flesh greeted his nose and he gritted his teeth, pain spiking through his body.

"Fuck," he muttered. He'd hoped that the necklace would block the attack, but the agony in his shoulder suggested it'd only stopped the worst of it.

The whispers grew louder in his head, more frantic, but were still unintelligible. He needed to get close to King Pyro where his strength would be an advantage. He yanked out a knife and readied it.

"Do you smell it, Brownstone?" Pyro chuckled. "I smell your fear."

James spun and charged at Pyro, who threw two quick fireballs that blasted right through his coat and burned his chest. He slammed his knife into Pyro's shoulder. The metal melted seconds later, but the force of the blow sent the other man sailing back howling in pain.

The bounty hunter tossed his burning duster to the ground and followed up with his two remaining grenades. They exploded in rapid succession, stunning King Pyro for a second but not killing him.

James glanced down at his chest and narrowed his eyes. Unlike his still painful shoulder and leg, his chest was only reddened and there was very little pain. Either the king's attacks were growing weaker, or his skin was growing stronger.

As if answering him, the whisper in his head became more insistent.

"Let's finish this, you piece of shit," James shouted, yanking off his burned tactical harness and dropping it to the ground. The guns and knives wouldn't do shit for him, so there was no point in risking one of them blowing up or melting right next to him.

King Pyro put his hands close together and a fireball grew in front of him.

"Now, Brownstone, you die."

26

James threw himself to the side. The massive fireball roared past him, its intense heat exacerbating the existing burns on his exposed body.

He had never thought of what it'd be like to be a stripper, but at this point only a few scraps of shirt remained, and his pants and boots had huge holes. Hell, even his underwear wasn't in the best shape.

In another situation the bounty hunter might have laughed about all that, but right now rage, pain, and deep breaths kept his mind focused on defeating his enemy.

His entire body ached, and he had wounds and burns all over. The amulet necklace had saved his life and protected him from the worst of his enemy's attacks, but it hadn't completely saved him from harm.

It didn't fucking matter. There was no way he was letting King Pyro get away again while he was still breathing.

No one I love will ever again get hurt, if I have anything to say about it. That fucker is going down.

James charged and slammed his fist at full strength into King Pyro's chest. The other man flew backward, smashing through a front window and crashing into the street. The bounty hunter stepped through the shattered glass, glaring at the fallen criminal with murder is his eyes.

"You're done, you sonofabitch," he rumbled in his deep voice.

There were dozens of cops, crouched behind their vehicles with rifles, shotguns, and pistols at the ready. Armed drones circled overhead, and at least twelve AET members in full armor were in position behind collapsible tactical shields.

King Pyro laughed as he hopped to his feet with blood running down his face. "A god can't be killed by a man, bitches!" A fireball blasted toward a nearby police cruiser, but the cops behind it fled just in time. The car exploded, raining down parts. Other officers rushed backward, even the AET members.

The bank robber followed by throwing fireball after fireball into the sky. Drones exploded and melted at their touch.

James blinked, watching the fireworks display in disbelief.

What the fuck?

For whatever reason, King Pyro's power kept growing. Maybe the man had been right, and his near death at James' hands had unlocked greater potential. Or perhaps the fear of death had let him dig deep.

He knew he had to end this shit soon.

The bounty hunter didn't care about the reason, only that it was happening. If this kept up, King Pyro would become unstoppable. James wasn't even sure how long his necklace protection would hold out.

"Everything burns in the end, Brownstone," King Pyro shouted. "Ashes to ashes, dust to dust."

James tilted his neck back and forth and cracked his knuckles. "They aren't gonna stop me this time, Adams. I told you not to threaten my family, and now you're gonna pay for that."

"Your family, Brownstone? Don't you get it? After I'm done with you, they're going to die nice and slow. I'm going to roast them alive, enjoying their screams." Pyro snorted. "I heard about what happened to your dog. That's going to be fucking merciful compared to what I'm going to do. I hope at least a few of them are bitches. Then I can have even more fun."

Dark whispers filled his head again. James didn't have to know the language to understand that the amulet necklace was telling him to finish King Pyro.

The bounty hunter charged, but King Pyro didn't even bother throwing any fireballs. Instead the man sidestepped and grabbed James' wrist. The flames licked at the bounty hunter's skin, burning despite the amulet's protection. Pyro yanked him close, trying to surround him with the flames around his body.

"Burn, bitch, burn!"

"I told you," James gritted his teeth as the pain in his wrist intensified and finished with a roar, "*no one threatens my fucking family!*"

The bounty hunter pivoted and slammed his free fist directly into King Pyro's throat, and the man collapsed, gagging. A ferocious kick sent the criminal spiraling into a nearby minivan.

"You keep ending up in cars, Adams," James remarked.

"Fuck...you," the other man managed to grind out.

The bounty hunter grabbed the still-burning man by his throat, ignoring the pain, and slammed him headfirst into the pavement three times. Blood splattered everywhere, and the flames died out.

"Brownstone," King Pyro, his face mangled, coughed up blood. He managed a weak chuckle. "Your eyes..."

"What *about* my eyes, you sonofabitch?"

"They aren't...human. It's okay...if a god gets beaten by a monster." He gagged on his own blood. "You're not human, Brownstone. Fucking...Oriceran...piece of shit."

The amulet's whispers grew louder.

James shook his head. "You're not a god, Adams. You're just a fucking criminal who got lucky, but now your luck has run out."

He slammed his fist into the man's head, caving in his skull, and he completed the job with another blow. He grunted as he straightened up and tried to wipe his bloodied hand off on what little remained of his pants.

It was over. King Pyro would never threaten anyone James cared about again.

"The king is dead," he muttered. "Long live the king."

James' body throbbed all over, and exhaustion had long since seeped into his muscles and bones. With his adrenaline fading, he even managed to discover some new aches and pain. The whispers from the necklace had gone all but silent. He stepped away from the dead flame master, picked up his tactical harness, and limped toward his truck.

Most of the nearby cops aimed their guns at him, including the AET members.

"Drop the weapons, get on your knees, and put your hands behind your head," shouted an AET member, his voice muffled behind his red-eyed goggled mask. He raised his rifle, ready to shoot.

The whispers in James' head returned, insistent in tone. He wondered if the damn cursed artifact was trying to get him to fight the cops.

Is that your plan? Berserker rage-shit? Fuck you. I borrowed your power, but I'm still James Brownstone. I call the shots for my body.

"Stay back," shouted someone else. "Brownstone's legit." The voice sounded familiar, but with his exhaustion and injuries James couldn't quite place it. "Leave him alone. He's a licensed class-six bounty hunter. There's a valid bounty out on Jordan Adams, and that was a righteous kill. It was an official dead-or-alive hunt."

The cops on either side of James kept their weapons trained on him, but those in front parted, providing him a clear path to his truck. He continued shuffling toward it, glancing over at an AET member hauling a rocket launcher out of the back of their armored van.

Could never be too careful, he guessed.

James managed a chuckle. He'd never been shot with a rocket launcher. He wasn't sure if even the necklace could protect him from something like that. He grimaced as a gust of wind blew dust into some of his exposed burns.

He glanced up. More armed drones had arrived, along with helicopters, both news and police.

A few more steps and he'd be at his truck. He

looked behind him. A line of cops slowly closed on him, weapons in hand. The AET members advanced behind several of their men with tactical shields. Most of the AET members carried stun rifles or assault rifles, and the rocket-launcher cop had been joined by a man with a heavy mini-gun—yet another weapon he'd never had the displeasure of personally experiencing.

Glad to see I'm worth the heavy ordnance. He could just see it. **Here lies James Brownstone. Cause of death: being turned into Swiss cheese**. More about the latest barbeque winner at five.

If James hadn't been beat to hell and back he might have been able to scatter the men without too much trouble, but taking them on when he was wounded didn't seem like a bright idea. He didn't like the idea of hurting cops, even if they took a shot or two at him.

Ignoring the cops, the bounty hunter pulled open the door of his F-350 and climbed inside. No rockets or bullets tore into his beloved vehicle.

Please don't shoot up my truck. It'd be hell to find this model still in good shape.

He took several deep breaths, then pulled out the energy and healing potions from the go-case in the back seat.

Thanks, Zoe.

James downed the energy potion, and after about ten seconds his exhaustion vanished.

He grunted, his mind now even more aware of his extensive wounds. "*Fuck* I hurt!"

After quickly pulling the stopper on the healing potion,

he downed the contents. It was surprisingly sweet, unlike the bitter energy potion.

The bounty hunter waited in his seat, looking down at his burned legs as the seconds ticked away. His skin began to repair itself before his eyes and the pain lessened, becoming more bearable. His wounds and burns shrank. After about thirty seconds not a single burn or wound remained on his body, and all his pain was gone.

"Yeah, that sucked," James muttered, reaching into the back.

He fished out another metal square from the go case and pulled the paper off the adhesive backing. With a deep breath, he yanked the amulet out of his skin.

Pain shot through his body, and the whispers became yells in his mind. Abrupt silence followed.

He held the amulet in his hand and slapped the metal square onto the back before letting it settle back onto his chest. The small army of cops outside might still decide he needed to join King Pyro in the afterlife, and now that he wasn't wounded, he might be able to escape with the necklace's help.

James reached into the backseat to pull out the t-shirt, pants, underwear, and shoes he'd brought. After the burns he'd suffered in his first fight with King Pyro, he'd half-expected to end up in burning scraps of fabric. He peeled off the remains of what had once been his clothing and footwear to slide on his new duds.

"What a fucking day. Too bad I didn't bring my Mexico coat." He snickered. "See, Shay, if I'd kept it, it would have gotten burned."

James thought about it for a moment.

That fucking coat had really been comfortable. He was going to buy a new one. Shay would just have to deal. He was a bounty hunter, not a male model.

He grinned at the idea.

The bounty hunter finally looked up. There were fifteen cops in front of his truck, but they didn't have their weapons out. They all stood with their backs to the truck, except for one familiar face: Sergeant Mack.

James opened the door and stepped out of the vehicle.

"It's okay, guys," Mack assured them.

The cops surrounding his truck started walking away, except for Mack. The sergeant wiped some sweat off his brow.

"You know, when I started this job," the cop began, "the worst thing we had to worry about was a terrorist with an automatic weapon or a bomb." He motioned toward the bank. "Now that crap almost seems quaint, like the shit you'd expect from school kids."

"Were you the one trying to get them to stand down earlier?" James said.

"Yeah." Mack snorted. "Next time use a damned bathroom to change, Brownstone. We didn't need to see your junk."

James could only chuckle at the absurdity of what had just unfolded. He leaned against his truck. "Well, AET didn't light me up, so that's good."

Mack shook his head. "You were going after a bounty. Fair game, and all that."

"Is Adams dead?" James frowned. "Because if he's not, I need to finish him off." His voice made it clear he wouldn't argue about it.

The cop gestured toward King Pyro's body. Several paramedics surrounded him, chatting and gesticulating, and four of the AET team had their weapons trained on the prone form.

"Yeah, he's dead. Kind of hard to live after having your skull caved in like that." Mack turned back toward James. "Look, I know you played a little stunt getting the bounty going. Not even sure if it's all that legal."

"So what happens, then? Am I going to be hauled in?"

Mack shook his head. "Nope. At least not today. The bounty's out there, so it doesn't make much sense for us to arrest you. Plus, I don't think anyone is all that hot on the idea of risking a major shoot-out with the guy who just took out King Pyro."

"I don't know, those AET folks seemed like they really wanted to take me on."

The cop stepped forward and looked over his shoulder at the AET guys. "Look, I'll be honest. Not everyone in the department likes having someone like you around."

James grunted. It wasn't like he hadn't had a few run-ins with cops before. It was why he'd spent years with little gifts like the donuts. He wanted them to understand that he was on their side.

Of course they were going to be afraid. Maybe Pyro was right, and he was a monster. He didn't fucking know anymore.

Mack held up a hand. "Don't sweat it, Brownstone. Most of us get that you're on our side. That asshole Adams killed cops getting away, and that's on top of everyone else he killed. You don't worry about AET or anyone else. Me and some other guys will make sure this all goes away in terms of the paperwork. There's just one thing I need from you."

"What?"

The cop gestured to the ground. "Pick up all your burnt rags, or I'll have to cite you for littering."

The men shared a laugh.

27

A few days later, James pushed through the door of the Leanan Sídhe. The Professor had been busy since his return from Mexico, so the bounty hunter'd had no chance to meet with him and receive his payment for helping Shay retrieve the Green Dragon Crescent Blade.

He spotted Shay and the Professor in the back and made his way over there, everyone parting to provide him a path despite the heavy and raucous crowd. A few people gave him a polite nod, but no one gave him stink-eye.

The bounty hunter sat beside Shay across from the Professor. "Long time no see, Professor."

"You've been busy, lad," the Professor said with a grin. "A necromancer and a pyromancer. I'm sure there's a joke in there, but I'm not drunk enough to figure it out yet." He winked. "But get the music going and the booze flowing, and I'll give it a try."

"We've both been busy." James nodded to Shay, ignoring the Professor's antics. "Hi, Shay."

She placed a briefcase on the table. "All three of us have been busy."

He eyed the briefcase. "That the jade from the Green Dragon Crescent Blade?"

Shay shook her head. "When you were busy running around beating up the Flame King or Ember Boy or whoever, I ran a few errands. Kind of a follow-up to Mexico. Something I worked out with The Professor."

James glanced between the two of them. "It was King Pyro, not the Flame King, and he didn't have a partner."

He noticed a bandage on the tomb raider's arm, but decided not to press the issue. Shay would tell him whatever he needed to know. For that matter, so would the Professor. Bounty hunting and field archaeology only occasionally needed to overlap.

The Professor accepted the briefcase and set it beside him. "You'll find your account has received a rather sizable deposit, Miz Carson." He slid a small jewelry box to James. "And this is for you, lad. You're lucky. It's not always easy to find one so easy to use. It took me a lot of effort."

James snorted. "You probably pulled it out from underneath your couch."

"Maybe," the Professor offered in response.

The bounty hunter opened the box. A silver necklace lay inside. It was elegant enough, but not too fancy. He cared less about the aesthetics than the magical potential.

Shay peeked over at the box, and he held it up. Her brow raised in question.

"It's a gift for Alison," James said, before tucking the box into a pocket. "I'll explain later."

"Okay," Shay said, content to wait.

The Professor rose and gave them both a nod. "Lad, Miz Carson, I have a few things to take care of at the bar."

"Like acquiring beers?" James asked.

"Aye, lad. Exactly. I've only had one tonight, and that's just horrible, isn't it?" The Professor winked, picked up the briefcase, and walked to the front.

Shay watched the Professor disappear into the crowd. "That parents' weekend thing is coming up, isn't it?"

"Yeah. Want to go? I can buy you a supersonic ticket if you don't want to spend the money. Let's just fly out this weekend to Virginia together. I'm sure Alison would love to see you."

Shay grinned. "Free is a very good price. Sounds like fun. It's a date."

James stared at her for a second, deciding not to bother asking if she was serious about her use of the word "date."

No, don't say anything. She'll just say something about me being gay or some shit.

He forced a smile and rubbed the back of his neck. Women could complicate the simplest things.

Alison waved happily from a table in the lunchroom as James and Shay tried to make their way through the thick crowd of kids and parents.

"Look at this place," James exclaimed, gazing at all the elegant wooden tables and booths. "This looks more like a fancy restaurant than a school cafeteria."

At least he didn't see that pretentious ferret.

"Nothing wrong with a little class." Shay grinned. "Not

everyone can survive off hole-in-the-wall barbecue. I can't believe you drove four hours there and back for it."

James grunted, regretting having told Shay about his trip to Jessie Rae's. If she'd just go to the damn place, she'd fall in love with the flavor just as he had—along with all the contest judges.

People shouldn't talk shit about stuff they didn't understand.

Some teen bumped into James, and he resisted the urge to glare at him.

"Sorry!" the kid exclaimed, and scurried off.

The bounty hunter had promised Shay he wouldn't try to intimidate anyone while they were at the school, but it was taking all his self-control not to stare down the punk kids and their parents and get them to scatter.

Crowds were annoying. Every time he was in one, he thought about the disadvantage he'd be in if a fight broke out—let alone a fight at a magic school.

The pair finally arrived at the table. Alison got up to give James a tight hug, and then followed up with Shay.

"Aunt Shay, Mr. James!"

"'Mr. James?'" He arched an eyebrow.

"Well, it's kind of between Mr. Brownstone and James. It felt weird calling you James, because you're old and all."

Shay laughed.

James grunted. "I'm not old."

The girl shrugged. "Older than me."

"Just use 'James.' 'Mr. James' actually *does* makes me sound like an old man."

Alison nodded. "Okay, James. It's still weird, but whatever you want."

They sat down at the table.

Shay glanced around. "How are your classes going so far? This is your first time with formal education, isn't it?"

Alison shrugged. "They told me that in terms of my academics I'm really advanced, so lots of lower-level college courses already. They're having me do a lot of that online." She sighed. "If only everything could be like that."

James and Shay exchanged glances and the bounty hunter asked, "What's wrong?"

"Magic's a whole different ballgame. I've been tested, but I'm like messing up all their normal ways of checking for that kind of thing."

"What do you mean?"

"They know I have magic, but for some reason it isn't showing up right. The way they explained it to me, I have really high capability but little ability, or something. I don't quite get it, and apparently they don't either." She sighed and shook her head. "So I'm not going to be doing much magic for a while."

Shay reached out to pat her hand.

James shrugged. "Magic's complicated. I wouldn't worry about it too much." He didn't want to suggest that it might be better if Alison didn't have to worry much about magic. After all, magic not only represented power, it also represented her link to her dead mother.

"The headmistress said she expects it'll change as I get older."

"There you go, then."

A meek-looking girl in glasses passed them, and Alison waved at her. The girl waved back but hurried along.

"That's one of my friends, Julia," Alison explained.

"She's got an affinity for air magic. She's still figuring what she can do, but she's got great hearing because of it."

Julia was already deep into the crowd at that point, but she turned and waved to the table with a grin.

"See?"

James chuckled. "It sounds like you've settled in here, then."

The teen looked down for a moment before nodding. "I guess I have. I'm still kind of getting used to it, but I've been making friends, and I like a lot of the teachers. Not all of them."

"There's always one," James said. "For me it was Sister Emily." He grunted.

Shay poked him with her elbow. "Don't put your baggage on her. And give Alison her present already."

James pulled out the jewelry box and opened it, revealing a jeweled pendant on a silver chain.

"Oh, that's so pretty," Alison exclaimed.

"And functional."

"Huh?"

"It's called an 'Aegis Pendant.' It's a kind of shield. You activate it by wanting to be protected and saying 'Aegis aeon.' Once you do that, it'll form a magic shell right around your body. It can take a decent punishment, magical or physical, but I wouldn't stare down an angry dragon." James tapped his head. "It's important to have both the words and the intent when you use it. It won't work without both."

Alison furrowed her brow. "I don't understand."

"You have to really *want* to be protected." James glanced over his shoulder. That air girl was probably hearing everything he said. *Fucking magic.* "It'll last for one hour once activated, unless it starts pulling energy from you. It has to be recharged."

"How exactly?"

"It'll automatically do it over a day, but the point is, don't play with it unless you need it. It draws on background magical energy or some sh— Stuff."

Shay chuckled. "Talk about overprotective."

"I love it," Alison replied. She hopped up and rushed over to pull him into a hug, and tears ran down her cheeks.

James blinked. "Why are you crying if you like it?"

Shay rolled her eyes. "Don't be such a doof, Brownstone. She's crying because she's happy."

Alison nodded quickly. "I'm going to go show my friend."

"Okay, you do that, kid."

Shay waited for Alison to disappear into the crowd. "What's the deal, Brownstone?"

James frowned. "What are you talking about?"

"You showed me that the other day and it was just a silver necklace, not some fancy expensive pendant. That cost a lot of money."

He shrugged. "I had that added, so others will see that necklace and know someone cares about that young woman. There's no money I can spend that will help her as much as others telling her how pretty she is."

Shay shook her head. "You're a damn enigma, Brownstone."

"Huh?"

"Clueless one second, wise the next."

EPILOGUE

A week later, James moved toward a park several streets down from his house. High chain-link fences surrounded the entire perimeter of the park, and the only access was through a single gate.

Trey and several of his boys sat at the front, next to a series of keyed lockers. Their colors were on display, but they had no obvious weapons. The only people in the park with weapons were Sergeant Mack and a few other police officers. Even though they were all in casual clothes, they had their guns and badges.

The cops stood near two large wheeled barbeque pits, smoking up a storm and cooking up a fucking feast. A band on a small wooden stage played some rock song that sounded vaguely familiar.

Children rushed around, laughing and playing. Bounce houses and bounce obstacle courses littered the park.

A family stepped into the park. Three gang members came right after, their colors showing they weren't Trey's boys.

The gang leader held up a hand. "Hold up, homies."

The other gang members squared their shoulders. "This park ain't your turf, bitch. You don't tell us what to do."

"No, but this is a community event, which means y'all can come in, because you members of the community. But this is about chillin', not killin'." Trey gestured to the locker. "So guns go in there."

The other gangbanger narrowed his eyes. "How do I know that shit is safe?"

"Because, bitch, this shit is protected ground. Like some fucking sanctuary where some hunchback can go and shit."

The other man looked toward the cops.

"Nah, not the cops," Trey said. "Cops ain't shit. This place is protected by *real* power."

"By you?"

"Nah." The gang leader lifted his shirt to make it clear he wasn't armed. "See, I ain't carrying either. This is a Granite Ghost party. Motherfucking James Brownstone. No one goes in packing but him or the 5-0."

"What's to stop me from poppin' your ass right now?" The gang member smirked. "Not trying to be mean, bitch, just curious."

Trey looked past them, grinning as he caught sight of James. "It'd be motherfucking righteous. People would be talking about Trey forever. It'd be like, 'Yo, bitches, you heard about how Brownstone killed all the Harriken because they iced his dog. And then, you bitches, you heard about how Brownstone killed all the gangbangers who thought they could cause trouble at his party?'"

James stepped forward. "Trey's right," he rumbled. "I

take it personally when people mess with my family. Ask the Harriken and King Pyro."

All the gang members turned around, visibly swallowing.

"Trey's your family?" the first gang member asked, shock on his face.

"When you are inside these fences with no weapons, you're my family. At least for today."

The gang members all pulled their guns out and hurried over to the lockers to deposit them.

"Today we family," Trey agreed. "Tomorrow shit is real again, motherfuckers."

They pulled out their keys and headed through the gate.

"How the hell did you do that?" Trey asked once the others were out of earshot.

"Do what?"

"Show up right as I was talking."

"I'm blessed, Trey." James shrugged and grinned. "Any trouble so far?"

"Nah, Mr. Brownstone. That was about the most heat we got all day." The gang leader grinned. "Except for all them kids pushing on the bounce houses. They the real thugs here."

James surveyed the park with a small smile. "I'm glad you were willing to accept this as payback for your favor."

Trey looked at all the family and friends in the park playing and enjoying themselves. "It ain't nothing, Mr. Brownstone. It ain't often that pigs will come to cook the pork for us." He grinned. "For one fucking day, we all know life will be safe."

James looked around. "That it will, Trey. That it will."

First, THANK YOU for supporting this new series about Mr. James Brownstone, a man who just wants a simple life of bounties and barbeque. At least, that is how I think of James Brownstone. One reviewer described him as a 'Catholic Bounty Hunter' and I thought that was unique.

Not that I had intended to write about a Catholic bounty hunter. My intent was to point out that the orphanage helped his life when no one wanted 'that little boy with the messed-up face' except those who were willing to see beyond his disfigurement and take care of him.

Now he is all grown up, and like so many of us he is a product of what we watch, feel, and learn as we grow up from the adults who help (or hurt) us as we attain adulthood.

Brownstone isn't any more or less religious than many in life. He is not sure if capturing bounties is a get-out-of-jail card—or maybe a pass on the greased slide right down to the fire.

Either way, he won't be changing his life's work.

He will find out the results at the end, so to speak.

Then we have Shay, who we learn more about in this book and the next Brownstone, but more importantly in her own series being worked on called *I Fear No Evil* which is being worked on as I type.

When Martha (Carr) and I were discussing what to name the series, we came up with it and figured it could be taken both ways:

"I fear no evil, for the Lord is with me…"

Or

"I fear no evil, *for I am the baddest bitch walking.*"

In the beginning of the series it is obvious that the *second* option is more appropriate. However, as it goes on we see that she is at least *trying* to find the person she might have become if she hadn't started down the path to becoming a hitwoman for hire.

And then there is Alison, who is in her mid-teens. She has lost her mother and father (may he rot) and is seeking an anchor in her life. We learn a little more about what is going on at the School of Necessary Magic here, and in the next Brownstone book.

Alison's series *School of Necessary Magic* will begin in about eight weeks, and four books are currently planned (more YA than Brownstone and Shay's series).

All these series are focused around how three people, each an orphan in their own way, come together as a family unit to protect and care for each other.

Each one of them stands separate and capable, but if they ever decide to work together?

I think the ground would tremble.

What about the future?

Right now, we have twelve books planned for Brownstone, twelve books planned for Shay, and four books planned for Allison in the Oriceran Universe. That's twenty-eight (28) wonderful books and "if" everything goes right, they will be published this year (2018).

Further, if you check out the new series (Leira 2.0 series called *Rewriting Justice*) you will see she is using the same logo we revealed with James Brownstone.

Why? Because the story of *Rewriting Justice* will explain how we get the bounty system that James is part of twenty years later.

It's about what an Austin Police Detective goes through to realize that the world isn't set up to handle special criminals. It will be coming to you in a couple of months (we hope) as well.

Looks like it will be an Oriceran Summer ;-)

Thank you SO MUCH for your crazy reviews, wonderful support, and encouragement each time we get one of these books out.

Looking forward to more, and more barbeque soon!

Ad Aeternitatem,

Michael Anderle

BBQ NOTES - MIKE ROSS
WRITTEN APRIL 19, 2018

Michael Anderle here. Remember in the *BBQ Notes* in the back of *Feared by Hell* where I asked you to check in the back of the next book to see if I was able to talk Mike Ross into sharing a recipe with us?

I sent him some questions and my request, and he responded to not just the questions—he included a recipe! WOOHOO!

QUESTIONS:

Michael: What is your favorite meat to cook, and why?

Mike R: Ribs. I like the color of the ribs, and the bones are beautiful. Nice deep reds and blacks. Plus, they are one of the more versatile meats. You can make them do whatever you want.

Michael: What is the favorite meal selected at Jessie Rae's by the customers?

Mike R: Maniac fries!

Michael: Who came up with the spices and the dressing for your waffle fries, which are a personal favorite of mine?

Mike: All sauces and rubs were created by Jessie Rae and me.

RECIPE:

Smoked butter:

Melt some whipped butter in the smoker in a safe dish. Melt it on a super low heat like 180, using a heavy smoke.

Add your favorite BBQ rub to taste.

Mix well and cool. Keep mixing while it cools.

Use for potatoes, mashed or baked. You can also use it on any vegetable, but corn is the best!

CONNECT WITH MICHAEL ANDERLE

Michael Anderle Social
Website:
http://kurtherianbooks.com/

Email List:
http://kurtherianbooks.com/email-list/

Facebook Here:
https://www.facebook.com/OriceranUniverse/
https://www.facebook.com/TheKurtherianGambitBooks/

Made in the USA
Las Vegas, NV
19 May 2022

49097546R00184